A CORPSE IN CHRISTMAS CLOSE

MICHELLE SALTER

Boldwood

First published in Great Britain in 2024 by Boldwood Books Ltd.

Copyright © Michelle Salter, 2024

Cover Design by Rachel Lawston

Cover Illustration: Rachel Lawston

The moral right of Michelle Salter to be identified as the author of this work has been asserted in accordance with the Copyright, Designs and Patents Act 1988.

Every effort has been made to obtain the necessary permissions with reference to copyright material, both illustrative and quoted. We apologise for any omissions in this respect and will be pleased to make the appropriate acknowledgements in any future edition.

A CIP catalogue record for this book is available from the British Library.

Paperback ISBN 978-1-83561-289-7

Large Print ISBN 978-1-83561-285-9

Hardback ISBN 978-1-83561-284-2

Ebook ISBN 978-1-83561-282-8

Kindle ISBN 978-1-83561-283-5

Audio CD ISBN 978-1-83561-290-3

MP3 CD ISBN 978-1-83561-287-3

Digital audio download ISBN 978-1-83561-281-1

Boldwood Books Ltd
23 Bowerdean Street
London SW6 3TN
www.boldwoodbooks.com

To Southgate

1

'Wear a dress.'

My boss, Elijah Whittle, issued this order while lighting a cigarette and reading a crested itinerary with the heading:

7 November 1923: Presentation of the Freedom of the City of Winchester to His Royal Highness, the Prince of Wales

I'd been assigned to cover the event for *The Walden Herald* along with Robbie Roper, Elijah's favourite freelance photographer.

'What's wrong with these?' I glanced down at my navy wool trousers as I stood to crank open the window a fraction more. 'They're new.'

'Don't you want to look your best for the prince?' Elijah blew smoke across his desk, adding to the layer of fog that already filled the newspaper's two offices.

I rolled my eyes. 'Perhaps he likes women in trousers.'

'He likes anything in a skirt from what I've heard,' Robbie called from the outer office. He'd taken his camera apart, and its various components were strewn all over my desk. He was now attempting to put it back together again from the comfort of my chair.

The sewing machine oil he was using on the camera mingled with tobacco fumes, and I wrinkled my nose at the curious odour.

'Queen Mary doesn't approve of women wearing trousers.' Elijah buttoned his tweed jacket over his waistcoat and gave an exaggerated shudder at the cold air blowing in through the window. He reached for his Homburg hat, which had been resting on the windowsill, and crammed it over his sparse grey hair. 'You'll need her blessing if you want to snare her son.'

'I doubt he cares what his mother thinks.' Both King George and the prime minister were known to be concerned about Prince Edward's reckless behaviour and blatant womanising. If he could ignore them, I was sure his mother's views of propriety meant little to him. 'And I have no desire to snare a prince.'

Elijah waved his cigarette in my direction. 'Wouldn't you like to be crowned Queen Iris? I can picture you as a royal dictator, wielding power over us humble menfolk.'

Robbie snorted at this.

'I'd rather have warm legs while I hang around outside Winchester Station. What time does he arrive?' I pulled over a chair, with no choice but to wait in Elijah's smoke-filled den until Robbie had finished his camera repairs.

Elijah checked the itinerary. 'The royal train is due at eleven o'clock. There'll be a Royal Air Force guard of honour waiting for him on the platform when he arrives. After that, he'll be driven to the Guildhall and presented with the Freedom of the City by the mayor. Then he's being taken to Stanmore, the new council housing estate, to plant a commemorative tree. Try to get some pictures of that, Robbie.'

'Will do.' Robbie's six-foot frame was an advantage when vying for the best position in a scrum of photographers and reporters. Usually, I was the only female in the pack and didn't stand a chance of keeping up with him. Fortunately, his height along with his copper hair made it easy for me to spot him in a crowd.

'You can take a break when he's visiting the Royal Hampshire County Hospital, as they won't let you in, and lunch is a private affair with the Lord Lieutenant at the castle. You'll see him again at two o'clock when he's attending a short service at the cathedral. At two-thirty, he's going to Winchester College to watch a football match that kicks off at three. His last engagement is in the college chapel where they're holding a service to consecrate a new altar as part of the college's war memorial.'

'Who'd want to be a prince,' Robbie muttered.

'The football match will be your best chance to get an informal shot,' Elijah advised. 'Something amusing when he chats to the pupils would be good. And if he pays particular attention to any females...'

Robbie's grunt indicated he didn't need telling. He'd been doing the job long enough to know where to point his camera and when to click.

Elijah turned to me. 'Find out what he says to them and write a few words on how witty and amusing he is.'

'Say he's not either?'

'He's the future king of England. Anything he says will be deemed to be the funniest or cleverest thing anyone's ever heard.' Elijah stubbed out his cigarette. 'Then it's back to Winchester Station. The royal train is due to depart at half past five.'

I was beginning to realise why Elijah had no desire to accompany us. It was a packed schedule, and we'd be traipsing around Winchester all day. Apart from a few words on how charming and gracious the prince was, and a comment on the enthusiastic reception from cheering crowds, I'd have little to write. Most of our readers would just want to see Robbie's photographs.

'Take the car,' Elijah instructed.

Horace Laffaye, owner of *The Walden Herald*, had purchased a four-seater Austin Twelve motor car that we shared with the printworks below. While Elijah and I occupied the upstairs space, Laffaye Printworks took up all the rooms and the basement beneath the newspaper's offices.

I could see by Elijah and Robbie's faces they were waiting for my inevitable question.

I obliged. 'Can I drive?'

I liked to think my skills as a motorist were improving, though I lacked experience. When my father had purchased a car, he'd begun to teach me to drive. But after a few heated altercations, my stepmother had suggested he might not be the best tutor for me. I could see her point. My relationship with my father was fractious at the best of times and our spats behind the wheel were unlikely to improve it.

'It's up to Robbie,' Elijah replied with a grin, knowing he was passing the buck.

Robbie pulled a face. 'If the roads are quiet, you can have a driving lesson on the way there. Make sure you're at the studio by nine.'

* * *

The following morning, I inspected the contents of my wardrobe. My hand hovered over a green velvet winter dress I'd had for some years. Then I turned and picked up the woollen navy trousers I'd slung over the back of a chair. Elijah would never know.

I went down to the kitchen to find Ursula boiling a kettle. She was usually first up in the morning.

I'd been lodging at 13 Victoria Lane for three months now, ever since my father had remarried in the summer. I'd been reluctant to live with the newlyweds, so when my friend, Millicent Nightingale, had suggested I take rooms with her and her great-aunt, Ursula, I'd leapt at the chance.

'There's a letter for you.' Ursula pointed to where the post lay on the kitchen table. 'From your London boyfriend.'

I squirmed. Scrutiny of my private life was something I thought I'd leave behind when I moved out of the family home. But, of course, whoever you share a house with soon becomes familiar with your habits.

In this case, it was my correspondence with someone I'd met during the war that had attracted Ursula and Millicent's attention. I'd hoped they would assume it was a woman. But Ursula was too sharp for that.

'A clever young man,' she declared after examining the clear, precise handwriting on the envelope.

And she was right. The problem was, he was a married, clever young man.

'I'll read it later. I have to get to Robbie's.'

Ursula smiled, causing the lines around her eyes to deepen even further. Her wild grey hair was tucked beneath a turquoise headscarf and she wore a heavy woven midnight blue dressing gown. The ensemble made her look like one of those spiritualists or clairvoyants that had been so popular since the war. And, unfortunately, Ursula did have a knack of seeing into your soul.

I thought she was going to question me about the letter, but all she said was, 'Eat a good breakfast. Winchester will be busy. You might not get anything else until later.'

'And remember you're staying in town.' Millicent entered the kitchen dressed for school in a tweed suit with brown leather brogues, her unruly dark curls pinned into a neat bun. 'Daniel's going to drive us over to Winchester this evening for Percy's penguin talk.'

Along with Millicent, Percy Baverstock had founded the Walden Natural History Group and occasionally gave talks on whatever creature was his latest wildlife passion.

'It's going to be a long day.' I joined Ursula at the stove, and together we boiled eggs and toasted thick slices of bread while Millicent filled her satchel with the exercise books she'd been marking late into the previous night.

Ruth, a pretty young woman of seventeen whom Millicent had once taught, arrived just as I was leaving, at a quarter to nine. Thanks to Ruth, the larder of 13 Victoria Lane was kept filled and the house was always clean – if not tidy.

I noticed Millicent and Ursula glance at my letter as I plucked it from the pile of correspondence on the kitchen table – and knew I had to be careful.

As much as I pretended to myself that my relationship with Marc was innocent, I knew I'd face some uncomfortable questions if anyone were to find out about our meetings.

I hurried along Victoria Lane and turned onto Walden high street, pulling the belt of my mustard-yellow overcoat tighter around me. I'd covered my bobbed hair with a navy beret but a cold wind still pinched my ears.

R. Roper Photographic Studio was a few doors up from Fellowes Emporium, and the Ropers lived in a flat above their business.

As well as freelancing for a few regional newspapers, Robbie was a skilled portrait photographer who counted Horace Laffaye and local Member of Parliament, Mrs Sybil Siddons, amongst his clients. Robbie knew how to capture his subjects to their best advantage, and a particularly flattering shot of Horace had secured him a job with *The Walden Herald*.

The shop window displayed examples of Robbie's work – photographs of family groups, glamorous head-and-shoulders shots, and full-length portraits. The studio behind the shop was filled with an assortment of props and screens painted with exotic backdrops.

Robbie's wife, Ellen, answered when I rapped on the glass

door. She ran the studio and took bookings, leaving Robbie to concentrate on the photography.

'Come in. He's nearly ready.' She handed me a paper bag. 'I've packed sandwiches and fruit cake. There's enough for two.'

The couple's eight-year-old twins, John and Julia, appeared from behind the counter.

'Is there any cake left?' John dragged a large brown bear behind him. I recognised it as one of the props Robbie used when photographing children.

'You can have some after school.' Ellen ruffled his hair. 'And put the bear back.'

Robbie emerged from the studio dressed in a thick brown corduroy jacket, carrying his camera and tripod over his shoulder. He grinned when he saw me. 'I thought Elijah told you to wear a dress.'

'He won't know. Too cold for dresses.'

'You'll never become Queen Iris in trousers.'

Julia's eyes widened. 'Are you going to be queen?'

I shook my head. 'Unlikely.'

'She wants to be a racing car driver,' Robbie quipped.

'Do you?' John jumped up and down in excitement. 'So do I!'

'Your father is implying that I sometimes drive too fast. But that's only because I'm still getting used to the car.'

'Are you having another driving lesson?' Ellen smiled at her husband as she held open the shop door for him, and he kissed her on the cheek as he manoeuvred past with his camera and tripod.

'Will you teach us?' the children chorused.

'When you're old enough,' their father promised. 'But not in a brand-new car owned by Mr Laffaye, though it will probably have a few dents in it by then if Iris's driving is anything to go by.'

I pulled a face, making the children giggle, and thanked Ellen for the sandwiches and cake.

We loaded up the Austin Twelve, which still smelt of new leather, and Robbie let me drive it out of Walden. He was happy enough to guide me through the quieter country roads but when we reached the outskirts of Winchester, he made me pull over and swap seats. Although I was gaining confidence, I tended to panic when faced with vehicles coming in the opposite direction.

'It's going to be chaotic enough in the city centre without letting you loose.'

And it was. Crowds lined the streets and bunting hung across shop windows. We reached the railway station at ten-thirty, and Robbie took the last place in the motor enclosure. He hooked his camera and tripod over his shoulder and jostled for a position amongst the other photographers on the platform. I managed to tuck in behind him, although I knew I wasn't going to get a clear view of the prince.

The royal train pulled in at eleven o'clock and the brass band began to play. The Lord Lieutenant of Hampshire and Major General J. E. B. Seeley moved forward to greet the Prince of Wales as he stepped onto the platform. I hastily scribbled a few notes describing the khaki military uniform he was wearing as Colonel of the Welsh Guards.

Robbie was able to capture a half a dozen shots before the prince was escorted to a Rolls-Royce and driven to the Guildhall. Only the official photographer was allowed inside, so there was more hanging around while the ceremony took place. The mayor was presenting his royal highness with the Freedom of the City decree encased in an oak casket made from eight-hundred-year-old beams taken from Winchester Cathedral.

Once the presentation was over, Robbie and I headed back to

the car to follow the royal party to Stanmore, a new garden suburb erected under the national building scheme.

This was something I could get my teeth into. The government had promised to provide 'homes fit for heroes' for the soldiers returning from the Great War. Five years on, and councils were still struggling to clear away city slums and replace them with good quality housing.

After she became only the third woman elected to parliament, my friend, Mrs Siddons, MP, had managed to secure central government funding for a housing project in Walden. In 1920, she'd organised the construction of a small collection of houses in Crookham to replace the caravans and shacks that had sprung up close to Lord Timpson's ancestral home of Crookham Hall.

Stanmore was a more ambitious project. It was an estate of five hundred and sixty medium-sized red-brick houses surrounded by trees and gardens.

Robbie took his place on the landscaped lawns and photographed the prince planting a commemorative tree in a pre-dug hole.

'We won't get anything more until after lunch,' he said as we trudged back to the car. The prince's next stop was the Royal Hampshire County Hospital on Romsey Road, about a mile outside Winchester. Then it was back into the city centre for a brief private luncheon with the Lord Lieutenant in the Great Hall of Winchester Castle. 'I'll park at The Westgate Hotel. We might be able to pick up some princely gossip from the pack.'

'Kevin Noakes is usually the only one who talks to me.'

As a young female, I was generally ignored by the middle-aged male journalists who worked this patch. Kevin, a flirtatious young reporter at the *Hampshire Chronicle*, was the exception.

I liked to think it was because he supported more women in

the profession, but I'm not sure his motives were that pure. After divulging some titbit, he'd usually ask if I wanted to go for a drink or to the cinema with him. If he thought I'd feel obliged to say yes, he was much mistaken. To his credit, he was always good-natured when I turned him down.

Robbie managed to find a space on Castle Hill between The Westgate Hotel and the castle's Great Hall. A few years earlier, I'd attended a trial at the assizes in the Great Hall and was familiar with local journalists' nearby haunts. Reporters would drink in The Westgate Hotel on the opposite side of the road to the court-house. You could see the entrance to the court from a bench in the bay window of the hotel. Whoever was designated this seat would make it worth the while of a clerk to come out and wave when the jury had reached a verdict.

Local journalists were given preference by the hotel's propri-etor as they were regulars, and Robbie and I knew we wouldn't get a look-in. We perched on a wall outside the castle to eat our sandwiches and when I spotted Kevin heading into the bar, I fished some money from my purse and dashed over to him. He agreed to get us some drinks and returned with three glasses of beer and a sandwich for himself.

'Cheers, mate.' Robbie took a swig. 'Any gossip from this morning?'

Kevin took a seat beside me on the wall, careful not to snag the trousers of his smart gaberdine suit. 'He was seen presenting a pretty nurse with a bunch of violets he'd been given by one of the crowd. But we weren't allowed to take photos inside the hospital.'

'Imagine how he must feel, knowing people are watching his every move.' I knew I'd hate it, although this didn't stop me from reading about his love life in the gossip columns.

'I heard he went to Finsbury Park Cinema in disguise. He

took a young lady to a showing of *Safety Last*! Have you seen it? It's supposed to be really funny.'

I shook my head, knowing what was coming next.

'It's on at the Picture House on the high street. If you haven't got to get back to Walden, we could go and see it tonight.'

I'd read some good reviews of the Harold Lloyd romantic comedy and wouldn't have minded seeing it. But I didn't want to encourage Kevin. It's not that he wasn't good-looking. In fact, he was quite appealing, with mischievous blue eyes and neatly cropped blond hair. What irked me was that at twenty-four, the same age as me, he'd managed to secure a more senior position in a bigger newspaper than I had. Apart from the typists in the office, there were no female staff at the *Hampshire Chronicle*.

Admittedly, this wasn't Kevin's fault, and I always tried to be friendly. But not too friendly.

'I can't tonight, I'm afraid. I'm going to a talk on penguins.' I didn't realise how ridiculous this would sound until I said it.

Robbie sniggered.

'Okay. I haven't heard that one before.' Kevin picked up our empty glasses and took them into the bar of the hotel.

A few reporters were beginning to gather outside the Great Hall and Robbie and I realised it was time to get back on the trail of the prince.

'Penguins?' Robbie chuckled. 'Not interested in young Kevin, then?'

'When I can have the Prince of Wales?' I replied as we returned to the car.

Robbie decided we should drive straight to Winchester College and wait there while his royal highness attended a service in the cathedral. The college football match was his best chance of capturing a lively shot of the prince, and he wanted to secure a good position.

Much of the college's architecture dated from medieval times and the courtyard was particularly impressive. I was fascinated by a face that a stonemason had carved into the roof of the archway into the college. When you enter, the face appears to smile as though pleased to see you, yet when you turn to leave, your viewpoint changes, and it shows sadness at your departure.

Only boys were admitted into college halls and, once inside, I realised I was probably going to be one of the few females present that afternoon.

Robbie set up his camera at the edge of the playing fields, and we waited for the match to start. Once the prince arrived, he was ushered into the royal box and seated with distinguished former pupils of the college.

Robbie nudged me. 'Isn't that your friend, Percy?'

I squinted over and gasped. 'Good God.'

Percy Baverstock, dressed in his best grey suit, was seated next to the Prince of Wales. And whatever he'd just said had caused the prince to throw back his head and bellow with laughter.

3

'Is he a former pupil?' Robbie asked.

I nodded. 'Percy was brought up in Winchester, and his family still lives here. I knew he was back for a visit, as he's giving the talk on penguins tonight. But I didn't know he'd be here today.'

'Seems to be getting on well with his royal highness.'

The prince was still chuckling as he went onto the pitch to meet the players. I dreaded to think what Percy had said to cause such merriment.

I waved, hoping to catch Percy's attention, but he was too engrossed in conversation with the prince's equerry. It was Kevin who waved back and came striding towards me, the whiff of his cologne reaching me before he did. He always wore a little too much.

'They'll be playing Fifteens,' he informed me.

'Fifteens?'

'It's a football match played under the Winchester Code.'

He began to explain the rules of what was regarded by some

as the oldest football code still in existence, and I realised I was in for a dull afternoon.

Despite Kevin's long-winded explanation, as the game between Commoners and Houses progressed, I only had the vaguest idea of who was winning. I hoped Elijah wasn't expecting me to provide a write-up of the match.

The prince's last engagement was to attend a service in the college chapel where the Bishop of Gloucester was to consecrate the new altar and screen that formed part of the college's war memorial.

The other reporters and photographers hurried towards the chapel, but Robbie and I decided to stay put.

'We won't get much more now.' Robbie stretched, massaging his back. 'I've got enough to keep Elijah happy.'

I was willing to call it a day. Every inch of me was stiff with cold, and I was glad I'd worn my navy slacks instead of a skirt and stockings.

While Robbie was fiddling with his camera, I opened my satchel to fish out my powder compact. My cheeks were red, and my hair was askew beneath my navy beret.

'Don't worry, Iris,' said a cut-glass voice. 'You could never be mistaken for a boy.'

I heard Robbie give a sharp intake of breath and glanced up to find myself staring straight into the blue eyes of the Prince of Wales.

'I, er, I...' Words failed me. I had no idea how to respond to this strange statement. Fortunately, he didn't seem to expect a reply.

My mouth gaped, and to my amazement, he winked and flashed me a smile before sauntering away. The noise of the camera told me Robbie had leapt into action and was snapping for all he was worth.

The prince's equerry hurried forward to usher him towards the college, and Robbie emerged from behind his tripod, hooting with laughter. In the distance, I could see Percy grinning and waving inanely.

I was tempted to make a rude gesture in his direction but didn't want to draw any more attention to myself.

'Iris and the prince. I think your friend, Percy, set you up.' Robbie was still shaking with laughter as he hoicked his camera and tripod over his shoulder.

All I could do was make a spluttering sound in response while Robbie cackled all the way back to the car, gleeful at what he hoped he'd captured on film.

I trudged after him across the muddy playing fields and by the time we reached the Austin Twelve, the shock of my royal encounter had worn off sufficiently for me to see the funny side.

'I've a good mind to heckle Percy during his talk, only his parents will be there.'

Robbie grinned. 'I think it would take a lot to throw him off course. How are you getting home afterwards?'

'Daniel Timpson is coming with Millicent and Ursula. He's going to drive us all home.'

'First a prince and now a lord.' Robbie gave an exaggerated wink. 'You move in such sophisticated circles.'

After his father's death, Daniel had inherited his title as well as the family's ancestral home of Crookham Hall.

I helped Robbie pack away the equipment in the boot of the car and watched him skilfully manoeuvre his way out of the college grounds. While the other photographers were driving towards the railway station, hoping for a final shot of the prince before he departed on the royal train, Robbie sped off in the opposite direction.

When someone reached for my arm, the waft of cologne that hit my nostrils told me it was Kevin.

'Aren't you heading back to Walden too?'

'I told you. I'm going to a talk on penguins this evening.'

'I thought you were joking. Who's speaking?'

'A friend of mine. Percy Baverstock. He works at the Natural History Museum, and he's a member of the Society for the Promotion of Nature Reserves. You should come along – he's really entertaining. There are still tickets available.' I thought Percy might appreciate some press coverage of his talk. And if he didn't, his mother, Hetty, would certainly be thrilled at seeing her son's name in the newspaper.

I could tell by Kevin's expression an evening spent listening to a talk on penguins wasn't appealing to him.

He hedged his bets. 'I'll see if I can get away from the office. What time does it start?'

'Seven o'clock. At Abbey House.'

The *Hampshire Chronicle* offices were at one end of the high street and Abbey House at the other. It was less than a ten-minute walk between the two.

'Okey-dokey.' He turned and waved. 'I'll see you later. I'm heading to the station now for the finale.'

I debated whether to go in search of Percy but decided to walk up to the high street and get a cup of tea instead. It was nearly dark, and the temperature was dropping even further.

I strolled along College Street, pausing outside the house where Jane Austen had died over a hundred years before. All was quiet now the reporters had moved on to the train station, and with its ancient buildings, it was easy to picture the street as it had been in Austen's day. Her final resting place was in the nave of nearby Winchester Cathedral under a memorial stone that celebrated 'the extraordinary endowments of her mind'.

Further down the road, the red, white and blue bunting draped across the front of P & G Wells Bookshop flapped in the wind. Judging by the window display of books on royal history, the bookseller had hoped to capitalise on the prince's visit.

I left College Street and went through Kingsgate, stopping on the corner by St Swithun's Church. I noticed a few reporters had gathered further down St Swithun Street and were turning left into what looked like a tiny side road. When I caught up with Kevin, he was telling his photographer to go on to the railway station without him.

'What's going on?' I asked.

'There's a police car and an ambulance outside Christmas Hall.'

I had no idea where this was, so I hurried after him as he set off with the other reporters into a narrow cobbled road enclosed by the grey-stoned medieval walls the city was famous for.

At the end of the close, a figure I recognised stepped out of one of the dark sedan cars. Superintendent Cobbe had previously been based in Aldershot but was now spending most of his time at police headquarters in Winchester. The rumour was he was in line to be made Chief Superintendent of Hampshire.

The superintendent adjusted his trilby hat and nodded to his sergeant to lead the way. A dense hedge of holly screened the path up to the hall, and they disappeared from view.

A few streetlamps were lit, but there was nothing to see. Two constables prevented us from getting any closer, and they refused to answer any questions shouted at them by reporters.

A ripple of excitement rose from the gathering crowd when two medics appeared from behind the hedge bearing a stretcher between them. The person they were carrying was covered from head to foot in a large white sheet.

Silence fell as they climbed into the back of the waiting

ambulance. The bystanders moved to one side to let the vehicle drive out of the tiny road.

'What is this place?' I asked, glancing around. 'I've never noticed it before.'

'Christmas Close,' Kevin replied. 'The hall belongs to the church. They sometimes hold prayer meetings there, but it's currently being used by the committee of Winchester Cathedral's Great War Fund. They raise money for Hampshire charities that support war veterans.' He clapped his hand to his mouth. 'Oh God. My landlady. She said she was coming here this afternoon.'

Kevin strode over to one of the constables. 'My landlady, Mrs Durling, was supposed to be here for rehearsals of the charity pantomime. Do you know—'

The constable held up a hand. 'I'm sorry, sir. I can't give out any information.'

'We need to close the road,' someone called from behind the hedge. 'Superintendent Cobbe's orders.'

The two constables immediately began herding the bystanders away from the hall. Kevin was reluctant to leave but I pulled at his arm.

'Why don't you go back to your lodgings to see if she's there?' I suggested.

He nodded, and we followed the other reporters out onto St Swithun Street.

'Kevin.' A woman of about fifty with greying blonde hair and dressed in a pink woollen coat waved at him from across the road.

'Mrs Durling.' Kevin rushed over to her. 'Weren't you supposed to be at the hall this afternoon?'

'They wouldn't let me in. Someone said a body's been found.' Mrs Durling started to tremble from shock or cold. Probably both.

'You must be freezing,' I said. 'Why don't we go up to the high street for a cup of tea?'

Kevin made hasty introductions and took Mrs Durling's arm. 'The Old Rectory Café should be open. Florrie will squeeze us in.'

After a little flirtation with Kevin, Florrie, a pretty red-haired waitress, managed to find us a corner table near the kitchen. It was a bit squashed but pleasantly warm and I was relieved to discover I wasn't the only one who was hungry as well as cold. The scent of salt and vinegar hung in the air, and we decided to indulge in an early supper of fish and chips, washed down with a pot of tea.

Once Bridget Durling had finished her meal and was on her second cup, I asked her about the pantomime that Kevin had mentioned.

'We hold one at the hall every Christmas to raise money for the cathedral's war fund. This year, it's *Cinderella*. I'm playing the fairy godmother. Rehearsals weren't due to start until five o'clock but I'd agreed to meet the leading lady at four to go over our lines. Jack, the caretaker, said he'd open up the hall and light the gas fires.' Her eyes widened. 'Do you think that's who it was? The body they found?'

'Jack Archer?' Kevin wiped his mouth with a napkin. 'I saw him talking to one of the constables outside the hall.'

'Oh, but that... That means... It must have been Rachel Lacey.' Mrs Durling's hand shook as she replaced her cup in the saucer. 'Our Cinderella.'

4

When we emerged from The Old Rectory Café, I heard the toot of a horn and someone calling my name. Percy pulled his Model T Ford to the side of the road and waved out of the window.

'Want a ride? You're coming to my talk, aren't you?'

I said goodbye to Kevin and Mrs Durling and hopped into the passenger seat.

'I'll come along later,' Kevin called. 'I need to go into the office first to see my editor.'

'Who's that?' Percy asked. 'A new boyfriend?'

I sighed. Percy sometimes had a jealous streak. 'He's a journalist for the *Hampshire Chronicle*. I've persuaded him to come and listen to your talk.'

He seemed to brighten at that. 'Good show. I need all the support I can get. I'm worried everyone will be pooped after all the princely goings-on today and will give it a swerve.'

'That reminds me, what did you say to him? How did he know my name?'

'I'm afraid I can't reveal my private conversations with his royal highness.' Percy tried to look innocent and failed miserably. 'Why? What did he say to you?'

'Something about me not being mistaken for a boy?'

He snorted with laughter. 'I thought you'd like to meet him, so I told him you'd worn trousers to attract his attention. I said you'd hoped to stand out from the other girls and were upset when you realised the college porter had only let you in because he thought you were a boy.'

'I did not want to attract his attention. I wanted to keep my legs warm,' I sputtered. 'What were you doing there anyway?'

'Wiggy, my old housemaster, put my name on the list. Believe it or not, I'm considered to be one of the college's success stories despite my lack of academic achievements.'

'Successful enough to be invited to meet royalty?'

'Admittedly, there were plenty ahead of me on the list. But old Wiggy knew I'd want to attend the chapel service for the consecration of the war memorial.'

Like schools and universities across the country, many of Winchester College's former pupils had been killed in the Great War. And Percy had lost some of his closest friends.

'Was it very moving?' I asked.

He sniffed. 'You know me. Not one to blub.'

This wasn't true. Even though he rarely spoke about the war, except to mention his great pals, I knew the pain of what he'd endured was never far from the surface.

'How long are you here for?' I noticed a suitcase on the back seat.

'I'm staying until Sunday. I meant to stop off at my parents' house before I went to the college, but I was running late. Wiggy, who arranged tonight's event, asked me to give my talk on penguins to the pupils. Went down a treat, if I say so myself. I was the star of the show until the prince turned up. Shame he couldn't come along tonight. I'm sure he'd enjoy it. He thought my impression of an emperor penguin was a complete hoot.'

Ever since Pathé News had presented a series of short films about penguins, they'd become a big hit with moviegoers who'd watched the reels before the main film began. There was now a craze for the creatures.

Percy slowed, and pulled up outside Abbey House, the official residence of the Mayor of Winchester. The mayor didn't actually live there, and the house was mainly used to host civic dinners and educational talks.

Percy's parents were waiting for him by the gate. His father, Clifford, was dressed in a formal tweed suit while his mother, Hetty, wore a flamboyant matching coat and dress in purple velvet.

'All this for me?' Percy quipped when he saw the bunting decorating the entrance. He kissed his mother on the cheek and slapped his father on the back.

'Iris. How lovely.' Hetty enveloped me in a floral-scented hug. 'Where's Millicent?'

I explained that I'd been in the city all day for the prince's visit and that Millicent was coming along with Daniel Timpson.

'Wasn't the prince a dream? I wore my fuchsia hat, which is hideous but eye-catching, and I'm sure he smiled at me when he left the Guildhall. I had to go by myself as Clifford thinks the royal family is a waste of our taxes.'

I'd first met Mr and Mrs Baverstock at a social event at the Natural History Museum some years before. Within minutes of chatting with Hetty and Clifford, I came to the conclusion that Percy had inherited his silly streak from his mother and his serious side from his father.

'Where's Freddie?' Percy was looking around for his younger brother.

'He'll be here.' Clifford turned to me. 'He's been working over your way.'

'In Walden?' I said in surprise.

Clifford nodded. 'At St Martha's Church.'

'Freddie's training as a stonemason,' Percy explained. 'With an old army pal of mine.'

'He's studying to become an architect,' Hetty added.

'Here's Daniel and Millicent.' Percy waved. 'Ursula, too. Game old bird.'

'Percy,' Hetty whispered. 'Don't be so rude.'

'She is, though. Wait till you meet her.'

I smiled at the sight of Lord Timpson strolling arm in arm with Ursula. I knew he'd rather have had his beloved Millie by his side, but he was nothing if not a gentleman. And a very attractive one at that, with dark blue eyes set under black lashes and thick dark hair. Mothers, seeking an advantageous match, had often pushed their daughters into his path. However, in my opinion, he'd shown extreme good sense by falling for my friend, Millicent, instead.

A young lady in a smart uniform showed us into Abbey House and led us upstairs to a packed reception room. Admittedly, it wasn't a huge venue, but Percy looked gratified by the turnout.

Rather than rows of chairs, the room was set out with separate tables that seated eight. Percy was whisked away to another room, and Mr and Mrs Baverstock, Ursula, Millicent, Daniel and I sat at a table close to the lectern. We were left with two spare chairs, and one was soon taken when a young man with a remarkable resemblance to Percy appeared.

'Here's Freddie.' Hetty waved him over.

Like Percy, Freddie had floppy brown hair and round dark eyes, though his face was thinner and more boyish that his brother's. He also had a serious and silly side, but tended to be more studious than Percy, with fewer displays of daftness.

'Hello all,' Freddie panted, his hair damp and his tie askew. 'Had to wait for Harry to get back before I could leave Walden, then I dashed home to change.'

The second empty chair was filled when Kevin Noakes made an appearance.

'Do you mind if my friend joins us?' I asked. 'He's a journalist for the *Hampshire Chronicle*. I mentioned the talk to him, hoping he might review it for the paper.'

Hetty clapped her hands together. 'I could show everyone at my bridge club.'

I took this as a yes and beckoned Kevin over. Introductions were made, and he took a seat.

'You must have had an exciting day,' Clifford remarked.

'I should say so.' Kevin's hair had been slicked back, and I detected a whiff of fresh cologne. 'Winchester has never been so lively. Royalty and a dead body in one day.'

'A body?' Hetty exclaimed. 'Where?'

'Christmas Close. By the cathedral.'

'Christmas Close?' Freddie stared at him. 'Where they're holding the pantomime?'

'That's right. The lady playing Cinderella was found dead outside the hall.'

Freddie inhaled sharply. 'Rachel?'

'Are they sure it's her?' I asked, alarmed by Freddie's expression.

'I shouldn't have said anything. The body hasn't been identified yet. But everyone's talking about it.' Kevin was watching Freddie closely. 'Did you know her?'

'Freddie's playing the handsome prince,' Hetty piped up. 'Poor girl. I wonder if the pantomime will go ahead.'

'I'm sorry,' Kevin said. 'You must have known her well.'

I could tell he was now interested in a much bigger story than penguins.

'Oh, n-no,' Freddie stammered, looking like he wanted the ground to swallow him up. 'Barely at all. I was just helping out at the hall. Building the set. I got roped into playing the prince, but I haven't learnt my lines or anything.'

The flush on Freddie's cheeks indicated he was better acquainted with Rachel Lacey than he was admitting. It sounded like more than just the pantomime had been going on. Perhaps they'd taken their roles a little too seriously.

Luckily for Freddie, the mayor appeared at that moment, saving him from further questions. At a signal for hush, the audience fell silent, and the mayor took his place behind the lectern. He began by saying what an exciting day it had been for Winchester and how honoured the city was by the royal visit.

I hoped he wouldn't dwell too much on the day's events as the Prince of Wales was a hard act to follow. Fortunately, he soon moved on to give the evening's speaker an eloquent and flattering introduction.

I was amused to hear Percy described as a 'distinguished' natural history expert. Anyone who'd seen him on the dance floor of the Foxtrot Club wouldn't associate him with that word, but the audience of Abbey House looked suitably impressed.

Percy took the mayor's place and glanced down at his sheaf of notes. He shuffled them around a bit, then seemed to discard them, stepping away from the lectern and leaning against it instead of standing behind it. He chatted to his audience as if he was propping up the bar of the Drunken Duck. And they loved it.

He was hilarious, although I'm not sure all of his jokes were intentional. He somehow managed to combine his love of penguins with his love of movies and described how an emperor penguin walked in a similar way to Charlie Chaplin. When he proceeded to demonstrate, the audience were as entertained as the Prince of Wales had been earlier that day.

The talk ended to loud applause, and when Percy came over to our table, Kevin stood up and shook his hand, promising a rave review in the next edition.

I'd kept one eye on Freddie during the talk and could see he hadn't been paying much attention to his brother's antics. Rachel Lacey's death had clearly disturbed him, and his relief was evident when the evening came to an end.

Perhaps anticipating further questions from Kevin, Freddie was first out of the door when Percy finished thanking his guests and ushered his family from the room.

'I get the impression Freddie was smitten with Rachel Lacey,' Kevin said as he watched them go. 'She was quite a looker from what I've heard.'

'Do you know how she died?' I stood up, eager to follow Freddie's example and get home.

'The police aren't saying.' Kevin yawned as rose to move my chair back for me.

'Was she an actress?' Millicent asked, helping Ursula to her feet.

He shook his head. 'It's a purely an amateur production. She's a receptionist at Tolfree Motors. You must have heard of Gordon Tolfree. He lives in Walden, doesn't he?'

'We've heard of him,' I replied. We all knew who Gordon Tolfree was.

'He's in the pantomime too.'

Ursula gave a derisive snort.

'What?' I couldn't picture Gordon Tolfree hamming it up on stage.

'He's playing one of the ugly sisters. He's on the committee of Winchester Cathedral's Great War Fund.'

'Since when has Gordon Tolfree been involved with charitable causes?' I couldn't keep the scorn from my voice.

Kevin looked at me quizzically. 'Since he decided to stand in the election.'

Daniel, Millicent, Ursula and I gave a collective gasp and stared at him in horror.

Kevin was clearly confused by this strange reaction. 'That's the rumour. He's planning to stand as an independent candidate for Aldershot.'

Daniel let out a low groan, and Kevin eyed him curiously.

'We ought to be going.' Millicent reached for Daniel's arm.

Ursula followed her lead. 'Would it be possible to bring the car around to the front? My old legs aren't what they used to be.'

This was a lie. I'd seen Ursula dash to Fellowes Emporium in under five minutes when she discovered she was out of sherry.

'Of course.' Daniel took the hint and hurried to the door.

Ursula gripped Millicent's arm, and they made their way more sedately down the staircase, Kevin and I trailing behind.

Before I could follow them outside, Kevin put out a hand to stop me.

'Did I just put my foot in it? I forgot the Timpsons took over Tolfree Biscuits. I've heard the rumours about old Redvers Tolfree. Care to share any secrets?'

I considered this, then nodded. 'Okay. We'll speak again soon.' It wasn't something I wanted to talk about, but if Gordon Tolfree was standing for election, I'd need all the allies I could muster.

Outside, Kevin inspected the Timpsons' Daimler with interest. It was an old model, having belonged to Daniel's mother, but still a grand-looking car.

Kevin opened the rear door and helped Ursula and Millicent onto the back seat. I thanked him for coming and hopped into the front seat next to Daniel. I wanted nothing more than to get home and sit in front of the fire with Ursula and Millicent and a cup of cocoa. Or, after that bombshell, perhaps we'd crack open the sherry.

'I can't believe Gordon Tolfree's standing against Mrs Siddons.' Millicent waved politely at Kevin as we drove away.

'Revenge,' Ursula announced.

None of us had to ask what she meant.

'Constance is going to be furious.' Daniel gripped the steering wheel with unnecessary force.

For the past two years, his younger sister, the Honourable Constance Timpson, had been running the family business she'd inherited from their mother, Lady Timpson. And against all odds, she'd succeeded in making Timpson Foods even more profitable than it had been in their mother and grandfather's day.

She'd initially acquired a controlling stake in Tolfree Biscuits when Redvers Tolfree had needed help in keeping his family's business afloat. Then, after he was charged with embezzlement, he'd been forced to sell his remaining shares to Timpson Foods.

His son, Gordon, had always suspected that Mrs Siddons and I had helped Constance to uncover what was going on at the Tolfree & Timpson factory. And he was right. We had.

As a result, Gordon Tolfree, who seemed convinced of his father's innocence, hated all three of us.

5

Percy hooted with laughter when he saw the photograph on the front page of *The Walden Herald*.

Elijah had insisted on placing it in the most prominent position because it was the one picture from the Prince of Wales's visit that was unique. All the other photographs taken that day were broadly the same. But, in this one, the prince was smiling flirtatiously as he winked at a surprised-looking young lady. Unfortunately, that lady was me, mouth gaping, as I glanced up from my powder compact.

Hetty patted my arm. 'You must have stood out from all the other girls.'

'She always stands out from the other girls,' Percy chortled. 'Not always for the right reasons.'

'It was after the football match at the college. I was the only female there.' I diverted Hetty's attention from the picture by showing her the article I'd written on Percy's talk.

'He's mentioned in this one too.' Hetty pointed to a feature in the *Hampshire Chronicle*. Kevin had been true to his word and given Percy's talk a glowing review. 'I've shown everyone at my bridge club.'

Hetty had invited us to Sunday lunch to meet Harry Hobbs, an old army pal of Percy and Freddie's, as he and his wife, Victoria, would shortly be moving to Walden. Percy had collected Millicent and me that morning and driven us to his parents' red-brick cottage on Water Lane in Winchester. Their home overlooked a clear chalk stream of the River Itchen that flowed along the length of the lane.

'Well done, mate.' Harry slapped Percy on the back. He was a giant of a man, over six foot, with thick dark hair and bushy eyebrows. 'Sorry I missed it. Can you eat penguins?'

'I believe Mother's prepared beef,' Percy quipped, pouring his friend a glass of home-made beer from an enormous brown bottle.

Hetty sighed. 'If it hadn't been for the prince's visit and that poor girl's tragic death, you might have made the front page. I'm going paste all your press cuttings into a scrapbook and add any reviews of the pantomime that mention Freddie.'

Her younger son winced at this. Or it might have been because he caught sight of the headline emblazoned across the front page of the *Hampshire Chronicle*. It read:

Cinderella slain as she smoked

Millicent pulled a face. 'As she smoked?'

Harry's ready grin disappeared. 'Rach used to smoke outside the hall.'

'You knew her?' I asked.

'Known her for a few years, haven't we, love?'

When Harry turned to look at Victoria, I noticed a scar running down the side of his head, partially hidden by his thick mop of dark hair. Percy had told Millicent and me about the exploding grenade that had ripped into his friend's face. The injuries had changed his mood as well as his appearance, and Percy warned us that Harry was prone to fits of elation followed by melancholy.

'My brother, Oliver, manages Tolfree Motors,' Victoria explained. 'Rachel was the receptionist there.'

In contrast to her husband, Victoria was of slender build, with fine features and delicately arched eyebrows and bow lips. Her slightly pensive expression did nothing to detract from her beauty, giving her the look of a damsel in distress in a silent Hollywood film.

'Rach used to perform once a week in a bar, and I'd sometimes go along to hear her sing. Lovely girl,' Harry said before taking a large gulp of beer.

I noticed Victoria glance anxiously at Freddie, and I got the impression she didn't entirely agree with this statement. But she said, 'Poor Rachel didn't have it easy. She lost her parents at a young age.'

Before I could learn more, the Baverstocks' maid came in bearing a tray of dishes, and Hetty cleared the newspapers from the table while Clifford poured wine for the ladies. The aroma of roast beef, roast potatoes and a meaty gravy filled the room.

Over lunch, in typical Baverstock style, conversation covered an eclectic range of topics and stopped and started erratically. Hetty would hop from one subject to another, whereas Clifford liked to discuss politics and world affairs. He engaged Millicent in a debate on the forthcoming election while Percy, Freddie and Harry drank beer and reminisced about their army days.

'Will the pantomime go ahead after what's happened?' I asked Victoria.

She nodded. 'I expect so. Everyone's worked so hard. We've

been helping out too. Harry and Freddie built the sets, and I made the costumes. My brother, Oliver, is playing one of the ugly sisters and his boss, Mr Tolfree, is playing the other.'

'Tolfree's got something to do with it,' Harry suddenly growled. He'd obviously overhead our conversation and was now staring unseeingly into his beer, his brow furrowed.

Everyone fell silent at this unexpected statement.

Victoria touched his arm. 'It could have been anyone. We don't even know how she died.'

I was intrigued. 'You think Gordon Tolfree's involved in Rachel Lacey's death?'

Harry shrugged. 'I'll tell you when I have the proof.'

When it became evident he wasn't going to say anything further, Percy tried to lighten the mood by announcing he was going in search of more beer.

'Come on, Freddie, let's see what the old man's got hidden away in the cellar.' By the way he dragged his brother from the table, it was clear he wanted to ask him what was going on with Harry.

Ever the diplomat, Millicent steered the conversation away from murder by asking Harry and Victoria when they'd be moving to Walden.

'Next week. We can't wait, can we, Harry?'

Her husband nodded but didn't seem to share his wife's enthusiasm, and I noticed Hetty and Clifford were watching him with concern.

Before his head injury had invalided him out of the army, Harry had looked after Percy, Freddie and the other young men in his unit, even though he wasn't much older himself. With both their sons away fighting, it had been a frightening time for the Baverstocks, and I knew how fond they were of Harry. Their fears for their boys would have been shared by thousands of other families during the nearly five years of bloody conflict.

'You're already working over at Walden, aren't you?' I said to Harry.

He nodded. 'At St Martha's Church. Your vicar, Reverend Childs, is involved with Winchester Cathedral's Great War Fund and that's how he heard about me. Before that, I did some work at Crookham Hall. Beautiful place. I wish I could do more jobs like that.'

'Daniel mentioned you'd done some work at the hall for him,' Millicent said. 'He described you as a master craftsman.'

Victoria beamed. 'Stonemasonry is the family trade. Harry learnt from his father and grandfather.'

'We need to produce a son to carry on the business,' Harry announced, much to his wife's embarrassment. 'Hobbs & Son. Or sons,' he added hopefully.

Victoria coloured. 'Let's wait until we're settled in Walden and you have more work coming in.'

'Plenty of work in Winchester,' Harry retorted.

'You can still take jobs around here now you've got the van,' Victoria replied.

I got the impression this was a conversation they'd had before.

'We're moving to the estate near Crookham.' Harry gulped the remainder of his beer and held out his glass as Percy and Freddie returned with another bottle. 'I liked the new houses at Stanmore, but Victoria wants to get away from here.'

'Walden is so pretty with the canal and the lake. It will be nice to be somewhere quieter.' Victoria's forced smile gave me the impression there was more than picturesque scenery behind her desire to leave Winchester.

Lunch passed pleasantly enough after that, although I

detected a certain tension in the air. And it seemed to centre around Harry and Freddie. I said as much to Percy when we were back in the car.

'It's this bloody murder, if that's what it is. No one seems to know how she died.' Percy drove out of Water Lane but went in the opposite direction of the road to Walden.

'Where are you going?' Millicent asked.

'I'm taking you on a detour to Christmas Close.'

'Where that poor woman's body was found?' Millicent may have sounded sympathetic, but the gleam in her eye told me she was keen to view the crime scene.

'The hall will be locked,' he said, 'so we can't go inside. I just need to talk to you about something.'

Percy drove along the narrow Winchester streets, flags still hanging from many of the buildings. When we reached the city centre, we passed the cathedral – its high stone walls and mosaic stained-glass windows creating strange shadows in the fading light.

All was quiet when Percy pulled up outside Christmas Hall and the building was in darkness. We got out of the car and stood by the holly hedge that hid the entrance from view.

'I couldn't say anything in front of Ma and Pa. The thing is, the police have questioned Freddie about Rachel Lacey.'

'They're probably interviewing everyone involved in the pantomime,' Millicent said.

'It's more than that. Someone told Superintendent Cobbe about an incident that took place over there, under that porch. It's where her body was found.'

A flagstone pathway led from the pavement to the double doors of the hall. Close to the doors was an old-fashioned lych-gate-style porch. We walked over to it.

'What sort of incident?' I didn't like the sound of this.

'Freddie admitted that he'd had a bit of a crush on Rachel. She was jolly pretty by all accounts. Anyway, one evening after rehearsals, he followed her out to the porch and asked her if she'd like to go to the cinema with him.'

I could see where this was leading.

'She said something like: "I won't be around for much longer".'

'What did she mean by that?' It sounded like Rachel had had a horrible premonition of what was to come.

'It seems she was planning to move to London. When Freddie said that London's not that far, she told him she'd had enough of Winchester and enough of men.'

'Poor Freddie,' Millicent commented.

Percy dug his hands into his pockets. 'Freddie's enthusiasm for the pantomime waned a bit after that.'

'Tricky if he's playing the prince,' I observed.

'Victoria roped him into doing it – I think she regrets it now. Performing isn't Freddie's sort of thing. I get the impression the thought of being Rachel's prince charming appealed to him at first. But after that encounter, he felt a bit awkward.'

'The police can't think Freddie would kill someone just because they didn't want to go to the pictures with him.' I couldn't help glancing down, wondering where exactly Rachel's body had been found.

'I'm afraid that's precisely what they think. Someone in the hall must have overheard what was said.'

'Does Freddie have an alibi? Where was he that afternoon? It must have happened before five o'clock as the police were at the hall by then.' I thought back to the reporters scurrying into the close, abandoning their trip to the railway station to see the royal train depart at five-thirty.

'Stuck at St Martha's in Walden. He'd been there with Harry

since nine o'clock that morning. At about one o'clock, Harry said he wanted to move some furniture to the new house at Crookham. He took all their work tools out of his van and left them with Freddie at the church while he drove back to Winchester. Freddie's only got a motorbike, so he can't ferry the tools around himself. He had to wait until Harry returned with the van, otherwise it would have meant leaving their tools lying on the ground outside the church.'

'Did Freddie tell the police that?' Millicent asked.

Percy nodded. 'But St Martha's was quiet that afternoon, and there were no witnesses to say he was there. The police reckon he had enough time to ride to Winchester on his Triumph, see Rachel, then return to Walden.'

I frowned. 'Seems far-fetched to me. When did Harry get back?'

'Not until five o'clock. Freddie had been due to come here for rehearsals. He said he could spare an hour before scooting along to my talk. As it was, he just got back to Winchester in time to change and join us at Abbey House.'

I pulled my coat tighter around me. 'Why is Harry so sure Gordon Tolfree is involved in Rachel's death?'

'I asked Freddie about that when we went to get more beer. He said Harry's been in a strange mood ever since the murder. When they're working at the church, he keeps looking around as though someone's watching them.'

Millicent was staring along the cobblestoned road. 'The police seem to be working on the assumption that whoever killed Rachel Lacey knew she'd be here for rehearsals that afternoon. I don't imagine many people come into Christmas Close. That would indicate it was someone involved with the pantomime.'

I wasn't so sure. 'Rachel could have mentioned to anyone that she was going to be here. Harry said she sang in a bar. Maybe she attracted the unwanted attention of one of the customers.'

'Could you speak to your friend at the *Chronicle*? See if he knows what's going on?' Percy looked tense as he pushed his hair from his brow. 'I've got to get back to London tonight, and I'd appreciate it if you could both keep an eye on Freddie for me while he's in Walden. They're going to be working at the church for another few weeks.'

I nodded.

'Of course we will,' Millicent promised.

'Thank you, I do worry about him, especially when he's being daft over some girl.'

I smiled at his brotherly concern. Percy clearly saw himself as the sensible one, despite the fact that he was also well-known for his daftness when it came to the fairer sex.

Millicent began to shiver and Percy took her arm and led her back to the car. Before I followed, I examined the ground, unsettled by the thought that I could be walking over the spot where Rachel Lacey's body had lain.

There was nothing to indicate anything untoward had taken place here, although the holly berries squashed underfoot left an unsettling red smear on the weather-worn flagstones.

6

'Is it true?' Millicent was doing the rounds with the sherry bottle.

After hearing what Kevin Noakes had said about Gordon Tolfree standing as a candidate, Ursula had decided to call a meeting of the election committee – or the coven of witches, as we were also known. The gathering consisted of Mrs Siddons, Constance Timpson, Ursula, Millicent and me.

Millicent and I had prepared the parlour by clearing away piles of Ursula's books and journals and checking our supply of booze. Ruth had cleaned the grate and lit the fire, and the room was now warm and welcoming.

Books and sherry played a big part in life at 13 Victoria Lane. My favourite room in the house was Ursula's library. It was crammed full of books on every subject under the sun, from giant academic tomes to detective stories and a few racy novels. If the books were catalogued in any sort of order, I'd yet to discover what it was. But Ursula always seemed to know exactly where to find what she was searching for. Whenever I was called upon to research some obscure topic, I'd consult Ursula and she'd spring out of her chair and start rummaging around the shelves.

'It was confirmed today. He's standing as an independent candidate.' Mrs Siddons reclined in one of the high-backed leather armchairs. She cut a stately figure in a full-length burgundy silk dress and what appeared to be an amethyst Cartier bracelet on her wrist. With her perfect make-up and elaborately curled dark hair, she looked a decade younger than her fifty-something years.

Ursula, on the other hand, had never gone in for cosmetics, and every line on her seventy-eight-year-old face was testament to the adventurous life she'd led.

'He's only doing it to get back at us.' Constance Timpson had sunk into one of the two brown leather Chesterfield sofas. Most of the furniture in the house tended to be vintage rather than modern, having been purchased by Ursula at one time or another over the previous fifty years.

'Maybe.' Mrs Siddons swirled the rich amber liquid in her crystal glass.

Privately, I agreed with Constance. Gordon Tolfree was out for revenge. He blamed everyone for the loss of his family's business. Everyone but the real culprit: his father, Redvers Tolfree.

Tolfree Biscuits had once been famous all over the world. Founded by Isaac Tolfree in 1850, the company's decorative tins had become as famous as the biscuits inside them. The tins preserved the contents, allowing them to be sent abroad. Captain Scott had famously taken Tolfree Biscuits on his expedition to the South Pole.

During the war, the tin factory switched to munitions work and production of luxury biscuits was discontinued in favour of army biscuits to send to soldiers fighting overseas. After the war, sugar beet was difficult to get hold of and Tolfree Biscuits' fortunes declined as the price of ingredients rose.

When Constance had bailed out Redvers Tolfree, she'd

added the Timpson name to the famous brand. A furious Redvers had sought revenge by embezzling from Tolfree & Timpson – then died of a heart attack before the case could come to trial.

'Gordon doesn't stand a chance of winning. He has no experience of politics,' Millicent pointed out. 'So why has he entered into the running at this late stage?'

There was less than a month until the election, and we'd assumed the race would be between three candidates.

'It's a tactic to divide alliances. A fourth candidate will split the vote even wider,' Ursula replied. 'He probably knows he can't win; he's just hoping to exert some influence over the result.'

Mrs Siddons nodded. 'He thinks he can sway constituents who want to vote for a local candidate – but would prefer that candidate to be a man rather than a woman.'

I saw her point. Mrs Siddons was popular because she lived in the constituency and understood the concerns of the community – unlike the male Conservative and Labour candidates. However, some people were against women in politics, no matter how good they were. In fact, many still opposed women being allowed to vote.

'With a local male candidate, some voters will choose that option,' Ursula said.

Constance gave an exasperated sigh. 'The usual prejudices.'

As a business owner, Constance had experienced as much opposition as Mrs Siddons. When she'd introduced equal pay for female employees and allowed them to continue working after they married, she'd faced hostility from fellow factory owners and the male-dominated press. These radical practices had stirred up ill feeling, and she was accused of forcing ex-servicemen onto the dole queue. At a time of high unemployment, it had been easy to blame women for taking men's jobs.

Mrs Siddons' support of Constance had put them both in the firing line – literally.

'I still don't understand how Gordon will benefit personally by standing,' Millicent said. 'Is a small crumb of revenge worth all the bother?'

'Perhaps he hopes to restore the natural order of things. Men in control and women left powerless in the home.' If I sounded bitter, it was because I was.

Despite the efforts of suffragettes like my mother, the Representation of the People Act in 1918 had given the vote to all men over the age of twenty-one but only to women over the age of thirty who met a property qualification. I still didn't have the right to vote and neither did Millicent or Constance.

'The natural order,' Ursula repeated. 'That sounds like something a general or a clergyman might say.'

'The latter,' I retorted. 'Archie Powell once said it.'

In the silence that followed, I wished I'd never mentioned his name. He was a vicar whom Constance and Mrs Siddons had once considered an ally. Until he'd aimed a rifle in their direction in a bid to scare them into changing their ways. At the time, I'd also been close to him. Too close. And I still regretted the liaison.

'A member of Gordon Tolfree's staff was found dead in suspicious circumstances last week,' I said to break the silence.

'I read about that.' Mrs Siddons put down her sherry glass. 'How did she die?'

'The police haven't said.' I told her what I'd learnt about Rachel Lacey.

Mrs Siddons peered at me through the old-fashioned lorgnette spectacles she'd taken to carrying to avoid wearing glasses. 'I'd be interested to know what happened to this poor woman. Redvers Tolfree had a few skeletons in his cupboard. It wouldn't surprise me if his son is the same.'

'I'm planning to go into Winchester to see if my friend at the *Hampshire Chronicle* knows any more.' I thought about the funny little hall where the body had been discovered and added, 'I wonder why the road is called Christmas Close.'

We all looked expectantly at Ursula for an answer, and she didn't disappoint.

'There's a tiny hamlet in Hertfordshire called Cold Christmas. The name's supposed to have come about after a high number of deaths in the area during a particularly cold winter.' Her expression suggested she was running through the pages of her encyclopaedic mind. 'In this case, I suspect the name derives from its association with the cathedral and religious ceremonies that took place there.'

'The church still holds services in the hall, though it's currently being used to stage a fundraising pantomime. It's organised by Winchester Cathedral's Great War Fund – one of Gordon Tolfree's charitable causes.'

Constance raised her perfectly shaped eyebrows. 'Charitable causes?'

'According to my friend at the *Hampshire Chronicle*, Gordon is presenting himself as a clean-cut family man who does good work through the church.'

'He won't like being involved in a scandal then.' Constance smoothed out the contours of her fitted jacket. It was a gesture I'd seen before. Her precisely cut suits were her business armour and it indicated she was preparing for battle.

I agreed. 'Once the police confirm the body's identity, he's bound to be mentioned in the newspapers.'

'Percy's friend, Harry, is convinced Gordon's involved some-how,' Millicent remarked. 'Although he doesn't seem to have any evidence to support this.'

'If it is murder, it won't do much for Gordon's election

campaign, no matter how slight his connection with the victim,' Constance said. 'Not at a time when he's trying to put the family's disgrace behind him and re-establish the reputation of the Tolfree name.'

She was right. The press would print every piece of salacious gossip they could find on Rachel Lacey and the men she'd been acquainted with.

This made me think of Freddie, and I had a horrible feeling that Gordon Tolfree wouldn't be the only one whose name would appear in the newspapers.

7

'I thought I'd visit Winchester Magistrates' Court. See if anything interesting turns up.'

Hanging around the magistrates' court was normally only something I did when we were desperate for a story. This tended to be during the holiday season in August when nothing happened in Walden.

Elijah grunted. 'You're not that bored. What's the real reason?'

I told him about Sunday lunch with the Baverstocks.

'Go on then. Have a nose around, though I'm sure the police don't seriously think young Freddie would react violently to being turned down for a date.'

I took the train to Winchester and walked along the high street, lingering close to the *Hampshire Chronicle's* offices. I spotted Kevin coming out at lunchtime and was pleased to see he was alone.

He smiled when he saw me and ran a hand through his slicked-back blond hair.

'That was a cracking picture Robbie took of you and the prince. My editor pinned it up on the board and told Terry, our photographer, that's what he should have got. If Robbie needs any work, the *Chronicle* can always use him.'

I cringed at the thought of being pinned to a board and hoped it wouldn't be long before that particular edition of *The Walden Herald* was only of interest as a fish and chip wrapper.

Kevin lit a cigarette. 'What are you doing back here? No princes today unless you count me.'

'Elijah sent me to hang around the magistrates' court.' I pulled a face.

'That desperate, eh? Not much going in on Walden?'

'We're mainly concentrating on the election. Gordon Tolfree's decision to stand has caused a bit of a stir. Apart from that, the only excitement is the school choir's forthcoming carol concert.' I fell into step with him. 'Thanks for the piece you wrote about Percy's talk. His mother was delighted.'

Kevin grinned. 'I enjoyed meeting the Baverstocks. And Daniel Timpson. Or should I say Lord Timpson. He seemed like a nice bloke. You said you were going to tell me more about the Timpsons and Gordon Tolfree.'

I'd been prepared for this. 'Let's get a cup of tea and a sandwich.'

We went to The Old Rectory Café, bagging a table by the window this time. When Florrie, the red-haired waitress who'd served us before, brought over our tea and sandwiches, she gave me a sidelong glance.

'Thanks, Florrie.' Kevin smiled as she placed a plate in front of him. 'This looks just the job.'

'I added some of that mustard you like.'

'You make the best sandwiches in Winchester,' he replied with a wink.

I concentrated on my ham sandwich, trying to ignore their flirtation. The sandwich was very good, freshly baked bread stuffed with a thick slice of roasted ham and a dash of Colman's mustard.

When Florrie moved on to another table, Kevin began to question me about the Timpsons.

'The way Tolfree tells it, his father was ripped off by Constance Timpson. She slandered Redvers Tolfree so she could take over his business.'

'Not true. Redvers was the one doing the ripping off.'

I told him how Redvers had been stealing money from the company by falsifying invoices. It was a story that had been over-shadowed at the time by the discovery of a young woman's body at Carnival Bridge near Crookham. The victim had been an employee of Timpson Foods, and it was suspected her murder was an attempt to sabotage Constance and Mrs Siddons' plans for reform.

'Gordon Tolfree likes telling reporters his old man was set up.' Kevin demolished his sandwich and poured a second cup of tea.

'If that were true, why didn't Gordon take legal action against Constance Timpson?'

'Yeah. His story has too many holes in it. That's why nothing's ever made it into print. Whenever one of us asks what proof he has, he clams up.'

'Because anything he says will incriminate his father even more. If it had come to court, I've no doubt Redvers Tolfree would have been found guilty. Mrs Siddons and I helped Constance uncover the embezzlement, so Gordon blamed the three of us for the loss of the family's business and his father's death. In truth, Redvers Tolfree was entirely to blame for his own downfall.'

'Gordon's a bitter man. I think he knows he doesn't stand a

chance in the election – he's just hoping he can oust Mrs Siddons from her seat.'

'He won't succeed,' I said with a certainty I didn't feel. 'Who are you interested in? The Timpsons or Tolfree?'

'Tolfree. I keep hearing rumours that his business isn't what it seems to be. But when I ask around, no one has a word to say against him. As far as I can make out, he's exactly what he claims to be: a successful businessman who uses his wealth to help war veterans who've hit hard times.'

'Did Gordon serve? Redvers Tolfree once showed me the OBE he'd received from the king for his war work. He turned the company's tin-making operations into munitions factories and switched to making army biscuits to send to soldiers overseas. I don't remember him mentioning his son.'

'Gordon was in the infantry. A second lieutenant. Nothing remarkable about his war service. It seems he chose at an early age not to enter the family business. He loved cars and set up Tolfree Motors instead. I've met him a few times and he seems like a decent bloke. What do people in Walden say about him?'

I pondered on this. 'On the whole, he's well regarded. After his father died, he inherited Sycamore Lodge and he lives there with his wife and children. And his mother. It's big house, not far from St Martha's Church, and the family are regular churchgoers. His wife, Jennifer, is a member of Walden Women's Group – they help poor families in the district.'

'All respectable and unremarkable,' Kevin commented.

'That about sums it up. Apart from the accusations made against his father, I haven't heard of any other scandals.' I decided it was time to press him on the subject of Rachel Lacey. 'Unless you count the recent suspicious death of one of his employees. Have you found out anything more about what happened in Christmas Close?'

'The police aren't saying. Rachel Lacey's body is still at the hospital mortuary, being examined. Her sister confirmed it's her.'

I wondered why Harry was so convinced Gordon Tolfree was involved when there was no evidence to suggest this.

'How old was Rachel?'

'Twenty-seven.'

'Who found her and when?'

'Jack Archer, the caretaker, arrived at the hall at around three-fifteen. Rehearsals weren't due to start until five, but he knew Mrs Durling had arranged to meet Rachel there earlier to go over their lines. Rachel was wearing one of her costumes when she died.'

I choked on my tea. 'A pantomime costume?'

'Her ball gown, apparently.'

'How did you find that out?'

'Jack Archer told Mrs Durling. He came round to ask her to go to the hall this afternoon to help clean up. The police left the place in a mess.'

'Is the pantomime still going ahead?'

'I think so. Though some of the cast might be a bit reluctant under the circumstances.'

'I expect they've all been interviewed by the police,' I said, thinking of Freddie.

'Only the male ones, from what I've heard. Have they paid Freddie Baverstock a visit?'

Reluctantly, I nodded. 'His brother's worried about him. Apparently, Freddie once asked Rachel if she'd like to go to the cinema with him and she turned him down.'

He laughed. 'I'm sure they won't read anything into that. If I went around murdering every woman who's turned me down...' He flushed, clearly remembering he'd asked me out on a number of occasions. I also saw him glance over to where Florrie was standing.

At that, Kevin decided it was time he got back to the office, so we paid the bill and left.

Instead of heading to the magistrates' court, I walked to the cathedral and along to St Swithun Street. If Bridget Durling was going to be at the hall that afternoon, I might be able to have a nose around inside.

When I reached Christmas Close, I noticed again how easily you could walk past it without realising it was there. High stone walls hid it from view of the old cottages that lined St Swithun Street.

The only reason to enter Christmas Close was to visit Christmas Hall, which could only be seen once you'd turned into the close and walked a few yards along the cobblestones. Even then, you could just see the roof. From a distance, the entrance to the hall was hidden by a thick hedge of holly.

I walked up the path to the spot where Rachel would have stood smoking, shielded from the worst of the weather by the wooden porch and dense hedge. You wouldn't have been able to see her until you turned into the pathway.

'Hello,' I called as I went inside, my footsteps echoing on the wooden floorboards. Chairs were stacked in one corner, and the stage was empty.

Bridget Durling emerged from a door at the rear of the hall wearing a pink apron over her dress. A mauve scarf covered her hair and she carried a bucket and mop.

'Hello again. What brings you back this way?'

'I came to see how you are. Kevin mentioned you'd be here.'

'That's kind.' She left the bucket and mop by the stage and gestured for me to come over. 'Let's go into the back. It's warmer.'

I followed her through the door into a narrow hallway with

rooms leading off either side. The floor was damp and the smell of carbolic soap hung in the air.

'These are the dressing rooms.' She pointed to a door on her left. 'The gentlemen use that one. It's where the clerics change into their robes when there's a service being held in the hall. Further down is the office, and there are toilets at the back.' She swung open a white-painted door and gestured to a pair of wooden chairs. 'We use this as the ladies' dressing room because it's the biggest and we have the most costumes. Come and have a sit-down.'

I had to push past a long clothes rail crammed with brightly coloured garments to get to the chairs. They were positioned by a makeshift dressing table that looked like it had once been a desk.

'As you can see, we don't have much space. Good job it's only a small cast. I'd offer you a cup of tea, but Jack's very strict about when we can use the gas ring in the office.'

'That's alright. I just had lunch with Kevin in the café.'

She smiled. 'He's a lovely lad. Never a moment's trouble. Are you courting?'

'Nothing like that. We're in the same line of business. I work for *The Walden Herald.*'

'Oh yes. He mentioned that. You're the first female reporter I've ever come across.' She eyed me shrewdly. 'Are you here about Rachel's death?'

'And the pantomime. Our local vicar, Reverend Childs, is involved with Winchester Cathedral's Great War Fund, and my editor offered his support.' It was true that the vicar was helping with the war fund, although I wasn't sure Elijah would necessarily want an article about his work.

That mollified her a little. 'I've met Reverend Childs. A nice man.'

'I'm interested in Rachel's death, too,' I admitted. 'Freddie

Baverstock's brother, Percy, is a close friend of mine. We're concerned about Freddie.'

She made a tsking sound. 'The police seem to think one of the gentlemen in the pantomime could be responsible for Rachel's death. If that's the case, it's not Freddie. He's a sweet lad, and he had a soft spot for her. But then most of the fellas did.'

My eyes strayed to the rail of garish costumes and a thought occurred to me. 'Kevin said Rachel was found in her ball gown.'

'That's right.'

'Does that mean she was due to rehearse her scenes with the prince that evening?'

Mrs Durling smiled. 'She'd rehearse with whoever showed up. Rachel was in nearly every scene and could have put on any of her costumes, but the ball gown was her favourite. She looked beautiful in it, and she knew it. She rather liked male attention, if you know what I mean. She sometimes struck me as a bit lonely.'

'Anyone's attention in particular?' The only male members of the cast I'd heard about were Gordon Tolfree, Victoria's brother, Oliver, and Freddie.

'There was a chap she liked. Not in the cast. He worked on the set.' She lowered her voice. 'He's married.'

My heart sank. Victoria Hobbs had said at Sunday lunch that Harry and Freddie had built the sets.

'You think something might have been going on?' I asked.

Mrs Durling shrugged. 'I'm not sure. He seems such a nice man. Devoted to his wife. But... I kept seeing them whispering together.'

'You suspected they were having an affair?'

She nodded. 'I once overheard them chatting outside and Rachel said, "You don't want Victoria to find out, do you?"'

8

'Was Rachel the type to get involved with a married man?' I pictured Harry and his jovial laugh. He'd struck me as warm and kind-hearted – qualities that would have made him attractive to a lonely girl.

'I'd have said only if he was very rich. And this chap isn't. As I say, I'm not sure.' Bridget Durling stood up. 'I'll show you some of the sets. They're the best we've ever had.'

I got the feeling Mrs Durling was regretting mentioning what she'd overheard. If the police knew, they'd certainly want to interview Harry. And with his changeable moods, I wondered how he'd stand up to their questioning.

We went out to the hall, and Mrs Durling guided me to the canvas backdrops behind the stage. The artistry was astonishing, particularly the depiction of the ballroom, which dazzled with bursts of light from chandeliers glistening on the dance floor.

'Who painted these?' I asked.

'Freddie.'

'I had no idea he was so talented. They're wonderful. I can't wait to see the pantomime. I only wish I could have seen Rachel in her beautiful ball gown.' I experienced a wave of sympathy for this young woman I'd never met. I knew what it was like to feel lonely – and to form relationships that might be considered inappropriate.

Mrs Durling touched my arm. 'I wish you could have seen her too. It's going to be difficult to carry on with someone else in the role.'

We walked out to the front porch together.

'Have you found someone to replace her?' I pitied anyone taking on the role in such tragic circumstances.

'Mr Tolfree said he'll sort it out.' Mrs Durling sighed. 'It may seem callous but the pantomime always raises a lot of money, so we can't afford to cancel at this stage. A mention in your newspaper would help us to sell more tickets over your way.'

'I'll see what I can do. I need my editor to approve the article first.' I turned to go down the path when a gaunt man in a bowler hat and shabby overcoat appeared coming the other way. The man walked slowly, and the smell of alcohol and cigarettes reached me before he did.

'You here already? I'll go and put the fire on,' he said to Mrs Durling.

I hadn't seen or heard his approach and realised that it wasn't only the entrance to the hall that was hidden from view. If you were standing under the porch, you couldn't see anything beyond the end of the path. An attacker could easily have taken Rachel by surprise.

'That's Jack Archer, our caretaker and stagehand,' Bridget said when he was out of earshot. 'He's supposed to be the only one with keys to the hall, but he's not always around.'

A thought occurred to me. 'How did Rachel get in that afternoon?'

'We keep a spare key under the plant pot by the back door. It's how I got in today. Jack turns a blind eye because otherwise it would mean him vacating his spot at the bar of the Perseverance Inn to come and let people in. He's usually first in the pub when it opens.' She looked pointedly at her watch. 'And he stays there until it closes at three.'

'Kevin told me that Jack found the body?'

'Lying right under the porch. Rachel used to come out here to smoke. Jack doesn't like anyone smoking inside, what with all the scenery. Most of it's highly flammable. He's always going on about fire hazards in theatres. We keep telling him this isn't a theatre, though I suppose he's got a point.'

'Did Rachel have any injuries?'

'Not that Jack could see. She was just lying on the ground, looking strange, so he ran to the cathedral to use the phone in the vestry. Then he came back to wait for the ambulance at the entrance to the close. It's easy to miss unless you know the roads around here.' She glanced down at the flagstones and gave a shudder. 'He only realised she was dead when the medics started to examine her. He said it was like she'd just keeled over. Her cigarette and lighter were on the ground by her body and her clothes and handbag were in the ladies' dressing room. The police have taken them away. They'll probably give them to her sister.'

'Rachel was planning to leave Winchester, wasn't she?'

'That's right. She'd handed in her notice at work and at Crows' Nest.'

'Crows' Nest?'

'She lived with Mark and Tilly Crow. They run a boarding house called Crows' Nest on Upper Brook Street.'

'Where was she planning to go?'

'I'm not sure. I think she was going to try to find work as an actress in London. Her mother was on the stage, and Rachel wanted to follow in her footsteps.'

'Was she any good?'

'Not bad,' Bridget conceded. 'Probably the best of the cast, although she did have trouble remembering her lines. That's why I said I'd help her. If she was word perfect, I think she would have given a lovely performance. Poor girl. She could melt your heart with those big blue eyes of hers.'

With this sad image in my head, I said goodbye to Mrs Durling and strolled back into town.

What I'd learnt about Harry Hobbs disturbed me. Had he and Rachel Lacey been having an affair? I remembered how uncomfortable Victoria looked when Harry called Rachel a lovely girl. Had she suspected what was going on?

From what Percy had said, Harry would have been in Winchester on the afternoon of her death, collecting furniture from his flat to take to the new house in Crookham. If he'd known Rachel was at the hall, he could have gone there to talk to her, perhaps worried about what she might say to Victoria. Could they have had an argument that got out of hand? I pictured Harry towering over a frightened Cinderella. It was an unsettling thought.

Yet Harry was convinced Gordon Tolfree was involved in Rachel's death. Could he be trying to shift the blame?

I wondered if I dare risk a visit to Tolfree Motors before I caught the train home. It was on City Road, not far from Winchester railway station. But if I wasn't careful, I could end up face to face with Gordon Tolfree.

I decided to proceed with caution and hang around outside before I ventured in. As it turned out, this proved to be a wise move.

I was able to hide behind a sign propped up by the door, announcing:

1924 Wolseley just in. Your car taken in part exchange.

and peeked through the showroom window.

Superintendent Cobbe and his sergeant were talking to a man in a dark suit, seated behind a desk. I walked over to a row of cars and hid behind the one furthest from the building.

I'd been chastised on too many occasions by the superintendent for involving myself in matters that he considered to be none of my business. Lurking around Tolfree Motors after one of their employees had been murdered was hardly going to endear me to him any further.

When I heard the tingling of the bell ring as the door opened, I knelt behind a Vauxhall tourer pretending to examine the tyres. I stayed out of sight until the superintendent and his sergeant had driven away.

When I was fairly certain the only person left inside was the tall man at the desk, I ventured in. He glanced up at the sound of the bell and rose to his feet.

'Can I help you?' he asked in a deep voice. 'I'm Oliver Miller, the manager.'

I detected a slight resemblance to his sister, Victoria, in the delicate arch of his brows and the deep brown eyes, which were scrutinising me warily as if deciding whether I was a legitimate customer or not.

'I thought you must be. I met your sister the other day at Sunday lunch with the Baverstocks. She mentioned you worked here.'

His expression relaxed. 'Oh yes, they're friends of Harry's, aren't they? What can I do for you? Are you looking for a new or used car?'

I decided to stick to the truth as much as possible. 'I'm Iris Woodmore. I'm a reporter for *The Walden Herald*.'

His face hardened, and his wariness returned. 'If you want to know about Miss Lacey's death, I can't help you.'

I shook my head. 'It's Mr Tolfree I'm interested in.'

His eyes narrowed. 'What about him?'

I feigned surprise. 'He's standing to become the next MP for Aldershot. I thought it had been announced.'

'Oh, that. Yes, of course.'

The relief in his voice made me wonder what he'd expected me to say.

'I'm writing profiles on each of the candidates for the newspaper. Their background and what they think they can offer local people.'

'I'm afraid Mr Tolfree's not here right now.'

'That's okay. I'm sure I'll be able to arrange a meeting with him in Walden. I was on my way to the railway station and thought I might as well pop in and learn a little about his company for the article. Where do your cars come from?'

'All over the place. People bring us used cars, and we buy new models from Fitzherbert's Motors in London. We stock some of the most popular makes, like the new Wolseley, but the specialist cars we buy to order.' He glanced at his watch and gestured to an empty desk close to the door. 'I can't speak for long. We're recruiting for a new receptionist.'

'That was quick.' The words came out before I could stop them.

'It was arranged before Miss Lacey's tragic, er... death. I don't want you to think me callous. Miss Lacey had given us notice to leave her position here.' His eyes moved to peer over my shoulder, and I saw his expression change. 'Ah, you're in luck. Here's Mr Tolfree now.'

I swung around, wondering if there was any way to escape before he joined us. There wasn't. I'd have to brazen it out.

Gordon Tolfree was a more attractive version of his father. Redvers had looked a little like the king, with greying hair and a neatly trimmed beard. At only thirty-five, Gordon's hair and beard were still a rich chestnut colour, and he had a muscular physique under his well-cut suit.

His expression soured as soon as he saw me. 'Iris Woodmore.'

Oliver Miller's eyebrows lifted in surprise at the harshness of his boss's tone.

'Good afternoon, Mr Tolfree.' I tried for a pleasant smile.

'What are you doing here?'

'I heard you were standing in the election. I'd like to interview you for *The Walden Herald*.'

'Then make an appointment with my...' He trailed off as his gaze fell on the vacant receptionist's desk. 'Oh, go to hell.'

He stormed past us and went into the back office, slamming the door behind him.

Oliver Miller's surprise had turned to shock. 'I'm terribly sorry – he's not usually like that. Miss Lacey's death has clearly upset him.'

I smiled. 'I'm the one who's upset him. He didn't like some of the things I wrote about his father.'

Comprehension flooded Oliver's face, and he nodded. 'Ah yes, the late disgraced Redvers Tolfree. It is a sore point with Gordon. When he gets onto the subject, it's best to agree with whatever he says, even when...' He glanced over his shoulder to make sure the door was still closed. 'Even when it's obviously complete nonsense.'

'Is he a difficult man to work for?'

Oliver sighed, seeming to relax a little. Gordon's outburst had broken the ice between us. 'I don't have too many problems with him, but if he takes a dislike to someone, he can be...' He grinned. 'Well, I'm sure you know what he can be like.'

'I certainly do. How did he get on with Rachel Lacey?'

He shrugged. 'One minute she was the golden girl, then the next it was like she didn't exist.'

'That must have been difficult for her.'

'She'd had enough of it here. She said there was nothing left for her in Winchester and had made plans to live with her sister in London. It's terribly sad. It was going to be a fresh start.'

'Do you have any idea what happened to her?'

'None at all. The police haven't told us anything.'

'Was that Superintendent Cobbe I just saw leaving? He and I are old friends.'

'Really?' He didn't seem convinced by this.

'Was he here about Rachel?'

He hesitated. 'One of our cars went missing on the day she died.'

'Stolen from the forecourt?' I supposed it must happen on occasion.

'No. It was kept out the back. It wasn't for sale. It was an old-style Wolseley that Rachel and I used to run errands.'

'Rachel could drive?'

'Yes. She was an excellent driver. She would collect new models from Fitzherbert's for us. She'd take the train to the dealership in London and then drive the car back.'

I was curious to know more about this missing car, but when we heard a noise from inside the office, we both knew it was time for me to leave.

Without a word, I made for the door.

Oliver raised a hand in a quick farewell, then sat behind his desk, picked up his pen and pretended to be absorbed in paperwork.

9

At lunchtime the following day, I decided to keep my promise to Percy and see how Freddie was getting on. I also wanted to meet Harry again.

My mother's grave was tucked away in a quiet corner of the churchyard of St Martha's, close to an ancient yew tree, and I managed to buy some late roses from the greengrocers to take to her. When I got there, I found a fresh sprig of flowers had recently been placed against her headstone – hothouse lilies tied with green and white ribbon – the colours of the suffragettes. Her old comrades hadn't forgotten the sacrifice she'd made.

I picked them up and sniffed their pungent scent before placing them back on the grave alongside my winter roses.

I could see Harry and Freddie sitting on an old wooden bench eating their lunch. Both wore heavy leather boots, black corduroy trousers, and thick woollen khaki army jumpers. When I walked over to them, they shuffled up to offer me a seat.

They'd finished their sandwiches, and I brought out a tin of cake from my bag.

'Did you make it yourself?' Freddie asked, taking a piece.

'Baking is not one of my skills. It's from Millicent.'

Harry looked over to where I'd placed the flowers. 'Is that where your mother's buried? Freddie tells me you were only young when you lost her.'

I nodded. 'I was fourteen.'

'How did she die?'

I didn't reply immediately. It was a difficult question to answer, and I was surprised Harry had asked. He seemed to be in a reflective mood.

Freddie intervened. 'She died fighting for what she believed in.'

I had to smile at the conviction in his voice. He could be very like Percy at times.

'She was a suffragette,' I said to a mystified Harry. 'Some of her activities were dangerous.'

'Ah,' he said, as if this required no further explanation and held out a calloused hand for a slice of cake. 'Seeing you with those roses reminded me of Rachel. Whenever she used to go up to London to pick up a car, she'd buy flowers and stop off at the cemetery on her way back to visit her parents' grave. Her dad died when she was seventeen and her mum a couple of years later.'

'How sad. That must have been hard for her.'

'We were at war by then, so she joined the Women's Army Auxiliary Corps and ended up in Winchester. If things had been different and she'd stayed in London, she might have been a famous actress by now.'

I wondered if that was something Rachel had said to him. 'It sounds like you were fond of her.'

Harry nodded morosely, then stared at the ground. Guessing he wasn't going to offer much more, I asked Freddie to show me his motorbike. Parked next to it was a van with the words *Hobbs*

Stonemason painted on the side. I was sure it hadn't gone unnoticed by Superintendent Cobbe that both Freddie and Harry had the means to get between Walden and Winchester relatively quickly.

Freddie sprung to his feet, as if eager to put some distance between himself and Harry. He proudly showed me his gleaming green and black Triumph motorbike.

'I painted it myself.'

'You're a dab hand with a brush. I saw the pantomime sets yesterday. They're wonderful.'

Harry, who'd been gazing unseeingly down at his shoes, looked up at this. 'You went to Christmas Hall?'

'My editor wants me to write a profile on Gordon Tolfree now he's standing in the election. I needed more information on his charity work and involvement in the pantomime.' This wasn't strictly true. 'As Reverend Childs is involved with the war fund, we're going to publicise the event. I'll mention the whole cast and crew. Your mother will love it.'

Freddie groaned and slumped onto the bench. 'Oh God. Why did I ever say I'd do it?'

Harry squeezed his shoulder. 'Because you fancied Rachel, that's why.'

'And where did that get me? A trip to Winchester police station.'

'Idiots are looking in the wrong place,' Harry growled. 'They should come here to Walden.'

I remained standing by Freddie's motorbike so I could watch Harry's face. 'Here? Why?'

'Tolfree.' He pointed in the direction of Sycamore Lodge, the Tolfree family home.

'Why are you so convinced he had something to do with Rachel's death?' I asked.

'Because she was scared of him.'

Freddie blinked in disbelief. 'When did she tell you that?'

Harry turned away and began stuffing their sandwich wrappings into a tin lunchbox. 'Must have been one evening in the Blackbird Bar,' he mumbled. 'I can't remember when.'

'Is that where you and Victoria went to hear Rachel sing?' It was an innocent enough question, although I remembered Harry saying 'I' rather than 'we' when he mentioned visiting the bar.

'Victoria doesn't like going there. She thinks it's too dark and dingy and she's not much of a drinker. I used to go along and have a laugh with Rachel sometimes.' Harry's sheepish expression told me he knew he shouldn't have allowed himself to become so close to the young woman. 'It wasn't often. Victoria nags me if I go out too much. We need all our money for the new house.'

'Why was Rachel scared of Gordon? Had he threatened her?'

But my questions were in vain. Harry stood up. 'We have to get back to work. You'll get your story one of these days.'

With that, he walked away.

Freddie sighed in frustration and gave me an apologetic shrug.

Harry suddenly turned and called over his shoulder, 'You're in the wrong place. You should be poking around down there at Sycamore Lodge, not here.'

I hesitated. The only places I ever visited on Church Road were St Martha's and Elijah's cottage, which were both at the top end of the lane closest to the town. The only reason to venture further down the road was to call at Sycamore Lodge, and I knew I wouldn't be welcome there.

I left the churchyard and leant against the gate of Yew Tree Cottage, the home Elijah had bought in 1895 to use as a weekend retreat. At that time, he was living in London, working for *The*

Daily Telegraph, but he tried to escape from the city whenever he could. When he was sent on an overseas assignment in 1898, he'd rented the cottage to my newly married parents, and I was born there a year later. When we moved to London in 1913, Elijah came back to live in the house.

Aware Harry was goading me into investigating Gordon Tolfree, I decided to take him at his word. Sycamore Lodge was reached by a private track that started where Church Road ended, and I headed in that direction.

All was quiet, as there were no other houses this far down, only woodland on either side. I stopped at the entrance to the gravel track that led to the Tolfree family home, hearing the rustle of fallen leaves nearby. It sounded like someone was striding through them.

Even though there was no one in sight, I decided not to walk directly along the track. Maybe it was my nerves playing tricks on me, but I couldn't shake the feeling I was being watched.

I didn't want to risk another encounter with Gordon Tolfree, especially not when I was trespassing on his private land. He'd probably accuse me of snooping – and he'd be right. The only reason to take this route was to get to his house and he'd see through any excuse I made about dropping in on him. I wasn't exactly on his Christmas card list.

Instead, I made my way through the conifer trees that lined the track, enjoying the clean, pine-scented air. When I heard the rustling again, I stopped and glanced around. I couldn't see any movement and told myself it was probably a squirrel or a fox. Or maybe even a deer. There were plenty hiding in these woodlands.

In the distance, I could see Sycamore Lodge, a large, colonial-looking house built by Isaac Tolfree in 1860, when Tolfree Biscuits had been in its heyday. The lodge was designed to impress, with sweeping steps leading up to a pair of tall oak doors flanked by white stone columns. Two rows of symmetrical windows sat in white-painted walls beneath a red-tiled roof.

I saw someone moving about in one of the upper rooms and slid back into the cover of the trees, wondering why I'd let Harry talk me into spying on the Tolfrees.

If I was honest, it was my curiosity to see where Gordon Tolfree lived that had brought me here. He was a private man, hardly ever coming into town, except to attend church on Sundays. His wife, Jennifer, was more outgoing, although the whole family had been somewhat reclusive since Redvers' fall from grace, and his widow was rarely seen.

By standing in the election, Gordon had clearly decided it was time to enter public life once more. And judging by the expensive Rolls-Royce on his extensive driveway, he had the money to do it in style.

Having satisfied my curiosity, I was about to turn back when I spotted something glinting in the shadow of the pine trees. A large dark shape stood out against the forest of greens and browns.

Only when I got closer could I see that it was a motor car, positioned at an odd angle, as though someone had left it there in a hurry. The glass headlamps gleamed in the winter sunshine.

I glanced around, wondering why it had been parked there and not closer to the house. There was room enough on the driveway for a dozen cars.

It was a Wolseley, not a new model but in good condition. Hadn't that been the make of car Oliver Miller had said was missing from Tolfree Motors?

I peered inside but there was nothing on any of the seats. When I tried the door, it opened, and I noticed that the key was still in the ignition. Could whoever had left it there still be around?

Feeling a shiver of unease, I slid into the driver's seat and looked for anything that would indicate who the car belonged to. On the passenger side, there was a small glovebox, and I leant over to pull it open.

At first, I thought the compartment was empty, then I saw a tiny old-fashioned snuff box tucked into a corner. I took it out and pressed the catch to release the lid, expecting it to contain tobacco. Instead, it was filled with a fine white powder.

10

'Any news from Ben?' Elijah called from his den as I hooked my overcoat on the hatstand and dumped my satchel on my desk.

My childhood friend, Ben Gilbert, had spent two years with the metropolitan police but had recently returned to his hometown of Walden as a newly promoted sergeant.

The previous afternoon, I'd made a note of the Wolseley's registration plate and gone straight to the station house to report what I'd found.

'I stopped by to see him on my way in. The car's registration matches the one Oliver Miller reported missing. Superintendent Cobbe is going to pay a visit to Tolfree Motors this morning to speak to Gordon Tolfree and Oliver Miller. The superintendent told Ben to leave the car where it was for the time being as Mr Tolfree may have forgotten that he'd driven the Wolseley home.'

'With a tin of suspicious white powder in the glove compartment?' Elijah grinned. 'I presume Cobbe won't be returning that to Mr Tolfree?'

'It's been sent to a laboratory for testing.'

'Cocaine is my bet.'

I nodded. 'That's what Ben said. But why would Gordon Tolfree leave the car so close to his home with drugs in it and then tell the police it had been stolen?'

Elijah grunted. 'I need some coffee before I can unravel that one.'

I took the hint and went over to the gas ring to heat some water. Elijah didn't move from his chair, and our conversation continued at a louder volume.

'It's not looking good for our independent candidate, is it?' Elijah shouted. 'If he was trying to avoid a scandal, he's gone a strange way about it. Will Cobbe tell him it was you who found the car?'

'I'm not sure,' I called back. 'Why?'

'Because it's not going to improve relations with him, is it? He'll see it as another example of you attempting to incriminate his family. I might pay a visit to Mr Tolfree myself.'

'What for?'

'Because we need to cover his election campaign, and he'll respond better to me than to you.'

It was true. Gordon's animosity tended to be directed at me, even though Elijah was the editor and decided what went into the paper.

'If he wants to win this election, he's going to need to curry favour with local newspapers.' Elijah stopped, hearing footsteps on the stairs. We weren't expecting any visitors. 'Of course, he might come to us.'

'It's probably Robbie.' My eyes fixed on the door as it opened. If it was Gordon Tolfree, I hoped he hadn't overheard our conversation as he was coming up the stairs. I could do without another confrontation with him so soon after the last one.

A head poked around the door and sniffed the air. 'Coffee and cigarettes. The fuel of a dynamic newspaper editor.'

Elijah beamed at the sight of the familiar floppy fringe and lively brown eyes. 'Mr Baverstock! To what do we owe the pleasure?'

Percy bounded into the office. 'Do I need a reason to visit my favourite nosy parkers? I mean investigative journalists.'

I placed an extra cup on the tray and took the coffee through to Elijah's den. 'Shouldn't you be at work?'

'Yes.' Percy ignored the coffee, accepting Elijah's offer of a cigarette and a stiff drink.

Elijah got to his feet, fishing around in the filing cabinet for his not-so-secret bottle of whisky. Typical that he could rouse himself from his chair to fetch liquor for a guest but would wait for hours for me to arrive to brew the coffee.

Elijah raised the bottle towards me, and I shook my head. Eleven o'clock in the morning was far too early for whisky in my opinion.

'Why are you in Walden and not London?' I dropped into the chair beside Percy. It was rare for him to turn up in the office unannounced, and I assumed this was a social call as he was in casual flannels rather than a suit.

'It's about Harry. The police have taken him in for questioning.'

'Why?' I asked, though I could guess the answer.

'I don't know. I was hoping you might have heard something.'

Reluctantly, I told him. 'Someone I spoke to seemed to think Rachel was seeing a married man.'

'It wasn't Harry,' Percy snapped.

'The lady who's playing the fairy godmother kept seeing them whispering together at Christmas Hall. She once overhead them chatting outside and Rachel said, "You don't want Victoria to find out, do you?" Is it possible they were having an affair?'

'No. Absolutely not. You saw him with Victoria. They love each other.'

Although I believed that was true, there'd also been tension between the couple, particularly when they were discussing their move to Walden.

'What does Freddie think?' I thought of the exasperated look he'd given Harry the previous day.

'He doesn't think anything is going on. Well, he does, but not like that. At least, I don't think so. I'm—'

Elijah held up his hand. 'Stop waffling. What was the nature of Harry's relationship with Rachel Lacey?'

Percy hesitated, picked up his whisky, then put it down again. 'Harry's found it difficult to settle since the war. Victoria tries to keep him on the straight and narrow, but, well, he likes to let his hair down sometimes. Freddie says Harry used to drink with Rachel at the bar where she sang, and Victoria would get annoyed as they need all their money for the new house. Rachel probably just meant he wouldn't want Victoria to find out they'd been drinking together.'

'Mrs Durling thought Rachel had taken a liking to Harry. She intimated the relationship was closer than...' I searched for an appropriate word. 'Than was seemly.' I cringed at how prim that sounded.

Percy scoffed. 'Lots of women hold a soft spot for Harry – always have. He's a great bloke. It was like that during the war. All the nurses used to run around him – there was nothing in it. I told Freddie that.'

Elijah and I exchanged a sceptical glance. It was evident Freddie suspected there had been more to the relationship than Harry was saying.

'Where was Harry when she died?' Elijah asked, getting straight to the point.

'In Winchester,' Percy admitted. 'He and his wife have bought a house on the estate at Crookham. Harry's been moving their furniture in his work van. He left Freddie with the tools at the church and drove back to Winchester to pick up some stuff from their flat to take to Crookham.'

Elijah sighed, evidently feeling Harry didn't have the strongest of alibis. 'What time was this?'

'He left the church at around one o'clock and didn't return until about five.'

'Jack Archer found the body at approximately three-fifteen.' It didn't need saying that Harry would have been in Winchester at that time.

Elijah turned to me. 'Do you think Cobbe's serious about him? Or is he fishing like he did with young Freddie?'

'According to Kevin Noakes, the police believe someone in the pantomime was involved with her death, although they still haven't said how she died.'

Percy's mouth sagged, and I could understand why. Neither his brother nor his best friend had a solid alibi.

If Harry had been fooling around with Rachel, he couldn't risk Victoria finding out. This gave him a credible motive to murder his lover, but...

Something else was playing on my mind. It was Harry's suggestion that had led me to the clearing at Sycamore Lodge. Had he known what I might find? Was he right to be suspicious of Gordon Tolfree?

'The person most involved with the pantomime is Tolfree,' I said. 'He's funding it, directing it, and even playing one of the ugly sisters. And now his missing car has turned up by his home with cocaine in the glovebox.'

'What?' Percy choked on his whisky. He whistled when I told

him what I'd discovered near Sycamore Lodge. 'This sounds more like it.'

Elijah frowned. 'I can't see why Tolfree would do something as foolish as this when he's standing for election. I'm going to ask Horace to see what he can find out about him. In fact, I wouldn't be surprised if he has already. Horace is backing Mrs Siddons, so he probably did some digging when Tolfree said he was standing against her.'

Horace Laffaye, owner of *The Walden Herald* and Laffaye Printworks, had an extensive network of contacts in both high and low places – and he used his considerable influence to ensure the town stayed exactly the way he liked it.

'Unless killing Rachel was the only way Gordon could avoid a scandal,' I mused.

Elijah drew on his cigarette. 'Reverend Childs introduced me to someone who sits on the committee of Winchester Cathedral's Great War Fund. This chap invited me to come and talk to him regarding their charitable work and what they do with the money they raise. Perhaps I should take up his offer. See if I can find out a bit more about Tolfree's involvement and his donations.'

'And I'll have a word with Ben. As the car turned up on his patch, he should be able to find out more about the case from Superintendent Cobbe.'

Percy looked cheered by these suggestions. 'I'm glad Ben returned to Walden. He was like a fish out of water in London.'

I smiled. 'He's back where he belongs in the station house with PC Sid King.'

'And all is right with the world.' Percy's grin faded. 'Only it's not.'

11

The more I learnt about Rachel Lacey, the curiouser I became. She'd wanted to leave Winchester to start a new life in London. Or perhaps resume her old, pre-war life. Why had someone stopped her before she could make that move? Could it have been a jealous lover?

I considered what I knew about Rachel so far. She worked at Tolfree Motors during the day and sang at the Blackbird Bar one evening a week. I wondered if she'd volunteered to take part in the pantomime to fulfil in some small way her ambition to be an actress. Or had Gordon Tolfree persuaded her to be his leading lady?

Bridget Durling said Rachel lodged at a place called Crows' Nest on Upper Brook Street. If Rachel had spent time with Harry, perhaps someone at her lodgings might have seen him walking her home.

I caught a train to Winchester and strolled along City Road, passing Tolfree Motors. Inside, Oliver Miller was standing behind a young woman seated at the reception desk near the door. It was too risky to try to talk to him again. Gordon Tolfree could be in his office, and Superintendent Cobbe might have told him about my visit to Sycamore Lodge.

I kept walking until I reached the turning for Upper Brook Street.

Crows' Nest wasn't hard to find. The name of the house was displayed on a ceramic plate by the front door above a picture of a bird's nest. In the bay window was a sign saying:

Room to Let.

I knocked, and a young woman with dark hair tied back with a red scarf answered the door.

'Can I help you?'

'I'm sorry to disturb you. My name's Iris Woodmore. I was a friend of Rachel Lacey's. Are you her landlady? I'm trying to find out her sister's address.'

The woman scrutinised my appearance and evidently decided I looked respectable enough to cross the threshold. She stood back and ushered me into the hallway. In contrast to the dated exterior of the Victorian end-of-terrace, the interior was bright and modern. The duck egg blue walls of the hallway were decorated with colourful prints and a modern long-legged table stood against the wall.

'I'm Tilly Crow. Me and my husband own this place. We rent out two rooms upstairs and the basement flat below.'

I judged Tilly to be no more than thirty years old. She had smooth pale skin with flushed cheeks and bright green eyes.

'I wanted to send my condolences to Rachel's sister. But I don't have her address.'

'You wouldn't. She's only recently moved to London after her husband passed away. She lived in France before that. Hold on a moment while I find my book. Rachel wrote it down for me.'

Tilly returned and handed me a slip of paper with the words:

Mrs Grace Evans, 3 Longbridge Court, Lewisham.

written in a neat hand.

'Thank you.' The address was in an area I was familiar with as I'd lived in nearby Hither Green during the war and my grandmother and aunt still resided there.

Tilly shoved her hands into the pocket of her apron. 'Would you do me a favour? I don't like to ask, but the thing is, Rachel owed us rent. Could you mention it in a polite way in your letter? She hadn't paid us for nearly three months and had promised to settle up before she left.'

I realised this might provide me with the excuse I needed to call on Mrs Evans. 'My grandmother and aunt live not far from this address. I'm due to pay them a visit. Under the circumstances, perhaps it would be best if I spoke to Mrs Evans rather than write. I'll mention the rent to her.'

Tilly looked relieved. 'Thank you. That's so kind of you. As you say, it's a delicate matter and best addressed in person.'

'I saw the "Room to Let" sign in the window. You're advertising for a new lodger already?' Poor Rachel was barely cold before her room was being let and someone else was seated in her chair at Tolfree Motors.

'The sign was up before... before it happened.' Tilly became defensive. 'She'd given notice.'

'Of course. Would it be possible for me to take a look at her room?'

I could tell Tilly wasn't entirely happy with my request. If I hadn't just offered to help her with the matter of the rent, I think she might have refused.

As it was, she shrugged. 'If you like. It's on the first floor.'

I followed her up the stairs, not sure why I'd asked to see the room. The police would already have searched it and taken anything of interest.

When Tilly opened the door, I was surprised to see how empty it was. A single bed was pushed against the wall and it was furnished with a bedside table, wardrobe, chest of drawers and washstand. A floral scent hung in the air and I wondered if it were the last traces of Rachel's perfume.

'Have all her things gone?'

Tilly nodded. 'I packed them up and sent them to her sister. It was the least I could do. I was going to mention the rent in my letter, but what with her only recently being widowed...' She trailed off.

'To lose her husband and then her sister. So sad, after losing their parents at such a young age,' I murmured, hoping to find out more about Rachel's early life.

Tilly nodded. 'Rachel told me she was seventeen when her dad died. He was a carpenter who worked in theatres building stage sets. Her mother was a singer, used to take part in variety hall acts. They lived in Blackheath, and her father had a car so he could drive her mother to the big theatres in Central London.'

'Rachel never told me how she ended up in Winchester. I only really knew her through the pantomime,' I said.

'She joined the Women's Army Auxiliary Corps as a driver. She thought she'd stay in London but ended up at Morn Hill. Mostly she drove officers around in staff cars, though sometimes she got to drive those big trucks loaded with troops headed for the front.'

In the autumn of 1914, a vast transit camp had been set up at Morn Hill on the outskirts of Winchester. At one time, 50,000 servicemen were camped there. By the end of the war, millions of soldiers had passed through Morn Hill camp, most only staying for a few days.

'How did she learn to drive?'

'Her dad taught her. After he died, she took his place driving her mother to work. As long as you're over seventeen, you can apply to the local council for a licence.'

I nodded, remembering the look of horror on Elijah's face when I'd waved my newly acquired driving licence at him.

'Her mum died in 1915. Got a chest infection and never recovered. By that time, her sister was nursing in a military hospital. When she got shipped over to France as part of a VAD unit, Rachel had to move out of their lodgings. She couldn't afford to stay there on her own. I believe her sister wanted her to train as a nurse too so they could stay together, but that wasn't for Rachel.'

'I got the impression she would have liked to have returned to London after the war.' From what I'd heard about Rachel, this seemed a likely assumption.

Tilly nodded. 'She always thought she would. Then her sister married an officer and settled in France and Rachel was offered a job at Tolfree Motors, so she stayed here.'

'She seemed excited at the prospect of moving away from Winchester.' I decided to see if Tilly's view of Rachel's situation concurred with Oliver Miller's. 'She said it was going to be fresh start for her and that she'd had enough of things around here. But when I asked what was wrong, she was evasive.'

Tilly put her hands on her hips. 'I got the impression she was in some sort of trouble. She wouldn't tell me what it was. Men and money, I presumed. She earned extra by singing in a bar once a week, but God knows what she did with her wages because she was always skint.'

I nodded as though I knew this. 'I thought she might have

been seeing someone, but she didn't tell me who. Did a gentleman ever walk her home?'

Tilly shook her head. 'I never saw her with anyone.' Then she lowered her voice. 'This is just between you and me. I didn't mention it to the police because I had nothing to go on, apart from a woman's instinct. But my guess is she was seeing a married man.'

'An affair?' I tried to appear shocked. 'What made you think that?'

'I've seen it before. Coming home with flowers and chocolates – all smiles. Then no more flowers or chocolates and floods of tears.' Tilly gave a world-weary sigh. 'And no more money. I think she met some unsavoury characters in that bar.'

I wasn't so sure it was her job as a singer that had brought her into contact with unsavoury characters. I remembered what Oliver Miller had said about how Gordon Tolfree treated Rachel. One minute she was the golden girl, then he'd ignored her.

If their relationship had soured, could he have wanted her out of the way? Had Rachel become an inconvenient mistress who could potentially ruin his marriage? But then the same scenario could also apply to Harry Hobbs.

12

I'd taken the early train to Waterloo and then a bus to Lewisham, where I'd arranged to meet my aunt. She'd booked us both in to have our hair cut at Dolly's Hair Salon on Lewisham high street at twelve o'clock. Afterwards, we were going to have lunch at a nearby café before I returned home with her to spend what would undoubtedly be an excruciating couple of hours with my grandmother.

My first call of the day was to Mrs Grace Evans, although as she'd been living in France until recently, I wondered how much she'd know about her sister's life in Winchester.

Longbridge Court consisted of a few detached houses on the edge of Lewisham Park. Number three stood on its own at the end of the road.

I knocked on a black front door that was opened by a slim young woman with dark hair fashionably styled into a bob like my own.

'Mrs Evans?' I asked.

'Yes. How may I help you?'

'I was a friend of Rachel's. My name's Iris Woodmore.'

She stared at me blankly.

'Mrs Crow gave me your address. She asked me to pass on a message.'

At this, the door opened a little wider, and she stood back to allow me to enter into a narrow hallway. She was wearing slacks like me, only hers were wider in the leg and of a softer, more refined fabric than my thick navy trousers.

She gestured to an open door that led into the front parlour. 'Come and sit down.'

The only furniture was a pair of faded green chintz armchairs and an occasional table. Two large black trunks had been pushed against a wall, along with numerous crates and boxes. The room was clean and warm but there was an unlived-in feel to it.

'I'm afraid I haven't had a chance to fully furnish the place yet. Or unpack.'

I took the armchair nearest the window. This gave me a clearer view of the room and the photographs displayed on the mantelpiece.

'I'm sorry to disturb you. My aunt and grandmother live in Hither Green, and as I was in the area visiting them, I wanted to call and offer my condolences.'

'That's kind of you. What did you say your name was?'

'Iris Woodmore.'

'I don't recall my sister ever mentioning you.'

'I didn't know her well. We had mutual friends. Freddie Baverstock. And Harry Hobbs.'

Her face softened. 'Harry. Yes, she mentioned him in her letters. She was very fond of him.'

So Rachel had liked Harry. Curious to see how she would react, I said, 'He might be in trouble. The police have been questioning him about Rachel's death.'

Grace's eyes narrowed in surprise. 'They haven't even told me how she died. Why do they suspect this man?'

'They seem to think Rachel may have been seeing someone. Perhaps someone associated with the pantomime she was taking part in.' I didn't want to go so far as to say Rachel might have been having an affair with a married man.

Her brow furrowed. 'I told Superintendent Cobbe everything I knew about Rachel's life, but with me living in France, we weren't as close as we'd once been. I'm sure she said Harry was married. She wrote fondly of him but not in those terms. He wasn't her boyfriend. If anything, he reminded her of our father, though of course he wasn't that old.'

'Your father?' It was my turn to be surprised.

'She said he was a craftsman, like our father. Wasn't Harry the one who built the sets for the pantomime?'

'That's right.'

'Our father was a carpenter and used to work in set design, often in the theatres where my mother performed. She was a singer and actress.'

Grace's eyes drifted to the photographs on the mantelpiece. One depicted a family group of a mother, father and two young girls of about eight. Another showed the two sisters when they were older, perhaps around eighteen, dressed in hats and gloves with smart jackets.

I peered at it, eager for a glimpse of Rachel. I was curious to see the woman I'd learnt so much about. Both girls were attractive, with large eyes and full lips. Grace seemed tenser, whereas Rachel's expression was softer.

'Rachel used to love acting,' I murmured, feeling guilty at my deception.

Grace nodded and gave a hollow laugh. 'She was very good. And I suspect that's really what made her decide to take up my offer. More opportunities here in London than in Winchester. And I have a feeling she was short of money.'

'Hmm, yes. Mrs Crow mentioned that Rachel owed three months' rent. I expect she intended to settle up before she left.'

Grace groaned. 'I'll send Mrs Crow a cheque. The Crows were good to Rachel. They sound like decent people. I'm glad she had someone who cared for her.' She suddenly looked tired and rubbed her eyes. 'I should have done more to help her. I'm the older sister by two years. I never realised... And now it's too late. God knows what kind of mess she got herself into.'

'When did you last see Rachel?'

'She came to France for my husband's funeral. That's when I told her I planned to return to England. At first, she seemed reluctant to join me in London but then she came around to the idea. She was going to finish up in Winchester at the end of the year and then come to live here.' Grace Evans stared at the unopened boxes. 'I can't even bring myself to unpack. Or sort through Rachel's things.'

'It must be difficult. Losing your husband and then your sister. Both so young.' I was curious to know how her husband had died.

'Simon was forty-seven when he passed away. He'd been ill for some time. We met when he was injured in the Somme and brought to the field hospital where I worked. I carried on nursing him after the war. It was fortunate he had private means as he wasn't able to return to his job in London. We settled in a quiet part of Nice, so he could recuperate in a warmer climate.'

If Grace were two years older than Rachel, she would be twenty-nine. That meant there had been an eighteen-year age gap between Grace and her husband. I wondered if Rachel had been attracted to older men, too.

'Did Rachel ever mention Gordon Tolfree? Harry seems to think she was afraid of him.'

'Her boss?' Grace faltered. 'Her opinion of him had changed. She'd seemed keen on him at first. But recently, I got the impression things weren't so harmonious.'

'In what way?'

'I'm not sure. Once she described him as charming, then she began to see a different side to him. I got the feeling it had something to do with Tolfree Motors.' She shrugged. 'Perhaps it was just that Rachel had grown up. She seemed more worldly the last time I talked with her. I was going to contact Mr Tolfree about her funeral but I'm not sure I want him there.'

'I think Harry Hobbs would like to attend,' I said, though I wasn't sure if Victoria would be keen to accompany him.

She nodded. 'I'll let him know when I've made the arrangements. The service will be held here in London. Rachel would want to be buried with our parents.'

Tears began to fill her eyes, and I knew it was time to leave.

I rose from my seat. 'I'm so sorry for your loss. I won't take up any more of your time.'

Grace stood up. 'I appreciate you coming to see me, Miss Woodmore. Perhaps I should speak to Superintendent Cobbe again about Harry. And Gordon Tolfree.'

I left Grace Evans's flat wincing as I imagined the superintendent's reaction should she tell him I'd been to see her.

On the high street, I waited at the bus stop for Aunt Maud to arrive, and then we strolled arm in arm to Dolly's Hair Salon.

That afternoon, I forgot about Rachel Lacey, Harry Hobbs and Gordon Tolfree and spent an enjoyable few hours with my aunt. This was followed by a visit to my grandmother, which was more a case of endurance than enjoyment, thanks to her caustic tongue.

Just before four o'clock, I kissed them both goodbye and slipped out onto Brightside Road, hoping my aunt wouldn't decide to take an evening walk. It was risky meeting Marc so close to where they lived, but he'd written to say he wanted to go back to the place where we'd first met, and I hadn't been able to resist his request.

When I turned onto Hither Green Lane, I could see he was already waiting by the gates to the Park Fever Hospital. The sight of him aroused a combination of emotions I was becoming familiar with – excitement, tinged with guilt.

Without a word, he reached for my hand and started walking through the gates.

'We can't go in,' I whispered.

'No one will notice.'

He was right. A group of nurses scurried past us, not even looking in our direction. Marc kept hold of my hand, and I knew where he was heading. He was leading me to the place where we'd shared our first kiss.

I squeezed his hand. 'I'm not eighteen any more.'

'And I'm not twenty-four, though I want to feel as if I am.'

When war was declared only months after my mother's death, my father had sent me to stay with his parents in Exeter in Devon. My grandmother had been a volunteer at a refugee centre in Exeter, and it was there I'd had my first experience of helping to organise accommodation for the thousands of Belgian refugees arriving in Britain after Germany's occupation of their country.

When I reached seventeen, and there was no sign of the war ending, I insisted on returning to my home on Hither Green Lane. I joined a Voluntary Aid Detachment, and my first VAD post had been at the nearby Park Fever Hospital, which had been given over to housing Belgian refugees.

Marc Jansen had arrived at the hospital in June 1917. He'd been in the Resistance and escaped from Belgium to come in search of his family, who'd travelled to Britain at the start of the war. He knew they'd been put on a train to Devon, and with the help of my grandmother, I'd been able to reunite him with his wife and parents.

That should have been all there was to it. But during his time at the hospital, we became close. Too close.

I'd just turned eighteen and was still grieving the loss of my mother. Overwhelmed by the trauma I witnessed every day, I'd often go and hide in the water tower of the hospital for a few moments of respite. One evening, Marc found me there.

At first, we simply exchanged our stories. Then, unable to resist, we began to exchange kisses. We both knew it was wrong. Marc had told me from the start he was married, yet despite this, our meetings in the tower became more frequent.

Glancing around to check no one was watching, Marc pulled open the heavy oak door, and we hurried inside, laughing at the childishness of what we were doing.

When the door closed behind us, it shut out the noise and bustle of the London streets and suddenly everything was still. It was the first time Marc and I had been cloistered together in six years, and I had the urge to pull him towards me as I'd once done. Instead, we both took a step back, reluctant to repeat the mistakes of the past.

'I wish things were different,' he murmured.

How many times had he said those words since we'd been reunited? When Marc had left the hospital to travel to Devon to see his family before joining the Belgian Army, I'd never expected to see him again. I had no idea he and his wife had made their home in Exeter after the war.

I turned away from the intensity of his gaze. 'I thought things were different. But we seem to have gone back in time.'

The old brick tower was just the same as it had been six years ago. And so were my feelings for Marc. What had drawn me to him then was his strength and self-possession. I'd found his soulful brown eyes reassuring at a time when I was a troubled young woman in a chaotic world.

I'd soon come to realise he was tired of being the strong one. He'd only just finished his law degree when the Germans had invaded. In an attempt to keep his loved ones safe, he'd married his childhood sweetheart, Annette, in a rushed ceremony before helping her and his parents escape from their war-torn country.

'Do you regret meeting me again?' I asked, his familiar scent filling the narrow confines of the water tower.

'No,' he said softly. 'I know I should, but it would be a lie. I'd felt for so long that something was missing from my life. When I saw you again on the beach at Smugglers' Haunt, I knew what it was.'

I'd felt the same. After that meeting in July, when he'd told me of his plans to move to London to start a new job, he'd asked if we could meet occasionally. I'd agreed, and when his first letter had arrived, I'd found myself looking forward to seeing him with far too much longing.

At first, we'd just walked around Hyde Park, talking about our lives and families. But, like in the summer of 1917, our conversations had grown more intimate. We trusted each other and shared confidences without fear of being judged. Yet there was one subject we always avoided – and that was our relationship.

I asked the inevitable question. 'How's Annette?'

With no family of her own, Annette was totally dependent on Marc. She'd been only twenty when they married and she'd fled to Britain under the protection of his parents. Nearly ten years after their hasty wedding, Marc admitted both of them often wondered what course their lives might have taken if war hadn't ripped their country apart. Although they still loved each other, they felt their childhood romance may not have led to marriage if circumstances had been different.

'She's finding it difficult to adjust to city life. She wants to go back to Belgium to be with my parents, and they'd like that too.' He raised his hands in a helpless gesture. 'If it would make everyone happy, perhaps that's what I should do.'

'What about your job?'

Marc had become a partner in a law firm in Holborn and loved his work. When I wrote to him, I used this address.

'I don't know. I keep asking her to give it more time.' He rested his head on my shoulder. 'But does time really change anything?'

13

'What's wrong?'

I turned to find Sergeant Ben Gilbert walking along the high street behind me, wheeling his bicycle by his side. His jacket was buttoned up to his collar and his hat was pulled low over his eyes.

I'd wrapped myself in a thick claret-coloured scarf and added a matching knitted beret to protect my bobbed hair from the effects of the damp November air. 'Why should anything be wrong?' I muttered through layers of wool.

'I know the way you walk. Usually, you have your head up and stride along as though there's too much to do and not enough time. This morning, you're trudging along as if every step is an effort. You're unhappy, aren't you?'

I didn't bother to deny it. We'd shared too much sorrow to pretend to each other.

'Do you ever feel something is missing from your life?' As soon as the words left my mouth, I regretted them. 'Sorry, that was a stupid thing to say.'

'I know something is missing from my life. Something I'll

never get back.' He was referring to Alice Thackeray, our dear friend, whose death had broken both our hearts. 'We can talk about her, you know.'

'Sometimes I feel guilty,' I said. 'She didn't get to experience all the things I take for granted. And yet I still want more.'

We turned down Queens Road, and he leant his bicycle against the wall of Laffaye Printworks. The odour of ink and printing chemicals rose up through the grate in the pavement and hung in the morning fog.

'When I was in hospital, I met a nurse I liked. I've spoken to her a few times since I've been back. I think she likes me too.'

'I'd be surprised if she didn't.' I knew of many young women who were enamoured with the town's burly young police sergeant. The Honourable Constance Timpson was one of them. I touched his arm. 'Ask her on a date. You have to move forward. We all do.'

'I resisted it for a long time, running away to London.'

'You came back. Like me.'

I'd spent nearly a year travelling around Europe with a young man I thought I'd been in love with. But those feelings had changed when our adventure fizzled out.

'What about you? Why do you never go on a date with anyone? Percy, for instance. Or hasn't he forgiven you?'

I smiled. 'Just about. Enough to be friends, at least. I think it's best if I avoid dating for a while if I'm ever to be considered respectable again.'

Percy wasn't the only one to have reacted badly to my scandalous trip abroad. Before my travels, my habit of wearing trousers had caused the odd muttered comment from the staider residents of Walden. That was nothing compared to the disapproval I'd faced on my return.

What was missing from my life was Marc. But I couldn't have

him. And I knew I had to stop seeing him or my reputation would be ruined forever.

'Do you have news for us, or are you just in need of a cup of coffee?' I asked when Ben followed me through the door and up the stairs to the office, which reeked of yesterday's coffee and today's cigarettes. Despite the cold, I couldn't resist cranking open the window a fraction.

'Both. And before you ask, Harry Hobbs has been released without charge.'

I hurried to put fresh coffee on, eager to hear what else he had to say. It felt like old times, having Ben back, and when we were all huddled around his desk, I could tell Elijah was in his element.

Ben took out his pocketbook. 'Superintendent Cobbe wants you to publish an article about the car. Could you get Robbie to take a photograph of it with the registration plate showing? It's still in the clearing where you found it. We're trying to find out when it arrived in Walden. Ask anyone who saw it to contact the station house.'

Elijah grunted in satisfaction, relishing the opportunity to spice up that week's edition with some local intrigue. 'What did Tolfree have to say about it?'

'He said he hasn't driven it for months and has no idea how it ended up in Walden. He denies knowing anything about the substance found in the glove compartment.'

'Was it cocaine?' Elijah reached for his cigarettes. 'Is that why Cobbe's trying to track down the driver?'

'It was, but that's not why we need to know who was driving.' Ben paused. 'The car was seen turning into Christmas Close on the afternoon of Rachel Lacey's death.'

Elijah let out a low whistle. 'Who saw it?'

'The caretaker of Christmas Hall.'

'Jack Archer?' I said.

'You know him?' Ben asked in surprise.

'I met him briefly. Is he sure it's the same car? It could have been a similar-looking one. There were a lot of cars in Winchester that day. Mrs Durling told me Jack goes to the pub most lunchtimes and stays there until it closes at three. He might not be the most reliable witness.'

Ben made a note of this. 'He said he'd been waiting outside the cathedral to see the Prince of Wales arrive at two o'clock for the service. After the prince had gone inside, he walked to the Perseverance Inn on Canon Street. As he was turning onto St Swithun Street, he saw the car drive into Christmas Close.'

'Did he see who was behind the wheel?' I guessed this was too much to hope for.

'He's not sure, but he thinks there was a passenger as well as the driver. He said he recognised the car as he'd seen both Rachel Lacey and Oliver Miller driving it before. He presumed it was one of them going to the hall – it was gone when he came back later and found the body.'

'Who noticed the car was missing?' I asked.

'Oliver Miller. He realised it was gone when he was locking up on the seventh of November. He'd been busy all day inside the showroom as Rachel Lacey hadn't shown up for work, and he'd had to manage on his own.'

'Was he there all day?' Elijah picked up his pen and began making notes.

'He said he arrived at eight o'clock that morning and didn't finish until six o'clock that evening. Customers drifted in and out all day, and he didn't leave at any time.'

'And Gordon Tolfree?' Elijah's pen hovered in mid-air.

'He was there too. He arrived at about nine o'clock and then left at around one-thirty to go to the cathedral. He'd been invited to attend the service for the Prince of Wales. It lasted about half an hour before the prince moved on to the college. Tolfree stayed at the cathedral with the other guests for drinks afterwards. He says he was there until at least three-thirty, then returned to Tolfree Motors. Oliver Miller wasn't sure what time Tolfree came back as he was talking with a customer, but said they spoke before Tolfree left for the day at five-thirty. Miller closed up the showroom at six o'clock and that's when he noticed the Wolseley was missing.'

'Did he report it straight away?' I asked.

'No. Apparently Gordon Tolfree had left his Rolls-Royce at home and taken the train from Walden into Winchester that morning. Miller wasn't sure if Tolfree had decided to drive home in the Wolseley rather than returning on the train. It wasn't reported missing until Winchester police called at Tolfree Motors the next morning to interview Tolfree and Miller about Rachel's death.'

'Why didn't Tolfree drive to work that day?' Elijah reached for his cigarettes. 'It's not as if he's short of cars.'

'He said he'd decided to take the train because he knew the city would be busy and he'd be drinking at the reception in the afternoon and was also planning to meet a friend for a drink after work.'

'If he was at the cathedral that afternoon, he was only a few minutes' walk from where the murder took place. He would have had plenty of time to go to Christmas Close, kill Rachel, park the Wolseley somewhere nearby and then drive it home to Walden later.' I sketched a rough timeline in my notepad. 'What time does his friend say he left Winchester that evening?'

'Mr Tolfree was reluctant to give the superintendent the name of his friend.'

'Suspicious. Especially as Jack Archer thought he saw two people in the car,' I said.

It had taken Robbie and me about an hour and a half to drive to Winchester on the day of the prince's visit, and that had been with a stop. It might have taken the older Wolseley slightly longer, although not much.

'Has Superintendent Cobbe told you how she died yet?' Elijah was scrawling a similar timeline to mine on his blotter. 'The pathologist must have found something.'

'He did. Cocaine.'

'What?' Elijah and I chorused.

'She died of a cocaine overdose.'

'So it was self-inflicted,' Elijah said, shaking his head in disbelief. 'How did she take it?'

'The pathologist found a mark on her arm. It was injected into a vein.'

'Injected? Is that usual?'

I didn't know much about the drug, but I'd mainly seen it in tablet or powder form.

'It's usually smoked or snorted. Or taken as a tablet.' Ben glanced down at his notes. 'If you dissolve the powder in water and inject it into a vein, it gets absorbed into the system faster. And the effects of the drug are felt more rapidly.'

'What effects?' I knew it was taken medicinally for pain relief and wondered if it was as toxic as morphine.

'Seizures and organ failures with a high enough dose,' Ben replied.

I winced. 'And that's what happened to Rachel?'

'Yes. The pathologist thinks she would have convulsed. When she was found, her features were distorted, and her skin was blue. It's likely death occurred quickly. There were also traces of a barbiturate in her stomach. The pathologist suspects they were her own sleeping pills. Her landlady said Rachel occasionally took one to help her sleep on the nights when she'd been singing in the bar.'

'Is that where she'd been the night before?' I asked. 'Singing in the Blackbird Bar?'

'No. She returned to her lodgings after finishing work at Tolfree Motors and didn't go out again that night. She left for work the next morning and that's the last anyone saw of her. It would help if we knew what she'd been doing in the hours prior to her death.'

Elijah frowned, running a hand through his thinning grey hair. 'Does the pathologist think Rachel injected the cocaine herself?'

'He said it's possible. Taken that way, it's known to provide an almost instantaneous high.' Ben snapped his pocketbook closed. 'However, no needle was found at the scene.'

14

'Horace has invited us to afternoon tea,' Elijah announced.

My visits to Heron Bay Lodge were the only times I saw Horace and Elijah relaxing together in private, as theirs was a relationship that could never be made public. In the eyes of the world, they were employer and employee. In truth, *The Walden Herald* had been created out of love. Elijah wasn't a man suited to retirement, so when he left his job at *The Daily Telegraph*, Horace had presented him with the role of editor of his new regional newspaper.

Heron Bay Lodge was a stylish wooden-clad house painted in soft grey with a wide veranda overlooking Waldenmere Lake. I knew Elijah had a key, but for propriety's sake, we knocked and were shown into a reception room decorated in the palest of greens and fragranced by cedar wood burning on an open fire.

Horace had an enviable collection of art including landscapes by famous painters, but what interested me most was the arrangement of cartoons displayed on one wall.

The drawings weren't signed but I suspected the artist was Horace himself as they clearly showed his waspish sense of humour. We'd even printed some of the anonymous cartoons in *The Walden Herald*, yet Elijah still refused to tell me who the illustrator was. I was tempted to suggest Horace draw a cartoon of Gordon Tolfree, but I knew I'd only be met by their faux innocent denials.

'I've been asking a few questions about Mr Tolfree, our independent candidate,' Horace began. He sat erect on the edge of the sofa; the fabric of his trousers pressed so precisely that two perfect creases ran from his knees to his highly polished brogues.

Beside him, Elijah slouched back against the dark green leather, a whisky and soda in one hand and cigar in the other.

I'd sunk into a comfortable armchair in the corner, savouring my small glass of expensive dry sherry. Afternoon tea with Horace rarely involved tea.

Horace picked up a sheaf of notes from the glass coffee table. 'Mr Tolfree appears to be accumulating wealth rapidly but not at an unusual rate.'

Horace was in a position to know, having enjoyed a long career in finance. When he'd first settled in Walden, he'd given locals the impression of being a mild-mannered bank manager looking for a quiet retirement. His wealth soon put paid to that idea, and most people now knew he'd travelled the world and made his fortune on Wall Street.

He'd chosen to settle in Walden ten years ago, deciding the peaceful town should stay just the way he liked it. And he used his considerable influence to ensure that it did.

'When Redvers Tolfree died in December 1922, he was virtually bankrupt. I can't imagine he left much for Gordon,' Elijah commented, leaning forward to tap the end of his cigar into a green onyx ashtray. Horace didn't care for ash on his upholstery.

'Redvers' finances were somewhat depleted,' Horace confirmed. 'In fact, he'd have been declared bankrupt had he lived. By dying, he saved his family substantial legal costs, as the case would have gone to trial. All Gordon inherited was the house, Sycamore Lodge.'

'So all his money comes from cars?' Elijah swirled ice cubes around the heavy crystal tumbler.

Horace nodded. 'He got into the motor trade at the right time. He buys from a car distributor in London who has the pick of the latest models. Each year, there are more cars to choose from, and more people want to buy them. His accounts show a healthy profit, and, on the surface, everything is as it should be.'

'But?' I knew from the smile that hovered on Horace's lips there was more to come.

'There's a rumour something's going on within the business. That Tolfree Motors could be hiding another, not so legitimate, operation.'

'Cocaine?' I asked. It wasn't an unreasonable assumption given that the drug was found in one of his cars and one of his employees had died from a cocaine overdose. 'Kevin at the *Hampshire Chronicle* said the same thing. He's been hearing rumours that Tolfree Motors isn't all it seems. But whenever reporters start to nose around, they don't find anything out of the ordinary. No one has a bad word to say about Gordon Tolfree. He's considered to be a successful businessman who uses his wealth to help war veterans.'

Horace consulted his notes. 'His banking transactions don't indicate any other income than that accrued through car sales. Sycamore Lodge and the car dealership are all the assets he has. And there are no signs he employs any dubious accounting practices.' He gave a slight cough. 'Unlike his father.'

I frowned. 'So where are these rumours coming from?'

Horace shrugged. 'I've no idea. My investigations went the same way as your friend Kevin's.'

'What about his personal life?' Elijah asked.

'Until a month or two ago, he'd occasionally been spotted in the company of an attractive young lady, believed to be an employee of Tolfree Motors,' Horace replied.

'An affair with Rachel Lacey?' I said.

'An affair that ended abruptly,' Elijah mused. 'The usual reason for that happening is the wife finding out.'

'Or, in Mr Tolfree's case, it may have been prompted by his decision to stand for election.' Horace took a sip of his whisky and soda. 'Apart from this possible liaison with Miss Lacey, he doesn't appear to have any other vices besides enjoying the occasional drink, but then don't we all? In fact, his only affiliation seems to be with the church and Winchester Cathedral's Great War Fund, to which he makes generous donations.'

'No doubt in a bid to improve his family's standing in the community, though these donations are worth investigating in case there's something else behind them.' Elijah downed the remains of his whisky and soda and hauled himself up from the couch. 'Which is why we have an appointment at St Martha's.'

I finished my sherry, reluctant to leave the warmth and comfort of Horace's luxurious home for the chill of the ancient church.

Outside, it was cold and wet, and I pulled the belt of my overcoat tighter, knowing it would be impossible to get Elijah to walk any faster. When we finally turned into Church Road, it was nearly five o'clock and despite the gloom, the gas lamps hadn't yet been lit. It was a relief to reach the shelter of St Martha's, although I doubted it would be much warmer inside.

When I pulled open the arched wooden door, its loud creak shattered the quiet of what appeared to be an empty candlelit church.

Inside, I instinctively began to whisper. 'Who is it we're meeting here?'

'He's one of the vergers at Winchester Cathedral and on the committee of the cathedral's war fund,' Elijah whispered back. 'I get the impression this chap would like me to publicise the work they do and emphasise that the money they raise is for charities across Hampshire and not just in Winchester.'

'What's this man's name?'

'Mr Powell. He's an interesting chap. He was a chaplain in France during the war, though he's a layman now. The vicar introduced me to him.'

I stopped walking. My stomach lurched. 'What does he look like?'

'Tall, dark blond hair. About forty...'

I gripped Elijah's arm. 'We need to leave.'

'What?'

'Now. We need to leave here now.'

But it was too late. A figure emerged from behind the altar.

'Iris. How lovely to see you again.'

I cringed at the sound of the familiar low drawl.

Taking a deep breath, I stared directly into the predatory green eyes of Archie Powell.

15

I scrutinised his face, feeling a mixture of panic and fascination. The last time I'd seen Archie Powell, he'd been Reverend Powell. Thanks to me, he no longer had that title.

I realised our last meeting had been exactly a year ago, on a cold night in November 1922. I'd sat next to him on a pew in St Mary's Church in Deptford, where he'd confessed his sins to me. He'd hoped for my forgiveness but hadn't received it. I was curious to see what the past year had done to him.

The smoky perfume that filled my nostrils made me realise what was going on. Not only had Archie used Elijah to engineer this encounter with me, he'd chosen a time when the church would resemble that chilly night in St Mary's with flickering white candles and incense burning at the altar.

His smirk told me he knew I was fully aware of the scene he'd set. Although he could no longer wear the clerical robes that had been his attire that night, he was dressed in a black shirt and trousers that gave him an ecclesiastical appearance.

'We have solemn evensong at five-thirty.' He gestured towards the altar. 'Hence, the incense and candles.'

'I see.' Elijah glanced at me anxiously. I could tell by his reaction he had no idea what was happening. He'd never met Archie before.

'I'm so glad you could come, Mr Whittle. Iris was always talking about you.'

This was a lie. I couldn't recall ever mentioning Elijah to Archie except to say that he was my boss.

'You two know each other?' Elijah's tone indicated he knew he had to tread carefully.

'This is Archie Powell,' I replied. 'He was once vicar at St Mary's Church in Deptford and used to run Creek House.'

'Ahhh.' Elijah made a strangled noise of comprehension. He managed to recover with remarkable speed. 'Mr Powell, I thought you were still in prison.'

Archie's eyes narrowed, and I could see that the jibe had hit home.

The previous year, when the press had been stirring up ill feeling towards Constance Timpson and Mrs Siddons for promoting equality in the workplace, Archie Powell had felt it was his duty to scare them into returning things to their 'natural order' as he put it. He'd tried to achieve this by anonymously firing a rifle in their direction. His intention had been to scare rather than harm, but, unfortunately, Ben had got in the way of one of his bullets. Although it hadn't left any lasting damage, I would never forgive Archie for what he'd done.

'I've served my penance for those unfortunate episodes caused by shellshock. And God has brought me here.' His eyes flickered upwards as if, at that moment, he was in direct communication with his maker.

The court may have been swayed by Archie's previously unblemished record and his gallant conduct as an army chaplain during the war, but I knew the shots he'd fired hadn't been the result of any type of war neurosis. They were the actions of a man with a huge ego and a desire to control. And women, old and young, had been his targets.

'God has brought you to Walden?' I hoped my tone conveyed the cynicism I felt.

'To Winchester Cathedral,' he answered, as if this conferred some superiority on him.

'As a verger,' Elijah commented. 'Not an ordained priest.'

'I serve God in whatever way I can. I find I'm able to accomplish even more in a lay capacity.'

His voice was smooth, but I'd seen the flicker of anger in his eyes at Elijah's words. He was still furious at losing his elevated position within the church.

'And you've decided to do that in Winchester?' I'd rather Archie had stayed in London, where I was less likely to run into him.

'For the time being.' Archie gave me a sideways glance. 'I'm working with Winchester Cathedral's Great War Fund on plans to open a home for disabled and unemployed servicemen. Similar to Creek House but on a larger scale.'

'And proceeds from the pantomime will go towards your fundraising campaign?' Elijah's fingers fiddled with the buttons of his thick wool coat, and I could tell he was feeling the cold as well as itching for a cigarette.

'The diocese has been supportive of my work. I also have the backing of many local business*men*.'

If his emphasis of the word *men* was supposed to rile me, it failed.

'Gordon Tolfree is one of them, I believe,' Elijah remarked.

'He's become a friend. We're of similar minds on many things.' Archie smirked in my direction, and I took his meaning.

Those similar things no doubt included a shared dislike of me, Constance Timpson and Mrs Siddons. I could picture them together, plotting ways to get back at us over a late-night drink.

'It's kind of you to offer to publicise the pantomime.' Archie thrust a playbill into Elijah's hand. 'This gives the names of the cast members.'

Elijah held up the brightly coloured bill, and we read the cast list.

Cinderella: Jennifer Tolfree
The Prince: Frederick Baverstock
The Fairy Godmother: Bridget Durling
The Stepsisters: Gordon Tolfree and Oliver Miller
The Stepmother: Nancy Miller
The Baron: Archibald Powell

I was unnerved by Rachel Lacey's replacement. I was even more unsettled by the inclusion of Archie's name in the cast. 'You're in the pantomime?'

'We were short of volunteers, so I offered. You're welcome to come along and watch me rehearse.' He gave me a wolfish smile. 'It's a small part, but I like to think I have a commanding presence.'

I gave an unladylike snort. 'Were you due to practise your lines with Rachel Lacey on the afternoon she died?'

Archie sighed. 'Still seeing evil where there isn't any?'

'In your case, the evil I saw was real.'

I could tell from his expression he knew what I was referring to, and it wasn't just his illegal activities with a rifle.

Perhaps sensing things were about to get nasty, Elijah turned to leave.

'Thank you for your time, Mr Powell,' he said over his shoulder, waving the playbill in the air. 'I'll be sure to include a review of your performance. No doubt it will be as theatrical as this evening's.'

I gave Archie a hard stare before following.

'I'm sure you'll portray me as the arch-villain,' he called after us.

In the churchyard, I inhaled deeply, filling my lungs with cold air. I automatically glanced towards the dark outline of the yew tree overlooking my mother's grave. I was incensed that Archie had invaded my hometown like this.

Without a word, we trudged up Church Road to Elijah's cottage. He led the way for once, and I followed the light at the end of his cigarette.

Elijah's housekeeper was in the kitchen preparing him a hot supper. She'd lit the fire in the parlour, and it felt warm and safe after the sinister chill of the church.

Elijah poured us both a brandy and we sank into a pair of old leather armchairs and stared into the flames.

'I presume that was all for your benefit?' He lit another cigarette.

'He even timed it so the church had the same appearance as St Mary's on the evening when...' I hesitated. 'When he was arrested.'

That night, Archie hadn't known I'd already been to the police with what I knew. Before Ben and Detective Inspector Yates had arrived, I'd told Archie what I'd uncovered. Even then, he thought he'd be able to persuade me to forgive him and turn a blind eye to what he'd done. He knew I'd been attracted to him and had used it against me. But it was too late by that time.

'I need to tell Constance and Mrs Siddons about this.'

'You're afraid they're in danger?' Elijah took a long drag of his cigarette.

I shook my head. 'I don't think Archie would target them again. He's not that stupid. But they need to know he's around.'

'And so does Ben,' Elijah said.

My fury rose. 'How could Archie do this? How's Ben going to feel having to face him again?'

Elijah pondered this. 'I have a feeling Mr Powell will go and see him. If he hasn't already. Try to seek his forgiveness.'

He was right. It was exactly the sort of thing Archie would do.

'I'm going to call in at the station house first thing,' I said.

Elijah nodded. 'And I'll go and see Horace. See what he can dig up about Archie Powell. Find out why he's out of prison so soon.'

I picked up the playbill.

'Gordon Tolfree is very much the linchpin of this pantomime,' I said. 'Oliver Miller works for him, and I assume Nancy Miller is his wife. Victoria Hobbs is Oliver's sister and she and Harry are involved behind the scenes. And it was Victoria who persuaded Freddie to take on the role of the prince.'

'What about Bridget Durling?'

'Her only connection to Tolfree seems to be that they're both on the fundraising committee of the cathedral's war fund.'

He took the playbill from me. 'Jennifer Tolfree is an unlikely Cinderella.'

I knew what he meant. Whenever I'd seen Mrs Tolfree around town, her dark blonde hair was elaborately rolled into a chignon at the nape of her neck, and she always wore the latest fashions. She was several years older than her husband and it was hard to imagine her as a young girl dressed in rags, sweeping ashes from the grate.

'This pantomime could be quite amusing.' I smiled for the first time that evening. 'Poor Freddie certainly isn't getting the Cinderella he'd hoped for. It's quite a bizarre cast.'

Elijah stubbed out his cigarette. 'And Gordon's new friend, Archie Powell, is the baron.'

My smile faded.

Elijah regarded me with a serious expression. 'What about you? Are you in any danger from him?'

I hesitated. 'I'm not sure. I told the police where to find his rifle. He won't forgive me for that.'

'Are you afraid of him? You didn't tell me everything that went on between the two of you. You seem to have a very personal connection.'

I blushed. My indiscretions with Archie were not something I wanted to dwell on. After seeing him again, I remembered how intensely I'd been drawn to him. Even when every instinct told me he was bad news, I hadn't been able to resist. It may only have amounted to a few kisses, albeit heated ones, but it was not something I wanted to share with Elijah.

'How did it end between you?' he asked, as if reading my thoughts.

I shrugged. 'Detective Inspector Yates and Ben took him to Deptford police station for questioning. And I never saw him again until this evening.'

I remembered what Archie had said to me before Ben had gripped his arm and led him away. He'd leant in and pressed his lips to mine, whispering, 'We have unfinished business. Until next time.'

As I left Elijah's cottage, those words kept playing in my head. He'd offered to take me home, but I'd insisted I'd be fine on my own. It was only a five-minute walk along a well-lit high street to Victoria Lane.

But as I turned onto the high street, I glanced behind me. I had the same sense of being watched that I'd experienced when I was snooping around Sycamore Lodge.

What had Archie meant by unfinished business? I quickened my pace, the warmth of the brandy replaced by a chill of apprehension.

16

After a sleepless night, I headed to the station house. When Ben answered the door, he didn't seem surprised to see me.

'Come in. But be quiet. Sid's still asleep. He was up till late at the Drunken Duck. Breaking up a fight, not drinking,' he added hastily.

We sat in the parlour where a fire smouldered in the grate. The room was tidy, which meant that Mrs Gilbert, Ben's mother, had recently been in to clean. Or maybe they'd cleared up themselves in anticipation of a visit from Superintendent Cobbe. As this case now encompassed Winchester and Walden, Ben and Sid would have to be prepared for the superintendent to appear at any moment.

Ben settled himself into a chair. Despite the early hour, he was freshly shaven and dressed in uniform. 'Is this about Archie Powell?'

'You've seen him?'

'He paid me a visit last night.'

Elijah was right. Archie had sought out Ben. 'What time was that?'

'Around seven o'clock. Why?'

I had a feeling Archie had waited to spring the surprise of his return on me before alerting anyone else that he was in Walden. I also wondered if he'd seen me leaving Elijah's cottage and followed me.

'Elijah and I met him in St Martha's Church at about five o'clock. He must have come to you after evensong was over. What did he say?'

'He asked for my forgiveness.' He gave a grim smile. 'He even asked if we could be friends.'

I snorted in disgust. 'What did you say?'

'I told him that I didn't consort with criminals.' Ben spoke in his usual calm manner. 'And that I had no desire to be friends with someone who shoots a rifle at women.'

'What did he say?'

'He muttered some biblical quotation about forgiveness and claimed he'd only acted that way because he was suffering from shellshock. When I asked him to leave as I had work to do, he said he was sorry for what he'd done to me.'

'But not to Constance or Mrs Siddons?'

'I get the impression he feels that as they weren't physically hurt, no harm was done.'

I growled. 'I wish he'd get out of Walden. Go back to London or preferably even further.'

'So do I.' Ben spread his hands in a helpless gesture. 'But I'm afraid there's nothing we can do. He's served his sentence and he's free to go wherever he pleases.'

'Even to the hometown of the women he targeted?'

'There's no law to stop him. I can only intervene if he threatens someone.'

I shook my head. 'He won't do that.'

'Are you going to see Mrs Siddons and Constance?'

I nodded.

'Tell them that I'll make Superintendent Cobbe aware of the situation. And that Sid and I will be keeping an eye on Mr Archibald Powell. If he does anything even slightly threatening, we'll arrest him.' Ben was watching me with concern. 'Try not to let him get to you.'

'He hasn't,' I lied.

He smiled. 'Normally you'd have asked me about sightings of the Wolseley by now.'

I leant forward in my chair. 'Did someone see it?'

'The vicar.'

'Reverend Childs? When?'

'He says it was in the clearing when he cycled to evensong on the seventh, the day of Rachel Lacey's murder. He goes through the back lanes from his cottage to the church.'

'What time did he see it?'

'He says it was there when he passed at just before six that evening. And he thought he saw the tail lights of Harry Hobbs' van driving off when he got closer to the church, though he isn't sure about that. It could have been another vehicle driving along the high street.'

'But...' I frowned. 'Harry or Freddie would have seen it pass.'

'I'll be questioning them again. The Wolseley was first seen that day at shortly after two o'clock in Winchester when Jack Archer said he saw it being driven into Christmas Close. It takes approximately an hour and a half to drive from Winchester to Walden and the vicar claims the car was parked in the clearing when he cycled by at six o'clock. Who had possession of the car between those times – and why didn't either Harry or Freddie mention seeing it being driving down Church Road? One of them should have been outside the church when it went by.'

I left the station house feeling bewildered by what appeared to be an incomprehensible sequence of events on the day Rachel Lacey had died. Gordon Tolfree had been in Winchester that afternoon until at least five-thirty. There was no way he could have driven the Wolseley back to Walden in that time.

Then I recalled that during my encounter with Archie, he'd said he and Gordon were now friends. Could he have been Gordon's accomplice? Jack Archer had thought he'd seen two people in the car as it drove into Christmas Close.

Of course, there was always the possibility that the car wasn't connected to Rachel's murder, although that seemed unlikely.

I hurried along the lake path to pay my next visit of the morning. But when I called at Grebe House, Mr Grosvenor, Mrs Siddons' butler, told me she'd made an early start and was already on her way to the House of Commons. I left a message, saying that I needed to speak with her and Miss Timpson urgently.

Grebe House was in the advantageous position of overlooking Grebe Stream, and I couldn't resist following the flow of water as it curved its way into the lake at Heron Bay. I strolled over the wooden arch of Grebe Bridge and along the footpath that wound its way between Willow Marsh on one side and Sand Hills Wood on the other. Beyond the wood, stood Sand Hills Hall, once the home of my dear friend Alice Thackeray.

Sometimes, I'd stop here to remember her. Today, I hurried by. Too many emotions were threatening to overwhelm me. One of them was shame. My behaviour had sometimes shocked Alice, and I didn't like to dwell on what she would have said about my relationship with Marc. Even though I told myself it was an innocent friendship, Alice had known me well enough to have confronted me about my true feelings.

Instead, I carried on to Mill Ponds, and stopped outside the mansion to look across the lake. A low mist hung over the water, and a heron stood motionless in the reedbeds, watching for prey.

Mill Ponds had been on the market since General Cheverton's death over two years ago. The general's nephew, Nathan Cheverton, was desperate to sell it. But due to its tragic history, there were no takers.

It was a beautiful property and there was still a grandeur about the place, even though the roof and chimneys were in need of repair.

Mill Ponds had been used as an officer training academy during the war, and if walls could talk, its glowing red bricks would tell tales of official secrets and military strategies. It was sad to see it so neglected. Once, there had been talk of it being converted into a convalescent home for wounded servicemen, but it had come to nothing. The army hadn't been able to afford to put the plan into action.

I walked along the footpath that ran parallel to the railway line before curving around to where a few stands of residential roads trailed off from the lake. One of these was Chestnut Avenue, where I'd lived with my father and our housekeeper, Lizzy, until I'd taken lodgings with Millicent and Ursula.

I still came back regularly for meals, and in the months since my father's second marriage, I'd begun to develop a friendship with my stepmother, Katherine. On impulse, I decided to call in and see if I could grab some breakfast.

Only Katherine was home, as well-turned-out as ever in a simple gabardine dress, at an hour when most ladies of leisure would still be in their dressing gowns.

'Lizzy's gone into town to do some shopping, and your father took the early train to London. Come into the kitchen, and I'll make you some tea and toast. You look frozen.'

Gratefully I accepted the offer.

While she was boiling the kettle, I couldn't resist tasting some of the cake mixture that was resting in a bowl on the sideboard. The sweet and spicy aroma of syrup and cinnamon made me long for some of the pastries I'd had when I'd travelled through France.

'Lizzy's gone to get some more sultanas. We wanted to make a start on the Christmas baking.'

I hadn't even begun to consider Christmas, even though November was drawing to a close. Lizzy had always enjoyed the festive season without much encouragement from my father and me. This year, it seemed she had an ally in Katherine. I suspected Christmas at Chestnut Avenue was going to be different with my stepmother in residence.

'I howled with laughter when I saw that photograph of you with the Prince of Wales. Don't tell me you caught the prince's eye, and you're now being courted by royalty?' She poured boiling water into the old brown teapot. 'You're the talk of the Walden Women's Group.'

During the war, the ladies of the town had got together to help families struggling with their menfolk away fighting. Though the war was over, the loss of loved ones, unemployment and disability had left many families still suffering.

'The group's been working with Winchester Cathedral's war fund, hasn't it?'

'That's right. It was Jennifer Tolfree's doing. We're helping with ticket sales for the pantomime. They're trying to reach a wider audience.'

'What's she like?'

'Pleasant enough, although she can be a little prickly about certain things.'

'What sort of things?'

Katherine placed a plate of toast in front of me, then sat down and poured us both cups of tea. 'As you know, the family's fortunes have fluctuated over the last year or so.'

'Is she resentful?' I asked, reaching for the butter and marmalade.

'A little. I think she hoped her son, Luke, would inherit the Tolfree biscuit empire. Instead, he'll get a motor car dealership.'

'Does she believe Redvers was innocent?'

'Probably not. She doesn't talk about him. Since his disgrace, her social standing has fallen somewhat. She's the daughter of minor aristocracy, an impoverished lord or something. She married into trade, but at least it was a well-established business with a famous name. Tolfree Biscuits was a respectable company with a royal seal of approval. And Redvers got his OBE from the king. Being the wife of a car dealer doesn't quite cut it.'

'She's a snob?'

'You could put it like that.'

Katherine laughed when I told her that Jennifer Tolfree had stepped into the role of Cinderella.

'Pantomimes aren't exactly my sort of thing, but I'll have to get tickets just to see her dressed in rags.' Katherine's smile brought dimples to her cheeks.

'What's Gordon Tolfree like? I'm afraid I haven't seen the best side of him.'

'I've found him to be quite charming. In fact, I like him more than her. They'll both be at the school's carol concert. I think they want to show they have nothing to hide. Rumours are flying about this car that was discovered near Sycamore Lodge and one of his employees dying in mysterious circumstances.'

I told her about Rachel Lacey, and she gave me a speculative look.

'Why don't I spy on the Tolfrees for you?'

'What?' I nearly choked on my tea.

'See if I can find out any gossip.'

I took a moment to digest this and then nodded.

'That would be useful. There are rumours that Rachel Lacey was having an affair with a married man. It could have been with Gordon. Or it could just be talk. And it's the same with the business. There are rumours of something odd going on at Tolfree Motors, but no one seems to know what.'

Katherine's hazel eyes gleamed. 'This will make my work with the Walden Women's Group so much more interesting.'

17

During the afternoon, Mrs Siddons telephoned the office to invite me to call on her that evening.

On my way to Grebe House, I hesitated over whether to stop by the church to see how Freddie was doing. On the one hand, I wanted to keep my promise to Percy to look after his brother. On the other, I didn't want to risk running into Archie Powell again.

When I realised I was actually afraid of seeing Archie, I resolved to go to St Martha's. I refused to let that man make me feel scared in a place where I should feel safe.

I found Freddie and Harry working on the south wall of the church. Freddie seemed eager to talk to me about the car. Harry less so.

'I've been thinking.' Freddie put down his hammer and brushed sweat from his brow. 'I'd seen Rachel drive the Wolseley before and would have noticed if it had come down Church Road when I was here. In fact, I would have noticed any car. I don't remember seeing a single one that day.'

That didn't surprise me. There were only a few houses on Church Road and none of the occupants had cars. Elijah didn't drive, and the Austin Seven was generally parked outside the office unless Robbie or the printworks was using it.

'And you left at around five? When Harry arrived?'

'It was probably about a quarter past as I helped Harry put the tools back in the van.' Freddie pushed his floppy hair off his brow in a gesture so similar to Percy's it made me smile.

I turned to Harry. 'And you left at around six?'

'Thereabouts. I checked the stones Freddie had been working on first. I'm not sure what time it was.'

'You didn't see the vicar?'

Harry shook his head, and I noticed how tired he looked. He and Victoria had now moved into their new home at Crookham, and I supposed working at the church all day and sorting out the house in the evening was taking its toll.

'Reverend Childs says the car was in the clearing when he came by on his bicycle, and he thought he saw the tail lights of your van as he cycled up the road, although he isn't sure about that.'

Harry kept his eyes fixed on his work as he said, 'I think it must have arrived after I left, though I suppose it could have come by when I was in the church. I might not have heard it if I was hammering.'

I noticed Freddie looking perplexed. It seemed impossible that neither he nor Harry had seen the car being driven down Church Road. I suspected it had been dark, or at least getting dark, by the time it had reached Walden, and the glare from the headlamps would have been visible from wherever they'd been, even through the stained glass of the church.

'Why was it driven into the clearing?' I mused.

At this, Harry turned to scowl at me. 'Because Gordon Tolfree left it there after he killed Rachel.'

I shook my head. 'It's not possible for him to have driven it to Walden at that time. He was at Tolfree Motors until five-thirty.'

'Then he got someone to do it for him.'

'But what reason would he have for murdering Rachel? Had they been having an affair?'

'It was something to do with Tolfree Motors,' Harry muttered, turning back to his work. 'I'll tell you when I have the evidence.'

'You should go to the police with what you know and let them find the evidence.'

But Harry ignored me and began to gently tap a chisel with his hammer.

Freddie seemed exasperated, and I guessed he'd already had this conversation with Harry.

Feeling as frustrated as Freddie looked, I left them to their work, and strode around the corner of the church – straight into the arms of Archie Powell.

He put his hands on my shoulders and I suspected he'd been hovering out of sight, listening to our conversation. I stepped away, repelled by the scent of incense on his clothes. And something else. I might have been mistaken, but I thought I caught a whiff of brandy on his breath.

'What are you doing here?' I demanded.

'I don't think that's any of your business,' he replied with an infuriating smirk. 'But if you must know, I was chatting with Reverend Childs about a project we're working on together. He's a most forgiving man. What about you? Have you found it in your heart yet to forgive me?'

'No. Because I don't believe you're repentant.'

'That's something only God can know. Let's talk about you. You seem to have found yourself another mystery to solve.'

I decided to turn the tables. 'You must have met Rachel Lacey. Who do you think killed her?'

'I haven't the faintest idea. I don't fancy myself as an amateur detective. I leave that sort of thing to the police. I don't have lofty ideas that I can do a better job than they can.'

'I'm not trying to do their job. I'm simply looking into the facts so I can report them accurately.'

'Are you? Or are you hoping to protect Percy's little brother? I'm sure you and Mr Baverstock must have made up your differences by now. Didn't I say one day you'd settle down with a nice young man like Percy and have lots of bonny babies? Or is there someone else in your life? I know how fickle you can be.'

'You don't know anything about me,' I snarled.

'That's not true.' He reached out and tucked a lock of my bobbed hair behind my ear. 'We used to be so close.'

I flushed and backed away. 'Not any more.'

He pulled a face, pretending to be sad. 'Perhaps you and Percy won't have your happy ending after all. Not if his little brother is hanged for murder.'

I gasped. 'Don't be ridiculous. Freddie had nothing to do with Rachel Lacey's death.'

'Are you sure? He was very keen on her. You didn't see how upset he was when Rachel spurned him.'

I turned away, unwilling to continue this conversation.

'But I did,' he called after me. 'And I followed your example of running to the police. I thought it my duty to tell them what I heard.'

* * *

When Mr Grosvenor showed me into the drawing room of Grebe House, I found Constance Timpson was already seated.

'Is this about Gordon Tolfree?' Mrs Siddons indicated for Mr Grosvenor to pour me a glass of sherry.

'Not directly.' I held out my hand for the elegant crystal glass and took an unladylike swig. 'It's about Archie Powell.'

Mrs Siddons didn't react, but I saw Constance shiver as I described what had happened.

'And he's in cahoots with Tolfree?'

I could sense the simmering anger in Constance's low voice.

'He seems to be.' I told them about the playbill for the pantomime. 'And now Jennifer Tolfree's taken over the role of Cinderella.'

'Do you suspect Archie had something to do with Rachel Lacey's death?' Constance asked.

'He thinks nothing of frightening women.'

Mrs Siddons frowned. 'But murdering them?'

'Perhaps he learnt some new tricks in prison,' I said.

Constance's hand shook as she reached for her glass, and I wished I'd kept my mouth shut. She'd been in the firing line last time. Of course she'd be frightened Archie would try again.

Mrs Siddons sat motionless, contemplating the smouldering wood on the fire as if she was posing for one of Robbie's portraits. Although she showed no obvious signs of distress, I knew that controlling her emotions was something she excelled at. I was present on both occasions when Archie had played at being a sniper, and it had been terrifying for Constance and Mrs Siddons to find themselves his targets.

Eventually, Mrs Siddons spoke. 'What does Archie want?'

I'd been mulling this over since the previous day's encounter in St Martha's Church.

'I think he wants his reputation back. Being a priest mattered to him. He's probably hoping Tolfree can help him regain at least some of his former respectability.'

'Could we use this to our advantage? Perhaps you could write an article revealing Gordon Tolfree's association with a convicted criminal who once targeted his political opponent?' Constance had regained her composure and was now ready to employ the tactics that made her such a formidable businesswoman.

I considered this. 'I'll talk to Elijah. He's gone to see Mr Laffaye to ask him to investigate Reverend—' I stopped myself. I'd been about to say Reverend Powell.

'Let's see what Mr Laffaye's enquiries reveal first.' Mrs Siddons was aware of how extensive Horace's network of contacts was. 'I don't want to risk turning voters against me by seeming to cast aspersions on a rival. We need hard facts.'

Constance stood up and refilled our glasses from the sherry decanter. 'I'll have to tell Daniel about this.' She sighed. 'It's going to bring everything back.'

When Archie had been a war chaplain, he'd served shoulder to shoulder with Daniel on the frontline. Daniel even credited Archie with saving his life on one occasion. When it proved to be Archie who'd targeted his sister, he'd felt a huge sense of betrayal as well as shock and anger. I had a feeling the former Reverend Powell wouldn't be forgiven by the usually gentle and magnanimous Daniel.

'Why is he here?' I seethed, feeling a surge of anger on the Timpsons' behalf. 'Why hasn't he got the decency to skulk away to where no one knows his past? Instead, he's come to a place where he'll cause even more upset.'

'Perhaps he wants revenge. Like Gordon Tolfree,' Constance suggested.

Mrs Siddons gazed thoughtfully at me. 'If Archie does want revenge, I don't think it's on Constance or myself. I'm concerned he'll vent his anger at you.'

It was my turn to shiver. After what Archie had said earlier, I was afraid she was right.

18

Elijah and I were once again seated in the stylish reception room of Heron Bay Lodge. I was curled up in my usual armchair in the corner, enjoying the warmth of the cedarwood fire, while Elijah was slouched next to Horace on the dark green leather sofa.

Horace picked up a single sheet of white paper from the glass table and began to read.

'Archibald Powell was sentenced to a year's imprisonment but was released after ten months. He was incarcerated in Winchester Prison and while he was there, he was praised for his exemplary behaviour and for helping his fellow prisoners learn new skills.'

Horace's contacts included senior figures on the crown court circuit and in the police force. He also had the ear of several high court judges. I guessed he'd tapped his legal connections to get a record of Archie's detention and miraculous rehabilitation. He'd worked fast to get this information, and I suspected it was due to Elijah's concern at how Archie's reappearance was affecting me.

'How did he get a job as a verger at Winchester Cathedral?' I asked.

'By becoming friends with the prison chaplain who's associated with the cathedral,' Horace replied. 'The chaplain arranged for the bishop to visit the prison to see the work Powell was doing to rehabilitate his fellow inmates.'

I could picture it. Archie excelled at putting on a show for his superiors. I also knew I wasn't being fair. To his credit, it was in Archie's nature to help men who'd fallen on hard times get back on their feet.

'When he was released, the bishop found him a job,' Horace continued. 'And lodgings close to the cathedral.'

'After what he did?' I shook my head in disbelief.

Elijah grunted. 'The church looks after its own. They couldn't go so far as to have him back as vicar, but this is the next best thing.'

'And where does Gordon Tolfree come into it?' I pondered. 'He's been involved with the cathedral's war fund since its inception. Is that what put him in touch with Archie?'

'Perhaps he read newspaper reports at the time of Powell's incarceration and saw him as a kindred spirit?' Elijah suggested.

Horace nodded. 'I think that's the most likely scenario as Tolfree decided to pay Powell a visit in prison.'

Elijah puffed on his cigar. 'It was Tolfree who approached Powell?'

'According to my sources, he wrote to Mr Powell and, in response, received an invitation to visit the prison.'

'I can imagine that conversation,' Elijah said. 'They have a lot in common. Both are resentful about past events and want to re-establish themselves in society.'

'But do they want revenge?' Horace steepled his hands under his chin. 'That's the question.'

I considered this. 'Gordon blames Mrs Siddons and Constance Timpson for what happened to his father. If he's looking for an ally, who better than the man who targeted them? But I think Archie's more concerned about proving himself in the eyes of the church than seeking vengeance. Although he'll probably take any opportunity to get back at me as long as there's no risk of further damage to his reputation.'

The thought of Gordon Tolfree and Archie Powell plotting against me was unnerving, and I noticed Horace and Elijah exchange a concerned glance.

'It's worrying that only a month after Mr Powell's release, Rachel Lacey is found dead,' Horace commented.

'Hmm.' Elijah shook his head. 'He's not a killer. And as far as we know, neither is Gordon Tolfree. Both are keen to avoid scandal and present themselves as upright citizens. Would they risk injecting a woman with cocaine?'

'That depends on whether she posed a threat to them,' Horace replied.

'Jack Archer, the caretaker at Christmas Hall, thought he saw two people in the car that drove into Christmas Close. That was just after the Prince of Wales had arrived at the cathedral. Gordon could have taken the car from Tolfree Motors, picked up Archie and driven it to the close. Rachel Lacey might have been there already and they killed her, then Gordon slipped into the cathedral for the service. Or he might have sneaked out during the drinks party afterwards and done it then. Maybe Archie was at the service too, as he's a verger at the cathedral. If he was around, it could have been him who drove the car to Sycamore Lodge and left it there.'

Horace sipped his whisky and soda. 'I think I'll suggest to Superintendent Cobbe he might like to have a chat with both of them.'

'Good.'

I hoped a visit from the superintendent would rattle Archie, if nothing else. But the Wolseley still puzzled me. Why would Gordon Tolfree let Oliver Miller report it as missing if he knew it was in Walden?

* * *

I stayed at Heron Bay Lodge for supper with Horace and Elijah, and when I got home, I found Millicent marking exercise books at the kitchen table.

I wandered over to the stove. 'Would you like some cocoa?'

'Hmm, yes, please.' She stretched her back. 'Where have you been?'

I explained about our meeting with Horace while I warmed a saucepan of milk.

'Do you think Archie wants revenge?' She gathered up the schoolbooks and put them to one side.

'Only on me. I think Constance and Mrs Siddons are safe enough.'

'Doesn't that frighten you?' Millicent took the cake tin from the sideboard and cut us each a sliver of fruit cake.

'It did at first. But I don't believe he plans to physically harm me. He just wants me to suffer for what I did to him.' I placed two mugs on the table and dropped into a chair, suddenly aware of how tired I was.

'What was it like seeing him again?' she asked.

Millicent was the only person who knew the intimate nature of my relationship with Archie, although I was sure Elijah suspected.

'Uncomfortable.' This was an understatement. I remembered the chill that had passed through me when I saw him in the candlelight. 'Now I'm just angry at his disregard for his victims. All he cares about is himself.'

'It is a cruel thing to do,' Millicent agreed. 'Daniel's upset. He thinks he should confront him.'

I shook my head. 'He should leave any confronting to the police.'

'That's what I told him.' She sipped her cocoa. 'You know Ursula and I are going to spend Christmas with my father in Kent?'

I nodded, my eyes drooping.

'Daniel's offered to drive us there. He said it would be nice to meet my father.'

'Oh.' I'd long suspected that Daniel had marriage on his mind and this was a sure sign. 'How do you feel about that?'

'I love them both, and I'd like them to meet. I think they'll get along well.'

'But?' This was the first time Millicent had mentioned love, and it took me by surprise, though I should have seen it coming. I should also have noticed that these feelings didn't seem to be making her happy.

'If I married, I'd have to give up my work as a teacher.' She ran her fingers over the stack of exercise books.

I sighed in exasperation. It infuriated me that so many women had to leave their professions when they married. Millicent was born to teach and had the enviable trait of commanding respect from both pupils and their parents. Walden was lucky to have her.

'What are you going to do?' I felt guilty that I'd been so preoccupied with recent events, I'd failed to see how troubled Millicent was.

'Accept his offer.' Seeing my shocked expression, she added, 'His offer to drive us to Faversham. He's going to drop us off and return to Crookham Hall to spend Christmas with Constance and some other relatives. Then he's going to come back and stay in a hotel nearby so he can see in the New Year with us.'

I smiled. 'That sounds lovely.'

'You will be alright on your own, won't you?'

'I won't be on my own. I'll be at my father's. I called in the other day, and Katherine and Lizzy had already started baking. If Katherine has her way, it's going to be a lively affair.' To my surprise, I realised I was actually looking forward to it. 'I must find time to do some Christmas shopping.'

Millicent picked up the tea plates and took them over to the sink. 'What about your London boyfriend? Will you see him?'

'I've told you, he's just an old friend. Why do you call him my boyfriend?'

'Because of how you look whenever one of his letters arrives. And because you've never told Ursula or me his name. You will be careful, won't you?'

Millicent had no idea she'd met my London boyfriend only four months earlier. I wished I could confide in her about my relationship with Marc and my feelings for him. Instead, I just nodded.

If it had been anyone else other than Millicent warning me to be careful, I would have protested that I wasn't a child.

However, she knew that the year before, I'd let my desire for Archie override the part of my brain that told me I should steer well clear. I liked to think I'd drawn away from him before things had become too intense, though by responding to his kisses, I'd still gone further than I should have.

The situation with Marc was different, I told myself. But I still knew it was a mistake I shouldn't be making.

19

I tried to push Archie Powell from my thoughts and concentrate on Rachel Lacey.

Now we had more information about the circumstances of her death, I decided to pay another visit to Tilly Crow at Crows' Nest.

She welcomed me with open arms. 'Thank you for talking to Mrs Evans. She sent a lovely letter and a cheque for the rent that was owing.'

'I'm so pleased.'

'Come in. If you don't mind the kitchen, I'll make you a cup of tea. I've got lodgers in the parlour.'

In contrast to the modern hallway furniture, the kitchen had an old-fashioned cooking range and an antique oak table and sideboard.

'The house belonged to my husband's parents,' she explained. 'He inherited it after they died. We redecorated the rest of the house but left the kitchen the way it was. It's cosy enough, though I wouldn't say no to one of those new gas cookers.'

When she'd placed two teacups on the table and sat down to join me, I asked her when she'd last seen Rachel. I was still confused about the sequence of events on the day of her death.

'Before she went to work on the seventh. At least, that's where I thought she was going, but the police said she never turned up.'

'Did you notice anything out of the ordinary that morning?'

'She was dressed for work as usual, though she left earlier than she normally did. It was barely half past six, and she was out of the door.'

'Did she say when she would be back?'

'Not till late, as she had a rehearsal at the hall. I said I'd leave her some soup on the stove.' She sniffed. 'And I never saw her again.'

'Did the police tell you how she died?'

Tilly clasped her hands around her cup. 'I was ever so shocked. I don't know much about drugs. I still don't understand if it was something she took or if someone did that to her.'

'Had you ever heard Rachel mention cocaine?'

'Never. She came home a bit tipsy sometimes.' She paused. 'At least, I thought that's all it was.'

'Was that when she'd been singing in the Blackbird Bar?'

Tilly nodded. 'But she hadn't been doing much of that recently. She was busy with the pantomime rehearsals and preparing to move.'

'Did she say anything about borrowing a car?'

'The police asked me that. She didn't mention it, and I didn't see her with the Wolseley. Sometimes she'd park it outside when she borrowed it, but I didn't see it that week.'

'Did Rachel talk much about her plans? Do you think she wanted to go and live with her sister in London?'

Tilly sighed. 'I'm not sure. One night, I heard her crying. I knocked on her door, and she let me in. She was in a state; I thought she'd been drinking. Perhaps, looking back, it was drugs. Anyway, I tried to comfort her. I said I'd give her more time to pay the rent, even though I knew my husband would be annoyed with me. But I told her she'd have to sort something out if she was that hard up. That's when she said she'd written to her sister to ask if they could live together when Grace returned to England.'

'It was Rachel who asked to live with Grace?'

'That's right. I'm not sure she would have done it if things weren't going so badly. Although, saying that, every time the pantomime came around, it would fire up her ambitions to be an actress. She knew there'd be more opportunities for her in London than in Winchester.'

I was sure Grace had said she'd invited her sister to live with her when Rachel had gone to France for her brother-in-law's funeral, yet Tilly seemed to think it was the other way around. I wondered if Grace was trying to make it appear as if she'd looked after Rachel more than she had. Maybe she felt guilty now her sister was dead.

'Did Rachel say when her sister moved into Longbridge Court?'

'Not exactly. All I knew was she planned to leave here at the end of December. She had to stay until the pantomime was over. It always runs for a week between Christmas and New Year.'

I left Crows' Nest wondering who else Rachel might have spoken to about her plans. Perhaps she talked to someone in the Blackbird Bar.

I walked briskly to the high street to wait outside the *Hampshire Chronicle's* offices until Kevin Noakes finished work.

'Fancy going for a drink with me?' I asked when he appeared.

He eyed me suspiciously, his shoulders hunched beneath his tweed trench coat. 'What sort of drink? A cup of tea in the café while you wheedle information out of me? Or a few pints in the pub because you fancy me and want to get to know me better?'

I smiled. 'A glass of whatever they serve in the Blackbird Bar while we try to find out more about Rachel Lacey.'

He turned and started to walk in the opposite direction.

'Sorry,' I called after him. 'I can go on my own. I just thought you might—'

'The Blackbird Bar is on Hyde Street, which is this way,' he said over his shoulder. 'I might as well come with you. It's not as though I've had a better offer.'

I wrapped my scarf tighter around my neck and hurried after him.

When we reached Hyde Street, I looked in vain for a sign for the bar. Kevin stopped outside The White Swan Inn and motioned downwards.

It was then I saw a wooden board swinging from a bracket on the wall at waist height. A singing blackbird was pictured on a dark red background. Beneath it, an arrow pointing downwards had been painted on the wall.

Steep steps led to a metal basement door and when Kevin pushed it open, we were greeted by a wall of smoke and a cacophony of sounds. The pungent aroma of cigarettes and booze was overlaid with an assortment of ladies' perfumes and gentlemen's pomade.

I wasn't sure what I'd expected, but the Blackbird Bar wasn't it. In the corner, a man in a blue three-piece suit stood on a low wooden stage. Accompanied by a trio of musicians, he sang 'April Showers' to a largely unappreciative audience. Couples at tables chatted, more interested in each other than the efforts of Vince Duke and his Band, which was the name emblazoned on the front of the bass drum.

'What do you want to drink? Beer or something more sophisticated?' Kevin nodded towards a waitress carrying two cocktail glasses filled with a green liquid.

I pulled a face. 'I'll have half a pint.' I dug my purse out of my bag. 'Let me pay.'

He waved it away. 'Don't worry, I know it's not a date. I can't compete with the likes of the Prince of Wales. Or Percy Baverstock,' he said with a wink.

'Percy's just a friend.' I took off my woollen beret and started to unwind my thick scarf, feeling overdressed compared to the other women in the room.

'If you say so. Grab that empty table, and I'll bring them over.' Kevin turned to bestow his most flirtatious smile on a thin barmaid with large kohl-rimmed eyes.

Getting to the table was easier said than done. The walls were painted a dark red, and the few wall lamps offered little more than a soft glow. The black wooden floor felt sticky underfoot and I made my way cautiously over to a small round table close to the stage.

When the waitress who'd been carrying the cocktail glasses reappeared, I raised my hand to catch her attention.

'I'm a friend of Rachel Lacey's,' I began. 'Did you—'

'You're a reporter, same as your friend at the bar.' She nodded to where Kevin was chatting with the barmaid. 'We barely knew her so you can save your questions.'

She wasn't unfriendly, just matter-of-fact, so I risked one more. 'Didn't she have any friends here?'

'She only spoke to Norman, the manager. And I'd hardly call them friends. Rachel had a good voice and the punters liked her but I only ever saw her drinking with one chap. Tall bloke with dark hair and a scar on the side of his face. I saw them together a few times.'

I nodded and thanked her. So Harry Hobbs had been Rachel's only drinking companion.

Kevin brought over the beers in time to catch the end of the conversation.

'You got the same response as me,' he said after the waitress had walked away. 'I'm guessing the chap she was seen drinking with was Harry Hobbs. Mrs Durling told me about him.'

I was silent for a moment, wondering how much to reveal to Kevin. Things weren't looking good for Harry, and I didn't want to make them worse.

'Harry's convinced Gordon Tolfree is responsible for Rachel's death.'

'You know Harry Hobbs?'

'He's a friend of the Baverstocks. He and Freddie are working over at St Martha's Church in Walden.' I decided to tell Kevin about the mystery surrounding the arrival of the car in the clearing by Sycamore Lodge.

'Something's not right there. And the police aren't stupid. I imagine they'll be looking very closely at Harry Hobbs. What do you think of him?'

I struggled to answer, eventually saying, 'I can't make up my mind. I like Harry. But he's hiding something and I don't know what. Or why.'

I took a sip of beer, which was surprisingly good and I said so. Kevin was swigging his pint with relish.

'It's from the Winchester Brewery. They own over a hundred pubs around here, including this place and The White Swan upstairs.'

'Have you been here before?'

'Once or twice. It's got a bit of a reputation.' He shot me a look as I supped my beer. 'It's not somewhere I'd choose to bring a lady.'

Florrie wouldn't be treated to the delights of Winchester Brewery beer and Vince Duke and his Band any time soon, then.

'A reputation for what?' I asked.

He ran his hand over his slick blond hair. 'Live music and adulterous relationships.'

I glanced around and could see why. It was dark and discreet, yet Harry claimed he just came here to hear Rachel sing.

'What about drugs?'

'If you ask the right questions, they'll probably be on offer, but you could end up getting yourself in trouble if you don't know what you're doing.' Kevin had downed half of his pint and was now jiggling his knee up and down to the music. 'No one's sure if Norman, the manager, is dealing or just turns a blind eye to those who are.'

We watched with interest as a few couples took to the dance floor in front of the stage. An undercurrent of energy was more evident now the band was playing a lively jazz tune rather than a ballad.

Kevin moved closer to speak above the noise. 'Rachel was a good singer.'

'I thought you'd never met her?'

'I hadn't. But I saw her in last year's pantomime. I didn't know it was Rachel playing Bo Peep until Mrs Durling mentioned it the other day. I remember she wore a ridiculous hat and sang a song about sheep. She had a lovely voice. Strong and clear.'

I imagined playing Bo Peep and Cinderella in charity pantomimes wasn't what Rachel had aspired to. Nor was the Blackbird Bar exactly the London Palladium.

I scrutinised all the dancers to see if I could detect any signs of illicit drug taking. If there were any dealers present, I had a feeling they'd target some of the livelier couples rather than Kevin and me. But then I had no idea how these things worked.

It was a shame Percy wasn't around. He would have taken to the dance floor with gusto and tried to find out for me – and, knowing him, landed in a police cell for his troubles.

It would be impossible to discover anything without asking direct questions, which would be far too risky. I didn't want to attract the attention of criminals or the police and said as much to Kevin.

He nodded. 'Let's stick to working on assumptions for the moment. If you'd asked me where in Winchester you'd be able to buy cocaine, this place would be high on my list. Now we know how Rachel died and the fact that cocaine was found in a car that she regularly drove, I'd say she somehow found herself involved with a drug dealer.'

20

The following evening could hardly have been more of a contrast than my visit to the Blackbird Bar. Rather than the stink of booze and cigarettes, the sweet scent of fruit cake, mince pies and lemonade emanated from the town hall.

The Walden Elementary School Choir's carol concert was always held in the first week of December to kick off the town's Christmas festivities, and the great and good of Walden had gathered to hear the children sing.

Colourful paper chains decorated the walls, and a huge lopsided pine Christmas tree stood in the corner, topped by a smiling silver angel.

The Ropers were there with their children, and Elijah went over to Robbie to discuss the photographs he wanted of the choir. I had the task of establishing all the children's names. Fortunately, Millicent was on hand to assist.

Mrs Gilbert, Ben's mother, was in the kitchen adjoining the hall, setting out rows of cups and saucers and uncovering trays of mince pies.

Ben appeared at my side, still in uniform, although he'd removed his hat for the occasion.

'You know you asked me where Archie was on the afternoon of Rachel's death?' he said. 'It turns out he was in the cathedral for the service for the Prince of Wales.'

I tutted in disgust. 'I've a good mind to write to the palace to tell them they should be more careful about the company they keep. And afterwards? Was he at this drinks party?'

'He told Superintendent Cobbe he sat in quiet contemplation in the cathedral for a while before returning to his lodgings nearby.'

I lowered my voice, seeing Gordon and Jennifer Tolfree enter the hall. 'That means both he and Gordon Tolfree were only five minutes' walk from where Rachel was killed.'

Reverend Childs called for everyone to take their seats, and I left Ben hovering at the back of the hall and went to sit next to Elijah. I smiled at Walden's newest residents, Harry and Victoria Hobbs, as they sat in the opposite aisle. Victoria was wearing a chic blue crepe dress in the latest tubular style, which suited her slender figure, and I wondered if she'd made it herself. Mrs Durling had described her as a talented seamstress.

I turned to glance around the hall and realised it was filled with nearly all my close family and friends. I noticed my father holding hands with Katherine. They made an attractive couple, and after five months of marriage, still had the glow of newly-weds. Our housekeeper, Lizzy, was with them. She was gazing rapturously at Mrs Siddons' emerald silk dress and diamond necklace. No change there. Lizzy had always been an ardent admirer of Mrs Siddons' jewels and finery.

Mrs Siddons was accompanied by Horace Laffaye, her neighbour, who was immaculately attired in a grey cashmere coat and matching fedora hat. They would easily win the prize for the most smartly dressed couple in the room.

A few rows in front of me, I saw Daniel whisper something in Millicent's ear and she smiled up at him. If Percy was here, he'd be nudging me in the ribs and whispering, 'I told you so.' He liked to think that Daniel and Millicent's romance was solely down to his matchmaking. Constance sat next to them, looking elegant and understated in a navy fitted jacket and skirt. By contrast, Ursula was in a festive mood, her grey hair tucked beneath a bright red turban adorned with a sprig of holly.

Despite being surrounded by people I loved, I experienced a pang of loneliness. What would it have felt like to have been sitting there with Marc by my side? I wondered if that was how Rachel had felt about Harry. Had she wanted too much and paid the price for it?

I glanced across the aisle to where Harry and Victoria were seated. The look of tenderness they shared as they smiled at the children trooping into the hall brought the reality of my situation home to me. Marc's place was with his wife, Annette. The intensity of our feelings for each other had perhaps been understandable in the turmoil of war. We no longer had that excuse.

The sadness that I'd one day have to say goodbye to Marc brought an unexpected tear to my eye. As I brushed it away, I looked up and realised to my horror that Archie Powell was watching me. He was seated next to Reverend Childs at the front of the hall to the left of the stage. Once again, he was dressed in a black shirt and trousers in an attempt to replicate his former clerical garb. And he wore that familiar challenging expression, as if he could tell what I was thinking.

I turned to Elijah, who evidently shared my disbelief. Daniel appeared equally dumbfounded, and I saw Millicent reach out to hold his hand. Ben quietly moved from where he'd been standing at the back of the hall to sit beside Constance. She turned to him with a grateful smile, but he kept his eyes fixed on Archie.

When Constance had been under threat from the then-unknown sniper, Detective Inspector Yates had assigned Ben to protect her. She would love having her old bodyguard back, perhaps mistaking his sense of duty for affection. However, I knew Ben would be as immune to her charm as he'd always been, especially now the nurse from the cottage hospital was on the scene.

Mrs Gilbert, Ben's mother, was standing at the door of the kitchen with a horrified look on her face. Her shock was enough to make me want to stride over and try to forcibly remove Archie from the hall.

Before I could say anything to Elijah, the children launched into 'O Little Town of Bethlehem', and I seethed in silence.

I automatically clapped at the end of each song, but my mind was elsewhere throughout the concert. Thankfully, due to the children's ages, it wasn't overly long. At the end, I went to the front of the hall with Millicent to note down their names. Mrs Gilbert and Katherine had set out drinks and mince pies for the youngsters and this kept them in one place for long enough to achieve the task.

I studiously ignored Archie, who, to my annoyance, was now chatting with Harry and Victoria. They would know each other through the pantomime.

Harry appeared to be telling some tale, but I noticed Archie's eyes kept drifting to Victoria. She was a beautiful woman.

Millicent and I exchanged a meaningful glance.

'Why does he keep turning up?' I whispered. 'He must have known Constance and Mrs Siddons would be here.'

'He tried to speak to Daniel,' she muttered. 'But not to Constance.'

'The only person he's apologised to is Ben.' I looked to where Constance and Mrs Siddons were standing, flanked by Ben and Horace Laffaye. 'He seems to think the women he targeted don't count.'

When Harry and Archie went to try to push the precariously lopsided Christmas tree into an upright position, I sidled over to Victoria.

'Be careful of Archie Powell,' I said without preamble.

Her smile of greeting turned to a frown. 'Archie's been good to us. People should be more forgiving. You don't know what he suffered during the war. He admitted what he did was wrong, and he's paid for his mistakes.'

I ground my teeth. Archie Powell no more had shellshock than I did. He hadn't made a mistake or acted foolishly because of his shattered nerves. He knew exactly what he was doing when he fired those shots, and I didn't believe he was repentant.

'You don't understand—'

Victoria held up a hand to stop me. 'He's truly sorry for what he did, and now he's attempting to use his experience to help others. Archie's a good influence on Harry. He has a calming effect on him. Sometimes, I just can't get through, but Harry listens to him. I think it's because Archie understands what drives him to be a little wild at times and can help him overcome those impulses.'

This silenced me as I wondered what those wild impulses were. And if they'd led Harry into a disastrous relationship with Rachel Lacey that he'd later regretted.

Victoria smiled over to where her husband and Archie were wrestling with the Christmas tree. Archie had clearly charmed his way into the Hobbs' affections, and I could tell there was no point in trying to warn Victoria of his true nature. Instead, I asked how they were settling into their new home.

'Everyone in Walden has been so friendly. It's going to be good for us here. A fresh start. Harry's already had plenty of offers of work.'

'That's great...' I began, when Horace caught my eye, jerking his head in the direction of Reverend Childs. I excused myself and hurried over to where Elijah was taking the vicar to task.

'I'm surprised, Reverend Childs, at the type of people the church now welcomes into its fold.'

The vicar flushed. 'Mr Powell is a devout Christian and has helped many people with his ministering.'

Horace had probably meant for me to drag Elijah away. Instead, I decided to take up the reins.

'He's also a convicted felon and has damaged the lives of many others.'

'I think, Mr Whittle and Miss Woodmore, that you should, "let him who is without sin cast the first stone".' To emphasise his point, he placed his palms together as if in prayer.

Elijah's enjoyment of alcoholic beverages was well known, and I assumed this was what Reverend Childs was referring to. I'd never heard anyone hint at any impropriety in his relationship with Horace.

As for me, I knew the town thought me something of an oddity. After my trip abroad, my reputation was probably beyond saving even though I was living with a respectable schoolteacher and her great aunt. I remembered how, when I'd first told Percy I was going to take up Millicent's offer of lodgings, he'd queried whether my dubious reputation might sully her good name. I'd been insulted at the time. Now I thought about my friendship with Marc and felt guilty.

'Reverend Childs.' Mrs Siddons sailed regally into our midst,

Horace by her side. 'I think Mr Whittle and Miss Woodmore have a point. That man—' she fluttered her heavily mascaraed lashes in the direction of where Archie was standing '—once threatened me and Miss Timpson with a rifle. Yet you expect us to welcome him into our lives.'

'I understand your concerns.' Reverend Childs was now red in the face. 'However, I will not turn away a repentant sinner from my door.'

'The diocese may be happy to admit him into their ranks, but I'm not sure the school's board of governors will be so keen to have him ministering to their pupils.' Horace nodded towards the stage, where Archie was ruffling the head of a small boy.

'If you must know, I didn't invite him here this evening.' The vicar's tone was more placatory now, aware that Horace Laffaye and Mrs Siddons were arguably the most influential people in Walden.

Although the conversation was being carried out in an undertone, it must have been obvious who we were talking about as Gordon and Jennifer Tolfree decided to intervene.

Gordon Tolfree thrust out his chest. 'If you're discussing Mr Powell, I invited him here this evening. He's a respected member of the congregation at Winchester Cathedral where he's a verger and a valued committee member of the cathedral's war fund.'

'He's a criminal,' Elijah commented.

Jennifer Tolfree gave him a scathing look. 'Fortunately, not everyone in this town is so small-minded. The Walden Women's Group appreciate Mr Powell's contribution to our worthy cause. They've seen fit to forgive any past errors of judgement and you'd do well to follow their example.'

I was about to object to this description of Archie's crimes when an angry squeal made us turn to look at the stage where

Millicent seemed to be breaking up a fight over the last mince pie. This provided a welcome diversion as it was evident the conversation had reached stalemate.

'Please excuse us.' Jennifer gripped her husband's arm. 'We must get the children home.'

Gordon nodded to Mrs Siddons. 'See you on election day. May the best man win.'

Mrs Siddons gave her most gracious smile. 'Or woman.'

As Jennifer passed the Ropers, who'd been standing nearby, clearly enjoying the spectacle, she called, 'Mr Roper, I hope you'll be able to attend the pantomime's press day tomorrow?' It was a command rather than a request.

'Of course.' He gave a polite nod.

'Press day?' Elijah queried when the Tolfrees were out of earshot.

'It's the day the tickets go on sale. The cast get dressed up and go out onto the streets of Winchester to drum up interest. I go along to take photographs that they then use for publicity.' Robbie pulled a face. 'Free of charge.'

'It's my fault,' Ellen Roper said. 'Mrs Tolfree asks me every year, and she's a difficult woman to refuse. It's all for a good cause.'

The Ropers went to collect their children from the stage and the group dispersed, Horace escorting Mrs Siddons from the hall, and my father diplomatically steering Elijah away from the vicar. I drifted over to help Katherine clear up the discarded cups and plates.

She followed my gaze to where Archie was standing with members of the Walden Women's Group.

'I'm afraid the ladies are quite enamoured of him,' Katherine said as she began to stack dirty plates.

My heart sank. I could just picture Archie worming his way into their good graces. The sooner this pantomime was over with, the better.

'I keep him at arm's length,' Katherine continued. 'And, of course, poor Mrs Gilbert can't abide him.'

'I'm surprised the others aren't more loyal to her.' Ben's mother was a founding member of the group.

'They've been persuaded he's a tormented soul who only acted that way because of the suffering he'd seen during the war. Jennifer Tolfree eulogised him when she introduced him to the group. She thinks he's practically a saint.'

'Archie's good at ensnaring people.' I tried not to sound too bitter. After all, I'd willing responded to his flirtation.

'She's embarrassingly keen on him,' Katherine whispered. 'I'm surprised her husband hasn't noticed.'

I watched Gordon Tolfree chatting with his son and daughter and had to admit the way he held their hands as he led them from the hall was quite sweet. It was clear he adored them.

Jennifer Tolfree didn't appear to be in any hurry to follow her family as she carried on her conversation with members of the Walden Women's Group. I noticed she'd placed a proprietary hand on Archie's arm as if to establish ownership of him in front of the other ladies.

'I have some news for you.' Katherine waited until we were in the kitchen before continuing. 'When I was in Winchester for an extremely tedious meeting about the pantomime's press day, I heard Jennifer Tolfree saying that she'd encouraged her husband to sack Rachel Lacey.'

I placed the tray of cups I was carrying next to the sink and turned to her in surprise. 'Who was she talking to?'

'One of the other cast members. A lady called Nancy Miller.'

I nodded. 'Her husband, Oliver Miller, manages Tolfree Motors.'

'I'll try to find out more tomorrow at the press day.' Katherine glanced towards the kitchen door to make sure no one was listening. 'It seems Jennifer told Gordon he had to get rid of Rachel as she'd become a liability.'

21

The parlour of 13 Victoria Lane was often the venue for campaign meetings as it was in the centre of town. Mrs Siddons sometimes held parties at her home, but many of her supporters had no transport and it was a long walk in the dark to Grebe House.

Crookham Hall was also too far out of town, although I'm sure many of the people arriving at Victoria Lane would have travelled there if it meant they could see inside the Timpsons' ancestral home.

When the bell rang for the fifth time, I opened it to find Katherine on the doorstep.

'Come in,' I said. 'It's warm and cosy in the parlour. Perhaps a little too cosy. More people turned up than expected.'

Mrs Siddons swept in, armed with two bottles of sherry to bolster our dwindling supplies, and Katherine gratefully took a glass from Ursula.

Once everyone was settled, Mrs Siddons stood in the centre of the room.

'We only have a week until the election, and, as you know, there's a fourth candidate.'

There was general harrumphing at this.

Mrs Siddons continued. 'However, as far as I can see, Gordon Tolfree doesn't appear to have made much of an impression as an independent candidate.'

This led to a volley of exchanges from around the room.

'He doesn't have any policies.'

'All he's going to do is split the vote.'

Ursula banged her spectacles on the table. 'We need to target the conservative voters.'

If numbers were down, Mrs Siddons risked losing her seat to the conservative candidate. Labour had yet to get a foothold in this neck of the woods despite my father's support for the party.

Mrs Siddons held up a hand. 'Ursula is right. We need those wavering conservative voters to become liberal ones. This is our last week before the election, and I'll be visiting every corner of my constituency. Most people know me, but I want to forge deeper connections with all members of the community, and I need your help to do that.'

She explained that she wanted us to focus on local issues when we went door to door with her leaflets.

'Yes, people are interested in the wider problems we face. But what they really want to talk about is getting an x-ray machine for the local hospital or being able to keep their children in school for longer before sending them out to work.'

The leaflets that Millicent had helped to write and Constance had arranged to be printed were passed around, and there was an energy in the room that was satisfying to be a part of.

My only concern was Constance, who was staring unseeingly into the fire. For such a young woman, she had a tremendous amount of responsibility on her shoulders. She relied greatly on

Mrs Siddons' political influence and if the election didn't go our way, it would affect her more than anyone.

'Why do men hate us so much?' she asked when I went to perch on the old footstool by her side.

Ursula had also recognised that Constance was in need of support and headed over with the sherry bottle.

'Not all men.' Ursula handed me the bottle and sank onto the sofa next to Constance and took her hand.

'I have few male allies. And no suitors.' Constance gave a rueful smile. 'I used to loathe it when Mother introduced me to young bachelors she deemed to be *eligible*. By that, I mean rich. Now I'm considered a pariah and no man will come near me, rich or poor.'

I'd long come to realise how lonely it was to be a woman in a man's world. The previous year, I'd got to know a policewoman, and she'd experienced the same problem of becoming isolated because of her profession.

I topped up their glasses. 'What's the alternative? To stay at home and do as we're told?'

Constance's tinkly silver laugh sounded for the first time in ages. 'I can't imagine you ever doing that.' She took a sip of sherry. 'Ignore me, I'm just feeling tired at constantly having to fight.'

'Concentrate on one battle at a time,' Ursula advised. 'We didn't choose to take on Gordon Tolfree or Archie Powell. They directed their unwanted attention at us. They've left us with no choice but to defend ourselves.'

Constance sighed. 'How do we do that?'

'First, we need to ensure Mrs Siddons keeps her seat,' Ursula replied.

'Then we need to find out what the hell is going on at Tolfree Motors,' I added. 'Elijah and I have been doing some digging with Mr Laffaye's help. And, of course, Ben is on the case.' I smiled. 'There are some good men out there.'

Constance raised her glass. 'And some good women.'

'Very true.' I rose from the footstool and picked up the sherry bottle. 'And I'm just going to speak to one of them.'

Katherine and I took our drinks into the kitchen so we could talk privately.

'Did you go to Winchester for the press day?' I asked, closing the kitchen door.

'It was surprisingly good fun. The costumes are wonderful. Victoria Hobbs has done an amazing job, especially having to conjure up a new ball gown at short notice.' Katherine took a seat at the kitchen table. 'I must admit, I was sceptical about the group getting involved with the pantomime, but it does raise quite a bit of money. Tickets were selling fast, so I bought a pair. You will come, won't you?'

I pulled up a chair next to her. 'I feel unable to resist, even though I'm cringing at the thought of it.'

She laughed. 'That's how I feel, especially now I've met the rest of the cast. They make an odd bunch. Poor Freddie seems absolutely terrified of Jennifer Tolfree. I made a point of chatting with Nancy Miller. She has to play second fiddle to Jennifer, as Gordon is her husband's boss. They pretend to be on the best of terms, but I get the impression there's some resentment on Nancy's part. Anyway, Nancy hinted that Gordon had been rather too friendly with Rachel Lacey.'

'Did she say how she knew?'

'Not directly, though she was at pains to mention the fact that her husband practically runs Tolfree Motors single-handed.'

So Oliver Miller had been suspicious enough of Gordon's behaviour towards Rachel to mention it to his wife.

'Did Jennifer know what was going on?'

'Nancy thinks she'd begun to suspect, and that's why Jennifer encouraged Gordon to fire Rachel.'

'Sacked by the boss because she had an affair with him?'

It seemed the wealthy Tolfrees had got rid of Rachel with no consequences to themselves but possibly dire ones for her. Sadly, I suspected similar scenarios were played out in offices and factories all over the country.

'No. That's the interesting thing.' Katherine paused, clearly relishing her role as my spy. 'Nancy described Rachel as a drug addict. She thinks it was this that prompted Gordon to sack her.'

22

'Another letter from your London boyfriend.' Millicent tossed the envelope onto the breakfast table, giving me a meaningful look.

I licked marmalade from my fingers before picking it up and shoving it into my pocket. As a distraction, I told her and Ursula what Katherine had found out about the Tolfrees and Rachel Lacey.

'This young lady seems to have got herself into a hell of a mess.' Ursula bashed the top of her boiled egg with a teaspoon as if to illustrate her point. 'It's interesting that she tends to rely on older men. First Gordon Tolfree and then this Harry chap.'

'Harry's only a few years older than her. But funnily enough, her sister, Grace, did say that she thought Rachel liked Harry because he reminded her of their father. Both were craftsmen, able to design and build stage sets.'

'If she did have an affair with Gordon Tolfree and he ended it, then she found herself in debt; she might have decided to take an overdose,' Millicent speculated. 'Her singing and acting career hadn't gone the way she'd hoped. Perhaps she put on her favourite dress, the ball gown costume, and injected the cocaine?'

'But where was the needle?' I finished my toast and wiped my hands on a napkin. 'And moving in with her sister gave her the opportunity she needed to make a fresh start in a new place.'

'If she'd taken cocaine, she may not have been thinking clearly,' Ursula pointed out. 'Drug addiction can lead to all sorts of unpredictable behaviour.'

'When I spoke to Victoria Hobbs at the carol concert, she said something about Harry's wilder impulses. I'm not entirely sure what she meant by that.' I stood up and took my cup and plate over to the kitchen sink. 'I'm going to call in at the church at lunchtime and ask Harry outright if he knew that Rachel took cocaine. He's hiding something.'

Ursula's brow crinkled. 'You might run into that Powell man again.'

'I'm not going to let him stop me from going wherever I please. He doesn't scare me.'

Though, if I were honest, his repeated appearances in Walden were starting to make me edgy.

Millicent drained her tea and began to gather up her school-books. 'I'd come with you if I could, but I've got lessons all day.'

'I'll be fine.'

In the hall, I quickly opened Marc's letter and perused its contents. When I heard the kitchen door open, I tucked it into my satchel to read again later. I unhooked my woollen overcoat from the rack, wound my scarf around my neck and headed out of the front door.

Outside, there was a hard frost, and the grass verges at the side of the road glistened white. I pulled my gloves from my pocket and put on an unflattering knitted hat that Lizzy had made me many years before. I didn't envy Harry and Freddie working in freezing conditions, though I supposed in their line of work it was something you had to get used to.

I'd reached the high street when an ambulance came speeding by. Jim Fellowes, owner of Fellowes Emporium, stood outside his shop watching its progress.

I went over to him.

'What's going on?'

'A body's been found at the church.' He stared morosely after the ambulance. 'Too late for saving from what I've heard.'

My stomach lurched. 'Who is it?'

'They think it was one of those stonemasons who've been working there.'

'Which one?' My voice shook. 'Harry Hobbs or Freddie Baverstock?'

Jim shrugged. 'I don't know their names.'

Panic swept over me and I gripped my satchel and began to run. Millicent, who'd left the house shortly after me, came in pursuit. Through ragged gasps, I told her what had happened.

We must have made quite a sight, the prim schoolteacher and the odd reporter dashing full pelt along Walden high street. We turned left onto Church Road and came stumbling to a halt outside St Martha's. PC Sid King was standing by the lychgate talking to two medics who'd rushed from the ambulance.

'I'm afraid it's too late,' he was saying. 'But you'd better take a look. He's around the side.'

'Who is it?' I demanded. 'Who's dead?'

Sid held up his hand to stop us going any further. 'I don't know yet. A young lad was riding by on his bicycle, delivering newspapers, when he spotted him. He came straight to the station house to tell us. Ben telephoned the cottage hospital to send an ambulance and now he's trying to get hold of the vicar. It may be one of the stonemasons working at the church, but that's not certain, so—'

'We need to know if it's Freddie Baverstock,' I pleaded. 'Or Harry Hobbs.'

'We can help you identify who it is,' Millicent added.

'Freddie Baverstock is the younger of the two. He's twenty-six with brown wavy hair. He looks like his brother,' I panted. 'You remember Percy Baverstock.'

'I think we should wait until Ben—' Sid began.

'Harry's the older of the two. About thirty. He has brown hair, but it's much darker than Freddie's. And he's taller.' I realised that as Sid had never met Freddie Baverstock, this was a fairly hopeless description. 'Please just let us take a quick look.'

Sid hesitated. 'It might be distressing.'

'We have to know if it's Freddie,' Millicent told him.

Reluctantly, he nodded and gestured for us to follow.

'Come on, let's get this over with.' Sid led us around to the side of the church to where the old bench was. 'Don't touch the body.'

Millicent strode ahead, but I stumbled, my legs feeling like they were about to give way. Say it was Freddie? I couldn't bear to think of what that would do to Percy, not to speak of Hetty and Clifford.

The man was lying on the frozen grass close to the bench. He wore heavy leather boots, black corduroy trousers, and a thick woollen khaki army jumper. By the frost on his clothes, it looked as if he'd lain there all night.

The medics were kneeling beside him.

'Too late,' one of them said softly.

As soon as I'd glimpsed the figure on the ground, I'd been able to tell who it was by his hair and stature – and felt guilty at the wave of relief that washed over me.

'It's Harry Hobbs,' I heard Millicent say.

23

My relief at finding it wasn't Freddie was replaced by shock and sadness at the sight of Harry Hobbs. I remembered the jovial man at the Baverstocks' lunch party. And his beautiful, loving wife.

He looked so cold. His skin was blue, and his face was bloated and contorted into a caricature of its former shape. Around the nostrils, I noticed traces of a white powder. The left sleeve of his jumper was pushed up to expose white skin with bluish bruising in the crook of his elbow.

'Who is it?'

The sound made us jump and we turned to find Ben striding towards us.

'The man's name is Harry Hobbs,' Sid replied. 'Miss Nightingale has just identified him.'

Ben stared at the body for a long time before addressing the medics. 'Take him to the mortuary. Sid, make a search of the area. You two come with me.'

It had begun to drizzle but Ben steered us away from the

shelter of the church to the cover of the lychgate. Now the body had been identified, he clearly wanted us to leave.

'Poor Victoria,' Millicent muttered.

'Is that his wife?' Ben asked, taking out his pocketbook. 'I think I saw them at the carol concert.'

'Yes. Victoria Hobbs,' I replied. 'They've only just moved into one of the houses on the new estate at Crookham.'

'Did they have children?'

I shook my head, remembering how Harry had talked about a son joining the family business.

'It looked like Harry had taken cocaine,' I said.

I'd noticed his van was parked by the side of the road but there was no sign of Freddie's motorbike.

'A pathologist will make a thorough examination.' Ben fixed me with a stern look. 'Until then, I'd prefer you not to speculate on the cause of death.'

'According to gossip, Rachel Lacey was sacked from Tolfree Motors because she was a drug addict,' I said. 'And that she'd been having an affair with Gordon Tolfree.'

'Do you have any evidence to back up these rumours?'

'No. But there must be a connection between the two deaths.'

'Who told you that about Rachel Lacey?' Ben asked.

'My stepmother,' I replied. 'The Walden Women's Group has become involved in the cathedral pantomime. Katherine overheard conversations between Jennifer Tolfree and Nancy Miller, wife of Oliver Miller. She also chatted to Nancy when she went over to Winchester for the pantomime's press day.'

Ben rubbed his eyes. 'You got her to spy for you?'

I quickly changed the subject. 'How long will the pathologist take to report on the cause of death?'

He sighed. 'Given the similarities to Rachel Lacey's death, I imagine the superintendent will ask for it to be given priority. And yes, I'll let you know the results, if I'm allowed—'

Ben was drowned out by the roar of a motorbike.

Freddie's Triumph skidded to a halt, and he jumped off. 'What's happening? Where's Harry?'

I took a step towards him. 'Freddie, I—'

Ben held up his hand. 'Mr Baverstock, please would you accompany me into the church.' Then he turned to me. 'Make sure no one enters the churchyard until the body has been removed and PC King has finished his search of the area.'

'Body?' Freddie's bewildered eyes sought answers from Millicent and me.

'I'll wait here for you,' I called as Ben led him into the church.

A moment later, the medics appeared carrying a stretcher between them, and we watched in silence as it was loaded into the ambulance. Although Harry was covered by a white sheet, I was glad Freddie hadn't witnessed the removal of his friend's body from the churchyard.

'First Rachel and now Harry. What the hell is going on?' I muttered.

'Is it possible they both died of accidental drug overdoses?' Millicent queried.

'It seems unlikely to me. The same method of death, three weeks apart. And why here?' I stared at the gravestones. 'A churchyard is the last place you'd go to take cocaine. Or murder someone.'

Sid appeared from around the side of the church. He had a boyish face that made him look younger than his twenty-six years, and though he lacked Ben's natural authority, he was an astute policeman.

'Anything?' I asked, knowing he would have made a thorough search.

'Nothing by the body. No sign of a syringe. I'm just going to take a look in his van.'

We watched him open the rear door of the unlocked van and inspect its contents before checking the front seats. Eventually, he closed the driver's door, holding what appeared to be a small card.

Curiosity getting the better of us, Millicent and I walked over to see what it was.

'I found this on the driver's seat.' Sid held up an embossed business card.

Printed on one side in black lettering were the words:

Gordon Tolfree, Tolfree Motors, City Road, Winchester.

Sid turned it over.

6 p.m. at church

was scrawled in blue ink on the back.

24

I wasn't surprised to find Kevin Noakes lurking in the doorway of Laffaye Printworks the following lunchtime when I came out of *The Walden Herald* offices.

'You've been having all the excitement around here.' He threw the remains of his cigarette to the ground and crushed the burning end under his shoe.

'We have indeed.' I pulled on my woollen gloves and tucked my scarf into my coat, guessing I was in for another trip to St Martha's Church.

'Care to give me a guided tour of the crime scene?'

'Follow me.'

After the information he'd shared with me, I could hardly refuse, although it felt ghoulish to return to where Harry had lain.

When we got to St Martha's, Kevin gazed around the frost-covered churchyard.

'It's a rum one, isn't it?' he said. 'Quaint old church like this, in the middle of nowhere and some fellow dies of a drug overdose.'

'Walden is hardly the middle of nowhere,' I objected. 'And we don't know how he died. It could have been from exposure. It was a cold night.'

I didn't think this was the case, but it hadn't been ruled out.

'Does Robbie have any photos we can use?'

'Of what? The body?' I asked, appalled.

'Of it being carried out. Or a police van parked outside the church.'

I shook my head. 'He'll probably have some photographs of the church you can use, but none with bodies or police vans. They tend to spoil the atmosphere at a wedding.'

He chuckled. 'I'll call in at his studio and see what he's got. Tolfree's place is nearby, isn't it?'

'I'll show you. But let's try to keep out of sight as much as possible. He won't be happy with reporters snooping.'

'He can't stop us.' Kevin dug his hands into his trench coat pockets and strolled back to the icy road. 'He'll have to get used to it if he wants to be a politician.'

It was alright for Kevin; he lived in a big city not a small market town. He didn't have to face the consequences of antagonising a prominent local figure.

Reluctantly, I led him along the track to Gordon Tolfree's house.

'Very nice,' he said when he saw Sycamore Lodge. 'And he lives here with his wife and children?'

'And his mother. The house used to belong to his father. Gordon inherited it on Redvers Tolfree's death.'

'And where was the car found?'

I took him to the clearing. The Wolseley had been returned to Tolfree Motors, and there wasn't much to see. This didn't deter Kevin from exploring the nearby woods and retracing the route back to Sycamore Lodge. Like any good reporter, he was getting a feel for the place.

'Why here?' Kevin gestured to the clearing. 'Tolfree couldn't have driven it himself that afternoon as he was seen at the cathedral service and Miller says he was in his office later. If someone dropped it off for him, why not leave it on his driveway? Why swing it around and park it out of sight, here in the woods?'

'Because there were drugs in the glovebox?'

We began to walk back to the church.

'Do you think Harry Hobbs liked snow?' he asked.

'Snow?' I glanced up at heavy grey clouds.

'Cocaine,' Kevin said, then added self-consciously, 'It's what they call it in America.'

'I think you'll find the only snow in Walden is the icy stuff that falls from the sky.'

He grinned. 'Not exactly New York, is it? But you'd be surprised how many drugs are lurking in people's homes. Particularly the medicine cabinets of ex-soldiers.'

'It's possible,' I replied cautiously. Ben had forbidden me to speculate about the cause of Harry's death or mention the business card found in the van.

Kevin stopped outside the church and looked back along the road. 'It all feels too close to home for Tolfree to be involved. Yet I'm sure something's going on with his business.'

'If he is involved, where would he get cocaine from?'

Kevin shrugged. 'He buys cars and there's cocaine hidden inside them.'

'He's not importing vehicles from abroad. From what Oliver Miller said, he's mainly trading in used motor cars. And buying to order from a place in London. He mentioned a dealer called Fitzherbert.'

'That's a genuine car dealership. It's an amazing place in New Cross. You've never seen so many cars in your life. Some of them cost more than I'll earn in a lifetime. I go there sometimes and pretend to be a customer just to look at them. They do the basics – the Fords and Wolseleys that Tolfree stocks – but they've got some high-end stuff as well.'

'High-end drugs?' I suggested.

He nodded. 'Maybe. If he was getting hold of cocaine, it's most likely to have come from London. I doubt he'd be importing it himself. More likely trading with a dealer in the city.'

'Oliver said that Rachel used to do the pick-ups. And...' I paused for emphasis. 'This is strictly a rumour, but it appears Rachel didn't hand in her notice. Tolfree sacked her.'

He whistled. 'I'd say Rachel knew too much about the set-up. It could have been Tolfree who got her on to cocaine when they were having an affair.'

'It's plausible, although it's all hearsay. The drugs and the affair.'

It certainly wasn't anything Elijah would put into print.

'What about Freddie Baverstock?' Kevin asked.

My eyes narrowed. 'What about him?'

'I know you don't want to think it, but...' He began to count on his fingers. 'One, he worked with Harry Hobbs. Two, he fancied Rachel Lacey. Three, he's part of the pantomime. Oh, and four, he's the youngest of the bunch. He might have got a taste for cocaine in some of the jazz clubs that are springing up. You won't catch many older people in those kinds of places. They can't stand the music for a start.'

I shook my head. 'The staff in the Blackbird Bar didn't mention seeing Rachel with anyone but Harry. I'm sure Freddie's not involved, though I think he's aware something was going on between Rachel and Harry. I'm still not convinced it was an affair.' I decided to distract Kevin from speculating too much about Freddie by giving him another suspect. 'There's someone else in the cast that might have caught Rachel's eye. Do you know Archie Powell?'

'The disgraced vicar? He's one to watch. Mrs Durling sings his praises, but he sounds dodgy to me.'

I wasn't surprised to hear Mrs Durling had fallen for Archie's charm – and pleased Kevin wasn't as easily swayed.

'Dodgy is the right word. I'm curious to know how Rachel got on with Mr Powell.'

'My car's parked in town. Why don't you come back to Winchester with me and ask Mrs Durling? She's at the hall this afternoon. When I told her I was coming to Walden today, she asked me to find out how Victoria Hobbs is. She wants to send her a card.'

I nodded. 'Okay. Daniel, Millicent and I are planning to visit Victoria tomorrow. I can pass it on.'

Elijah wouldn't be thrilled about me skiving off work for the afternoon. But I couldn't resist trying to unearth something that might suggest a motive for Archie Powell wanting Rachel Lacey dead.

25

After paying a visit to Robbie's studio and calling in to see Elijah, Kevin drove us to Winchester and dropped me off at Christmas Close.

Jack Archer was standing outside the hall smoking a cigarette.

'Is that young Kevin?' He peered at the car as it turned around and headed out of the close.

I nodded, realising he must have poor eyesight.

'You're Mrs Durling's friend. Can't remember your name.'

'Iris Woodmore. From *The Walden Herald*.' I took a step back from the stale smell of beer and tobacco that clung to his clothes and gazed at the cigarette ends scattered on the ground. 'It must feel strange standing where Rachel died.'

He grunted. 'It did at first. But you can't smoke inside. I keep telling them. They don't seem to realise the fire hazards in a place like this. Do you know how many fires there have been in theatres?'

'My grandparents live in Exeter. They remember the terrible fire at the Theatre Royal in 1887.'

Jack looked triumphant. 'Precisely. One hundred and eighty-six people killed when a gauze curtain caught alight on one of the gas jets they used for the stage lighting.'

'Is that why you light the gas fires yourself?'

'They can be fiddly. I know how to light them safely. I keep telling them not to touch them till I get here. Rachel was the worst.'

I noticed the tremor of his fingers as he drew on his cigarette. I wasn't sure Jack was entirely safe with a match amongst flammable materials.

'Were the gas fires lit on the day you found her?'

'The one in the ladies' dressing room was. Turned right up, too. And she'd used the gas ring in the office.'

I made a tutting noise, trying to ingratiate myself with him. I wasn't surprised Rachel had lit the gas fire. I'd have wanted to warm up the dressing room before changing into a ball gown.

'Kevin told me about the car you saw that afternoon. You might have seen who killed her.'

'I'd been outside the cathedral watching the prince arrive. When he went inside, I walked through Curle's Passage to Cathedral Close. I came out by Kingsgate, and that's when I saw it turn into St Swithun Street and then into Christmas Close. It was that old Wolseley. I thought it must be Oliver Miller or Rachel driving.'

'You didn't check?'

'I hadn't had my lunch. I went back to the Perseverance Inn to see if they had any sandwiches left. Whoever it was could let themselves in with the key under the pot.'

I guessed Jack had gone to the pub to continue his lunchtime drinking rather than in search of food.

'You didn't see who was in the car?'

He shook his head. 'I think there were two people, though

I'm not sure. I only saw it for a moment or two. It wasn't there later. I went back at about three-fifteen to light the fires. Rehearsals weren't due to start until five, but I knew Rachel and Mrs Durling would be there earlier. That's when I found her.'

The pub had closed at three. That would have given Jack an hour's drinking time before walking the short distance between the Perseverance Inn and Christmas Close.

I went inside and was unsurprised to find Bridget Durling in a subdued mood. She was sitting in the ladies' changing room, writing on a card.

'Is that for Victoria Hobbs?' I asked. 'A couple of friends and I are going to visit her tomorrow. Would you like me to give it to her?'

'Thank you, love, that would be kind. I was going to give it to Oliver or Nancy, but neither of them has been in.' She took out her handkerchief and dabbed her eyes. 'It's so difficult to know what to write. I suggested we cancel the pantomime out of respect. But we've sold too many tickets. And I think Harry would have wanted us to use his sets.'

'I'm sure he would.' I sat down at the makeshift dressing table and looked at the rail of costumes. 'And I expect Victoria would like her costumes to be worn too.'

Mrs Durling gave a sad smile and nodded. 'She did a marvellous job. Some of them needed to be altered to fit Mrs Tolfree, and of course, she had to make a new ball gown, but the Walden Women's Group helped out. They were marvellous on press day. I think we've sold more tickets than last year.'

'Harry would be pleased so much money has been raised for the war fund.'

'It's to help men like him. It's sad this should happen after everything he went through. I know Harry could be a handful at times, but he was a kind man.' She sniffed. 'They're saying it's drugs, but Kevin seems to think there's more to it than that.'

'A pathologist is still examining Harry's body. I'm not sure the police know how he died yet.'

She sighed. 'Moving to Walden was supposed to be a fresh start for them. The same as moving to London was for Rachel. A sad waste of two young lives. It's like someone wanted to stop them from being happy.'

'Did you suspect either of them might have been taking drugs?' I asked.

'I didn't have an inkling, although I suppose I'm rather innocent when it comes to those sorts of things. Maybe that's what they were whispering about. When Rachel said "you don't want Victoria to find out", perhaps she meant drugs.'

It was the same conclusion I'd come to.

'I knew Harry had his demons,' Mrs Durling continued. 'The poor man had suffered during the war, but I thought he was getting better. Archie Powell was a steadying influence.'

I stiffened at that.

'How did Rachel get on with Mr Powell?'

Mrs Durling frowned. 'I don't think she liked him. She once made a comment about him being a hypocrite. He's been in prison, you know.'

'Yes, I know.'

'I try not to judge people. He's made mistakes, and now he's endeavouring to put things right. People should support him in that.'

'Are you saying Rachel didn't?'

Mrs Durling shrugged. 'She kept away from him, which was unusual. He's a handsome man and normally she liked to flirt a bit. I don't mean that in a vulgar way. I think she was just a bit lonely at times. She didn't have any family close by, and she never seemed to have any female friends. But she was pretty enough to always guarantee some male attention.'

'Did she get it from Archie?'

'They seemed to be wary of each other. I thought at first she didn't like him because he'd been a vicar. Sometimes she assumed people were judging her or looking down on her. She told me she thought he was a troublemaker.'

Rachel had been spot on in her assessment of Archie Powell, and I warmed to her because of this. Had she been around men long enough to know when someone wasn't quite what they seemed?

I left Christmas Close and walked towards the cathedral. From there, I retraced Jack Archer's route though Curle's Passage and Cathedral Close to Kingsgate. He must have seen the car turn out of Symonds Street and drive along St Swithun Street and then turn right into Christmas Close.

From this viewpoint, he would only have caught a fleeting glimpse of the occupants of the motor car. If his eyesight was poor, it was doubtful he'd ever be able to identify them.

I wandered through Kingsgate and onto College Street to pay a visit to P & G Wells Bookshop. Normally, I'd get lost amongst the shelves and come out with far too many books that I'd later regret buying when I had to walk home from the train station carrying them.

But today, I managed to leave the shop without making a single purchase. My thoughts kept drifting back to what Mrs Durling had said. Her comment about someone not wanting Rachel or Harry to be happy had stuck in my mind.

Did someone believe they should be made to pay for their sins? If that were the case, the person was likely to have a strong religious background.

I shivered, knowing from experience that Archie Powell was fond of delivering what he thought of as retribution.

26

I'd never been inside one of the new houses on the Crookham estate. And I wished my first visit wasn't under these circumstances.

A holly wreath adorned the front door, which was opened by Oliver Miller, formally dressed in a black suit and tie. He showed us into the lounge, where his wife, Nancy, was seated with Victoria. The arrival of Daniel, Millicent and me made the small room rather too crowded.

'It's kind of you to come. Nancy and I were about to leave.' Oliver Miller placed empty cups on a tray. 'I'll make a fresh pot of tea first.'

Daniel and Millicent sat side by side on the sofa while I examined the room before following Oliver into the kitchen.

The smell of fresh paint lingered in the air, and the walls were decorated with pictures and photographs that showed a young couple's pride in their new home. And their dreams for the future.

The kitchen was compact with a cleverly designed built-in larder and new gas cooker. I picked up a dishcloth and began to wash the dirty cups while Oliver put a kettle on the stove to boil.

'I know this isn't the time to ask. But was Rachel Lacey sacked?'

'You've heard about that?' He rubbed his chin and gave a slow nod. 'I believe so, though I wasn't privy to the details. She and Gordon came to some sort of agreement. I was just told she'd be finishing at the end of the year and to find a replacement before then. Gordon said he wasn't happy with rumours he'd heard about drug taking in the bar where she sang.'

'When did you last see her?'

'The day before she died. She worked her shift as usual. The following morning, she was supposed to have opened up, but when I arrived, the showroom was locked and there was no sign of her. I was annoyed because she knew we'd be busier than normal due to the number of people visiting Winchester that day. Before that, she'd been a good worker. Reliable and on time. But, well, I suppose you can't blame her. She was leaving, and she had a lot to arrange before her move.'

'Mr Tolfree was there to help, wasn't he?' I dried the cups and set them down on the tea tray.

'Some of the time. He left to go to the cathedral service in the afternoon, and I was on my own for a while.' Oliver placed a fresh pot of tea on the tray.

'You said that Gordon had treated Rachel as the golden girl one minute – then ignored her the next.' I watched him closely. 'Had they been having an affair?'

He hesitated before answering. 'They behaved professionally enough in the office... but it was clear something was going on. When it ended, he just wanted her to go away. And she did.'

I gave him a withering look and he realised what he'd said.

'I didn't mean that,' he snapped. 'I just meant that she agreed to go. To move to London with her sister.' Oliver picked up the tray and hurried from the room.

In the lounge, he kissed Victoria on the cheek and indicated to his wife that it was time to leave.

'I'll come back tomorrow,' Nancy promised. She was a pleasant-looking woman with neatly waved dark blonde hair and pale blue eyes. Her dress was similar to one I'd seen Jennifer Tolfree wearing, and I could imagine the two women competing in the fashion stakes.

I stood by the window and watched the Millers get into their car – a newer model of Wolseley than the one that had gone missing.

Oliver wasn't telling all he knew about his boss and Rachel Lacey – I was sure of that. But then why would he? He'd be scared of losing his job.

'I can't believe he's gone.' Victoria clutched the cup of tea Millicent handed her. 'Not my Harry.'

'I thought he was indestructible,' Daniel muttered.

Tears spilled down Victoria's cheeks. 'So did I. No one thought he'd survive his head injury. But Harry proved them wrong like I knew he would. I just don't understand what happened.'

I pulled over an occasional chair to sit by her. 'When did you last see him?'

'When he left for work the day before he was found. I handed him his packed lunch and told him to put his hat on. It was so cold. He kissed me and...' She wiped her eyes with a handkerchief. 'I can't believe I'm never going to see him again.'

'You must have been worried when he didn't come home,' Millicent said gently.

Victoria nodded. 'It's happened before. But that was in Winchester. He had friends there who would put him up for the night if he drank too much. The only pub he's been to around here is the Drunken Duck.' She turned to Daniel. 'It crossed my mind he might have been with you at the hall.'

'I hadn't seen him since he finished working on the east wing. I wish he had come to me.' Daniel rubbed his eyes. 'He could have talked to me about anything. Harry knew I would never judge him.'

Millicent squeezed his hand, and I suddenly wanted them to get married there and then. Time was too precious to waste, as the war had proved. Someone you loved could be snatched away before you had the chance to do all the things you'd planned.

Victoria stared unseeingly into her teacup. 'They think it was cocaine. I don't understand where it came from.'

None of us had an answer to that question.

'He spent the day at the church with Freddie,' she continued. 'How would he get hold of cocaine in Walden?' The pain and confusion in her eyes were hard to witness. 'I don't imagine you could get that in the Drunken Duck.'

It was highly unlikely, though I supposed Ted Cox, the land-lord, wouldn't be aware if someone was trading illegal substances in his establishment. I still doubted this was where Harry had obtained the drug.

'Had he ever taken cocaine before?' I asked.

'He was prescribed it during the war. He said it helped him to cope. Once he was back home, it was more difficult to get hold of, though occasionally he'd find someone in a bar who'd sell him some. I told him not to. It was illegal. I thought he'd stopped but...' She brushed away a tear.

'But he just stopped telling you?' I ventured.

She nodded. 'I never liked the Blackbird Bar. Too dark and dingy for me. Harry sometimes went there on the nights Rachel was singing. At first, I wondered if something was going on, though Harry swore there wasn't.'

'When did you guess?'

'It wasn't difficult. His mood would change.' She gave a fleeting smile. 'He'd be elated – like the old Harry. Then he became down. I thought the best thing to do was for us to get away from Winchester to somewhere quieter like Walden, where there wouldn't be the temptation.'

'Do you think he got the cocaine from Rachel?' I stirred my tea, picturing the pair of them whispering together in the Blackbird Bar.

Victoria nodded. 'I suspected she was taking the drug too. Then she lost her job. That set Harry off. He knew Rachel had been having an affair with Gordon. And he disapproved, but he thought it was wrong for her to have been sacked. Strange as it may seem, Harry was a devout Christian.'

'He was a good man. Always helping others, especially the younger soldiers.' Daniel's voice was hoarse with emotion. 'He'd try to keep everyone's spirits up even when... Even when things were really bad. And he always tried to see the best in people.'

'Thank you.' Victoria's eyes shone with tears. 'He was a good man, though sometimes he could be a little naïve. He believed Gordon was the villain, luring Rachel into his bed. I don't think it was like that.'

'You think Rachel was the seducer?' I was curious to understand how this odd relationship had come about.

'No. I'm not saying that. All I'm saying is I could see how it happened. They genuinely seemed to like each other; it wasn't just... physical, if you know what I mean.' Victoria blushed. 'It may sound silly, but I think Rachel was more suited to Gordon than his wife. She looked up to him, whereas Jennifer can be quite challenging.'

'Yet he still sacked Rachel.' I was irked by the way she'd been dismissed so casually.

'Harry thought that was despicable of him. And then when she died, he got it into his head that it was Gordon's doing.'

'Why was he so certain?' I asked.

'I don't know. He never gave me a proper answer when I asked him. I suppose because Gordon had fired her. He got annoyed with me when I said I didn't think Gordon had behaved that badly. If Rachel was taking drugs, he would have had no choice but to sack her. I told him at the time it was best for everyone that she move to London to be with her sister.'

Victoria had clearly wanted Rachel to leave. And I didn't blame her. But London wasn't that far. Could she have been tempted to ensure Rachel stayed out of her husband's life for good?

And what of Harry? Victoria's grief over his death was genuine – however, love was always a powerful motivator for murder.

27

I stopped typing when I heard the clump of what sounded like a policeman's boots on the stairs and looked at the door expectantly. Elijah tried to appear uninterested, though I knew he'd been anticipating a visit from Ben, too.

I hurried to make a fresh pot of coffee while Ben removed his hat, undid the top button of his tunic and settled in Elijah's den. Once we were all huddled around Elijah's desk, Ben took out his pocketbook and began thumbing through the pages.

I wasn't surprised when he confirmed Harry Hobbs had died of a cocaine overdose. I told him that Victoria Hobbs had suspected Harry was getting the drug from Rachel.

'How was it administered?' Elijah asked, picking up his pen.

'Inhalation and injection.'

'Why would someone inject and snort cocaine at the same time?' This was a whole new world to me.

'It seems unlikely,' Elijah commented. 'Overkill, if you'll excuse the morbid pun.'

'Is it possible that was Harry's intention?' It had occurred to me that Harry could have killed Rachel and then, out of remorse, used the same method on himself. 'Perhaps guilt over Rachel?'

Ben nodded. 'It's something we're looking into, although it's difficult to find any evidence. Officers in Winchester have been investigating any vehicles seen near Christmas Close when Rachel was killed. Unfortunately, there were more than usual due to the prince's visit. However, Harry's van would have stood out, but there are no reported sightings of it.'

'What does Cobbe think?' Elijah pushed aside a mess of papers in search of his cigarettes.

'He doesn't know what to make of it. With no syringe present, it's difficult to conclude these deaths were the result of an accidental overdose. He needs to find out what both Harry and Rachel were doing in the hours prior to their deaths. In Rachel's case, the last sighting of her was by her landlady when she left home that morning.'

My heart sank as I guessed that Freddie was probably the last person to have seen Harry alive.

'Victoria Hobbs said Harry occasionally went to the Drunken Duck. Perhaps he called in after work?' I said hopefully.

Ben shook his head. 'I've checked with Ted Cox and the regulars. No one saw him. And Freddie says Harry didn't mention going for a drink that night. He said he helped Harry load the tools into the van and left him at the church at around five o'clock. The only person they'd talked to that day was the vicar.'

'What time was that?' Elijah asked.

'In the morning. Reverend Childs didn't return to the church that day. But one of the ladies from the Walden Women's Group told me that Archie Powell was with them at the town hall that afternoon and said he was going to call in at the church on his way to the railway station.'

'And?' I asked.

'Superintendent Cobbe has spoken to Mr Powell, who said he stopped at the church and chatted with Harry for around fifteen minutes. He says he's unsure of the precise time, but he carried on to the railway station and caught the five-forty-five train to Winchester.'

'Did he see Freddie?' I had an ominous feeling about this.

'He claims he didn't notice if Freddie was still there or not.'

'He would have seen his Triumph motorbike,' I pointed out.

Ben raised his hands in a helpless gesture. 'Mr Powell says it could have been parked outside the church but he's not certain.'

'How unobservant of Mr Powell,' Elijah said dryly.

'Bastard,' I growled. 'He just doesn't want to admit that Freddie had already left because it makes him the last person to have seen Harry alive.'

Elijah picked up his pen. 'So what is it that Superintendent Cobbe wants us to report?'

'We'd like anyone who may have witnessed any suspicious activity around the church on the day of Harry's death, or even in the preceding weeks, to contact the station house.'

'What about the comings and goings at Sycamore Lodge?' The proximity of Gordon Tolfree's house to a car containing cocaine and now another death from an overdose of the drug couldn't be ignored.

'Do not mention Gordon Tolfree's home.' Ben gave me a warning look. 'Church Road and surrounding area is broad enough.'

Elijah scribbled a few notes in his jotter in spidery black ink. 'What time did Harry Hobbs die?'

'The pathologist couldn't be certain,' Ben replied. 'He'd been dead for at least twelve hours, maybe longer.'

'So Archie could have done it before he left?' I tried not to sound too gleeful.

'It's possible,' Ben admitted.

Elijah put down his pen and wiped black ink from his fingers. 'What motive could he have? And what about Rachel Lacey? I can't see any reason for Archie Powell to kill either of them. And surely the same person must be behind both deaths.'

'According to Mrs Durling, Rachel didn't like Archie. She avoided him, whereas normally she played up to good-looking men, especially older ones. Perhaps she and Archie had been friendly, then he found out about her drug taking. Archie only likes women when he's in control – if she rebelled, he might have been driven to punish her for it. Giving her an overdose could be his way of delivering retribution.'

Ben shrugged, obviously not convinced, but I was warming to my theme.

'Mrs Durling commented that both Rachel and Harry had been attempting to make fresh starts. Yet someone wouldn't let them. It's as though they were being punished for their sins. Archie always did try to justify his crimes by saying he was doing God's work.'

Elijah shook his head. 'I can't see it. The person who links Harry Hobbs and Rachel Lacey is Gordon Tolfree. She worked for him, and so does Victoria Hobbs' brother.'

'There could be other links that we don't know about.' Ben closed his pocketbook and tucked it into his tunic. 'Such as the cathedral's war fund and the cast of the pantomime.'

'Who are mostly all linked to Gordon Tolfree in some way,' I reminded him. 'Including Archie Powell.'

'Superintendent Cobbe has talked to everyone involved in the pantomime, and he'll be interviewing some of them again.' Ben drank the remains of his coffee and reached for his hat. 'Specifically, anyone close to both Rachel and Harry – and those who don't have an alibi for the time of either murder.'

I didn't like where this was heading.

Ben rubbed his chin, looking pensive. 'He also feels that someone of a similar age to Rachel and Harry is more likely to have known about their drug taking. I'm afraid he will be bringing Frederick Baverstock in for questioning again.'

28

Grace Evans didn't look pleased to see me when I knocked on the door of 3 Longbridge Court. I didn't care. I needed to find out more about Rachel if I was to help Freddie.

'I'm sorry to disturb you. I was in the area visiting my grandmother, and I thought I should tell you what's happened. It's Rachel's friend, Harry Hobbs. I'm afraid he's dead.'

Grace's eyes widened. She took a moment to digest this, then she held open the door. 'You'd better come in.'

The front parlour was emptier than it had been before. In fact, it looked bare, apart from a collection of boxes pushed against one wall. The photographs were still on the mantelpiece, but there were no other ornaments.

'What happened to him?' She gestured to the faded chintz armchairs.

I took the same one I'd sat in before, with the window behind me. 'He died of a cocaine overdose.'

'The same as Rachel?' Grace was wearing slacks, and she curled her legs up into the armchair. 'Superintendent Cobbe told me how she died.'

'Did you ever suspect Rachel took drugs?'

'Did you?' she countered, almost aggressively. 'You said you were a friend of hers.'

'I had no idea,' I muttered.

'Well, she would never have got involved with anything like that. I saw the effects of cocaine on soldiers during the war. Rachel wasn't that sort of girl.'

I wondered if Grace was qualified to make such a statement. She'd settled in France after the war and had seen Rachel infrequently. Would she have known what was going on in her sister's life?

'They're treating Harry's death as suspicious. They've been questioning Freddie Baverstock.'

'Why? What reason would he have?'

'Superintendent Cobbe seems to think someone in the pantomime might be involved. Freddie was closer in age to Rachel and Harry than the other cast members.'

Grace frowned. 'I gather he was playing the prince.'

'That's right. Were you aware of a friendship between him and Rachel?'

'No. I'd never even heard of him until you mentioned his name on your last visit.' Her eyes narrowed. 'But then I never heard Rachel mention you before either. You say you knew Harry Hobbs?'

'I met Harry and his wife, Victoria, through the Baverstocks.'

Her expression softened. 'His poor wife. Where was Mr Hobbs found?'

'In the graveyard of St Martha's Church in Walden.'

'Walden? At a church? Why on earth would someone go to a church to take drugs?'

'Harry was a stonemason. He was working at the church.'

'I see.' Her lips tightened. 'Doesn't Gordon Tolfree live in Walden? I've read about him standing in the election.'

'That's right. His home, Sycamore Lodge, isn't far from the church.'

'He seems a more likely suspect than this Freddie Baverstock. I hope the police are questioning him too.'

'I believe so, although they aren't saying much.' I realised I had to be careful. I could imagine Superintendent Cobbe's reaction if Grace went to him and mentioned my visit. 'I thought you ought to know about Harry's death as you may have expected him at Rachel's funeral.'

Her shoulders sagged. 'Thank you for coming to tell me. I held a private ceremony for Rachel at the chapel in the cemetery where our parents are buried.'

'I believe the cast are dedicating the pantomime to her and Harry,' I said. 'Are you planning to go and see it?'

She gave a sad smile. 'That's kind of them. I'll send a cheque to help their fund, but I don't think I could face it knowing it should have been her on the stage. And I don't want to meet Gordon Tolfree until the police find out what really happened to Rachel. Do you know who's playing Cinderella?'

'Mr Tolfree's wife, Jennifer, has taken on the role.'

This information caused her mouth to drop in disbelief and I decided it would be safer to change the subject.

'What made Rachel apply for a job at Tolfree Motors? Did she like cars?'

Grace nodded. 'After my father died, she learnt how to drive his car so she could take Mother to wherever she was working. It proved a useful skill, especially as she had no desire to train as a nurse like me. The Women's Army Auxiliary Corps was looking for drivers, and she ended up being sent to the big transit camp at Morn Hill. That's where she met Oliver Miller. He got her the job at Tolfree Motors.'

This was interesting. Oliver had clearly known Rachel for a long time yet he'd never mentioned that fact. I'd assumed it had been Gordon Tolfree who'd given her the job.

'She told me she'd always wanted to become an actress like your mother.' I didn't like my deception but I needed to find out more about Rachel's background.

Grace sighed. 'After our parents died, we were left with very little money. It was a struggle to make ends meet, and I certainly wasn't prepared to pay for singing or acting classes. Life on the stage was too unpredictable, and I wanted her to apply for more practical jobs.'

'What sort of jobs?'

'I tried to persuade her to get work in an office and gave her the money to go on a typing course. But... well, she used it to pay for singing lessons.' Grace shrugged. 'That was Rachel.'

'Did she want to leave Winchester and come here to live with you?' It was a small thing, but I still wondered whose idea it had been for the sisters to live together. Tilly thought Rachel had written to her sister to suggest it, yet Grace had said on my previous visit she'd put the plan to Rachel at her husband's funeral.

Grace smiled sadly. 'I think she was happy to move to London, though she seemed less sure about living with me again.'

I raised an enquiring eyebrow.

'I guess she thought I'd nag her to get a respectable job. And perhaps I might have done.'

'What do you plan to do now?' I asked.

'I don't know. I need time to think. Everything's changed so quickly.' She clutched a cushion to her chest as if to protect herself from further loss. 'I only came here to try to make things up with Rachel. Not that we ever fell out exactly, but we had drifted apart. Without her, there doesn't seem much point in being here.'

As I stood to leave, I noticed a few books lying on top of the boxes stacked against the wall. One of them was a road atlas of Aldershot and the surrounding area, including Walden. I guessed it must have been Rachel's.

'I'm giving her belongings to charity.' Grace took a handkerchief from her trouser pocket and dabbed her eyes. 'Then I'm going away. Perhaps abroad. Maybe back to Nice.'

I left 3 Longbridge Court wondering what might have happened if the two sisters had lived together. No doubt Rachel would have tried to find work as an actress – perhaps she'd already made some theatrical contacts. How would Grace have reacted to that?

I took a bus from Lewisham high street into central London and walked from Pall Mall to St James's Park. It was a favourite meeting place for Marc and me. He loved seeing Buckingham Palace and strolling down The Mall.

'I come from a small town in Belgium,' he'd once told me. 'I never dreamed I'd end up working in the city of London. Whenever I see famous landmarks like the palace, I realise how far I've come in such a short time.'

We'd arranged to meet at the Queen Victoria Memorial, and I found him standing by the fountain gazing up at the golden-leafed Winged Victory. When I reached him, he took my hand, and pulled me closer to kiss my cheek.

It was an innocent enough gesture, though I couldn't help glancing around to make sure no one had noticed. I don't know who I expected to see, but whenever I was with Marc I had the sensation of being watched. It was probably due to the guilt I felt when we were together. I'd never asked him directly if Annette knew of our meetings, but I was sure she didn't.

He stepped back to admire the green dress and matching coat I was wearing. 'You look nice.'

'I'm meeting Percy at his dancing club.'

I hadn't seen Percy since Harry's death, and when I'd written to him, he'd replied asking me to meet him at the Foxtrot Club. I doubted he was in the mood for dancing and I expected to find him drowning his sorrows.

Marc smiled. 'You should be going out with a lively young man like Percy. Not walking around a park with a dullard like me.'

I didn't reply. We'd had conversations like this before. Yet we still corresponded. And we still arranged to meet.

Marc's fingers touched mine as we strolled by the lake, watching a child feeding bread to an ever-growing circle of ducks.

'How is Percy?' he asked. 'And his younger brother?'

'I'm worried about Freddie.'

I told him what had happened with Harry Hobbs.

He frowned. 'Where is this cocaine coming from? That's what the police should be trying to find out.'

'How would someone go about buying cocaine? I imagine it would be easier to get hold of in London than somewhere like Winchester.'

The extent of my knowledge of the drug came from a controversial movie I'd seen the previous year. Originally, the film had been called *Cocaine* until the censors decided to change its title to the less shocking *While London Sleeps*. It told the story of a man seeking revenge on gangsters after his daughter dies from an overdose.

'Word gets around, I suppose. What to ask for in a particular

nightclub or pub. I expect it's the same in towns and cities every-
where but on a smaller scale than in the capital.'

'Do many drug dealers get prosecuted?'

Marc shook his head. 'Not many. I've dealt with a few. It's
difficult to find anyone who'll testify against them. People buying
drugs don't want their source to vanish. They could also face
prosecution themselves.'

'There are rumours something secret is going on at Tolfree
Motors. But no one is willing to reveal what they know.'

'That could be your answer. Cocaine is being brought in
through the business. Perhaps Rachel Lacey was selling it in the
bar where she worked.'

'And someone killed her for it.'

'They might have been worried she would go to the police.'

'I can't see why she would,' I said. 'She'd only get herself into
trouble.'

But it would explain why Rachel was so keen to leave
Winchester and start a new life in London.

'The manager of Tolfree Motors mentioned a dealership
called Fitzherbert's Motors.'

Marc stopped abruptly. 'Ian Fitzherbert?'

I shrugged. 'He just said Fitzherbert's. Why?'

'I've come across the name Ian Fitzherbert on numerous
occasions. He runs legitimate businesses but has links to criminal organisations.'

'What sort of organisations?'

'People who deal in drugs and prostitution. Ian Fitzherbert
doesn't get his hands dirty; he pays others to do that for him. And
if they get caught, he foots the bill for their legal fees. Decent law
firms steer clear of him, but there are plenty of solicitors out
there who'll happily take his money.'

Could Rachel have been involved in drug dealing? It was

sounding more likely, which made me think we'd been looking too close to home for her killer.

We found an empty bench on the quiet side of the lake by Birdcage Walk, and Marc took my hands in his.

'My parents are coming over from Belgium to stay with us for the holiday,' he said. 'I won't be able to see you again before Christmas.'

I squeezed his hand. 'I don't mind. Of course you must spend time with them.'

'We could meet between Christmas and New Year? I have to return to work after Boxing Day, but it will be quiet in the office. Perhaps we could go for a drink together to celebrate the coming of the new year?'

'That would be lovely,' I said, though the thought made me sad. Was another year of clandestine meetings all we had to look forward to? Something had to change. I had to change. I just wasn't sure how.

29

Marc and I drifted around the park and when it was dark, he insisted on walking with me to Soho.

When we reached Gerrard Street, he stood back and gave a small wave as I pushed open a red door and descended the steep staircase to the Foxtrot Club.

In the basement, I gave my coat to the cloakroom attendant and went in search of Percy.

The band were playing a lively jazz tune, and couples were weaving across the dance floor, the heat from their bodies adding a sweaty perfume to the smoky ambience. There was no sign of Percy in their midst, and I was relieved I wouldn't be suddenly called upon to dance. My own attempts to master the new jazz moves usually ended up being unintentionally comical.

To my surprise, I saw Freddie's pale face peering from around the side of one of the booths. He waved at me, and I hurried over to find Percy stretched out next him on a red velvet banquette.

Percy swung his legs off the seat and sat upright so I could squeeze in beside him. The black varnished table was covered in empty glasses, and he and Freddie looked more than a little the worse for wear.

'Has Superintendent Cobbe spoken to you again?' I asked Freddie. He didn't have the air of a man who was being hounded by the police.

He shook his head. 'I've been staying at Percy's flat. I needed to get away.' He picked up his glass and swallowed the remains of an amber liquid.

I hoped the superintendent didn't think Freddie had run away.

'My parents will let us know if the police call,' Percy said, as if reading my thoughts. 'And I can run Freddie back to Winchester in the car.'

I nodded, reaching out to take Percy's hand. 'I'm sorry.'

His head fell forward to rest on my shoulder, and I instinctively pulled him toward me in a hug.

Marc's words came into my mind: 'You should be with him. Not with me.'

For a moment, I thought Percy was crying. Then he lifted his head, signalled to the waitress and ordered a bottle of cheap champagne.

When it arrived, he insisted we drink a toast to Harry, and we raised our glasses in a despondent gesture.

'He knew something,' Freddie whispered conspiratorially, his floppy hair falling over his forehead.

'Yes, but what? Why was he being so bloody mysterious?' It had been obvious Harry was hiding something from the way he'd been so sure of Gordon Tolfree's guilt.

'I've been thinking about it, and I'm certain it has something to do with the car. The Wolseley you found.' Freddie paused to hiccup. 'I'm sure he must have been at the church when someone drove it down the track to Sycamore Lodge. It didn't go past when

I was there. Yet the vicar saw it when he came by on his bike at six and thought he glimpsed Harry's van driving off. Harry must have seen something.'

'Didn't he say he might have been hammering or inside the church some of the time?' I remembered Harry hadn't looked up from his work when he mumbled this comment.

Freddie shook his head. 'He wouldn't have been hammering at that time of the evening. It was too dark, and it would have been dangerous to carry on working. And there was nothing that needed doing inside the church. All our work was outside. I checked with Reverend Childs when I went back to finish the job.'

'Why would he lie?' The only reason I could think of was that Harry was protecting someone.

'You should tell the police,' Percy advised.

I stayed silent. Superintendent Cobbe would come to the same conclusion as me. And if Harry was protecting someone, the three most likely candidates were his wife, his brother-in-law: Oliver Miller, or his young friend: Freddie Baverstock.

I sipped my champagne, then said, 'There's another possibility.'

They both looked at me.

'A box of cocaine was found in the glove compartment of the car. Could Harry have met with whoever was driving the car? And...' I wondered how to phrase this. 'Made a deal?'

By their silence, I guessed they'd considered this possibility. And they weren't rushing to say Harry would never do such a thing.

'Why was he so convinced of Gordon Tolfree's guilt?' I continued. 'Before the car was found, he was already sure it was him. Did he ever talk about Tolfree Motors or mention the name Fitzherbert?'

'Fitzherbert. Who's that?' Percy took a swig of champagne.

'It's probably nothing. Mar—' I stopped myself. 'A solicitor I know told me about a businessman with criminal connections who could have a link to Tolfree Motors.'

Freddie ran his fingers through his hair. 'A businessman in Winchester?'

'No. Here in London. He's been linked to drugs and prostitution.'

Percy frowned. 'Who's this solicitor you've been speaking to?'

'It's nothing. It's probably just a coincidence.' I decided to ask a sensitive question. 'Harry suffered a brain injury during the war, didn't he? Was he sometimes unhappy...?'

'No.' This time they replied in unison – and with force.

'That's why I asked you to meet me here. To try to help you understand.' Percy took another swig of champagne and then sat up straighter.

I waited, but he seemed to be struggling to find the right words. Freddie stared morosely into his glass.

Eventually, I asked, 'Understand what?'

'We lost so many friends,' Percy muttered.

'In the war,' Freddie added unnecessarily.

'We made a pledge.' Percy banged his glass on the table. 'We'd live our lives to the full in honour of our fallen comrades.'

'Eat, drink and be merry, for tomorrow we die.' Freddie raised his glass, then took a large gulp.

I'd heard Percy say something similar in the past. It was shortly after I'd first met him. We'd been larking about by Waldenmere Lake on a hot summer afternoon, and he made one of his sudden switches from silly to serious. Having come back from the trenches in one piece, he said it would be wrong to squander his good fortune. He felt it was his duty to dance with as many pretty girls as would have him, and I understood this sentiment.

'What is it that Harry liked to do? Drinking and dancing? Victoria thought he might have occasionally taken cocaine with Rachel at the Blackbird Bar?' I glanced around the club, wondering if the exuberance I'd assumed was due to the effects of booze or enjoyment of the music could actually be down to something else. Couples were gyrating on the dance floor, and groups were huddled around tables, laughing and drinking. Were any of them high on cocaine? I suddenly felt incredibly naïve. On the few occasions I'd met Percy here, it had never occurred to me that people could be taking drugs.

I looked at Percy and Freddie, wondering if either of them had ever indulged in cocaine.

As if in answer to my unspoken question, Percy lifted his glass. 'Freddie and I like a drink and a dance – but we've never had an appetite for drugs. The old Harry would never have touched them either. He only got a taste for cocaine during the war after he was injured.'

'Victoria said he was prescribed it in hospital.'

'It didn't need to be prescribed.' Percy ran his finger around the rim of his champagne glass. 'You could get it anywhere. At least you could at the start of the war. The army gave it out.'

'What!' I choked on my drink.

'There was this tablet called Forced March,' Percy explained. 'It contained cocaine and cola nut extract. It was supposed to boost your endurance, but it gave you a buzz at the same time. Some chaps liked it too much. They got their friends to send them more. You could even get it in Harrods.'

'It was banned around the time I joined up in 1916,' Freddie added.

'I remember reading something about it.'

My mind flew back to June 1916. I'd just turned seventeen and had insisted on leaving Devon to return to London. The newspapers had been full of outrage over the widespread use of psychoactive drugs like cocaine and opiates in the armed forces. *The Daily Mail* published a story on a kit that was sold in Harrods as a present to send to your loved ones on the frontline. It contained cocaine, morphine, syringes and needles.

'So how did Harry get hold of it?'

'Selling cocaine, morphine and opium to the British Armed Forces was banned in 1916, but it was still available to civilians. They only made it completely illegal in 1920.'

'And Harry took it?' I yawned, starting to feel the effects of the champagne.

'He said he'd stopped, then... then I asked him about Rachel.' Freddie stared at the couples on the dance floor. 'He knew I liked her, and she'd turned me down. I began to wonder if it was because of him. Victoria was concerned, too. That's when he told me about the cocaine. He said Rachel got it when she went to London to pick up a car. She'd sell it to the manager of the bar and keep some back that she'd take herself and share with him. He said it was harmless and that having a bit of fun now and then helped him to cope with things.'

We were back to the strange relationship between Harry and Rachel. He'd called it harmless, yet that seemed to have been far from the truth. Could it have become deadly?

Percy and Freddie were adamant that Harry would never have taken his own life. But if he'd been involved in Rachel's death, guilt might have driven him to it.

I wasn't going to mention this theory tonight. Instead, I asked, 'Do you think Harry could have taken an overdose by accident?'

'He knew the effects of cocaine. And that injecting it could be fatal. He wouldn't have done that to Victoria. Or to me and Freddie.' Percy's eyes grew misty. 'Or to the chums we lost. We were given the chance of life and to risk it like that would dishonour the memory of those who didn't survive.'

I nodded, understanding what he was telling me. If it hadn't been an intentional or accidental overdose – someone had murdered Harry.

30

Even in grief, Victoria Hobbs was a beautiful woman. Her large, mournful eyes made her look even more like a silent movie star. She'd loved Harry – that much was clear. But love could lead to murder.

Harry's funeral was held at St Martha's Church, and it was hard to shift the memory of his frost-covered body lying only yards away in the frozen churchyard.

Millicent and I sat with the Baverstocks, taking up a whole pew of the church. Hetty leant on Clifford's arm for support, raising a handkerchief to her eyes while Percy and Freddie stared miserably at Harry's coffin.

There was a particularly poignant moment in the service when Reverend Childs described Harry's war service and his miraculous recovery from his near-fatal head injury. I instinctively reached out to Percy when I saw his lip tremble and his eyes close, and he kept a tight grip on my hand for the rest of the service. All the time, I was aware of Archie Powell's eyes on my back and the sweet, smoky fragrance of incense that seemed to have permeated the cold stone walls of the church.

Snowflakes fluttered in the air as we followed the coffin out to the churchyard. After the burial, supported by Oliver and Nancy Miller, Victoria thanked each mourner for coming and invited everyone to raise a glass to Harry at the Drunken Duck in celebration of his life.

I gritted my teeth when I saw Archie put his arm around Victoria's shoulder.

'He likes her,' Millicent whispered.

'I noticed it at the carol concert,' I whispered back. 'He couldn't take his eyes off her.'

While Victoria exchanged a few words with Archie, I sidled over to the Millers.

'I spoke to Rachel Lacey's sister recently,' I said. 'She told me you met Rachel during the war when she was posted to Morn Hill.'

'That's right. She was an excellent driver and I was a good mechanic.' Oliver smiled at the memory. 'We made a first-class team.'

'They used to call him the fixer,' Nancy said with pride. 'He could put anything back together again.'

'Did you employ Rachel just because of her driving skills?' As I said this, I realised it might sound like I was implying he'd given her the job for other reasons, such as the fact she was an attractive young woman.

'Gordon employed her on my recommendation,' Oliver replied stiffly. 'Rachel knew her way around cars, and she was a good worker too. Conscientious before…'

'Before she was fired?'

He nodded. 'You couldn't blame her. It was an awkward situation.'

Nancy gripped her husband's arm. 'And poor Oliver was stuck in the middle of it.'

I nodded sympathetically. 'That must have been difficult. You said Rachel and Gordon had been close before he found out about the drugs.'

Nancy snorted in an unladylike manner. 'More than close.'

'Like I said, they were professional enough in the office, but I suspected something was going on.' Oliver shrugged. 'Then it all turned sour.'

'You didn't tell the police that Rachel had been sacked?' I tried not to sound judgemental but failed to keep the disapproval from my voice.

Nancy leapt to her husband's defence. 'We can't afford for Oliver to lose his job.'

Oliver held up his hands in a helpless gesture. 'Gordon swore it had nothing to do with Rachel's death.'

As she'd died from an overdose of cocaine and she'd been sacked because he'd found out about her drug taking, this piece of information clearly was relevant. But I could appreciate Oliver's predicament. No wonder Nancy was resentful of Jennifer Tolfree lording it over her.

Oliver led his wife away, obviously wanting to avoid further questioning. I watched the couple escort Victoria to a waiting car and wondered if Oliver had known the true nature of Harry's relationship with Rachel.

I was about to go in search of Millicent when I spotted Kevin Noakes lurking in a corner of the churchyard. A thick scarf was wrapped around the collar of his trench coat, and his gloved fingers gripped a cigarette.

I strolled over to him.

'Is it murder, suicide or accident?' he asked.

'No one seems to know for certain. Could you do me a favour? Rachel Lacey met Oliver Miller during the war when they were both posted to Morn Hill. I'm curious about the time they spent there together. They obviously got on well enough for him to recommend her for the job at Tolfree Motors.'

He took a last drag on his cigarette before throwing it to the ground. 'I know some chaps who were based there. I'll see what I can find out.'

'Apparently, he was known as the fixer. His wife claims it was because there wasn't a car he couldn't repair.'

'Interesting.' Kevin grinned. 'Maybe that wasn't all he could fix. I'll ask around.' He glanced over to the handful of people still standing by the entrance to the church. 'Is Tolfree here?'

'No. He's kept away. I'm guessing it's because he doesn't want to be connected with anything disreputable. Everyone knows Harry's death is drug related. He's hoping to keep his reputation intact, at least until we go to the polls on Thursday.'

Kevin's eyes gleamed. 'I'm afraid his reputation will have taken a nosedive by then.'

'Why? What's he done? Have you found out where the drugs are coming from?'

Kevin shook his head. 'I've got proof of his affair with Rachel Lacey. They used to meet at a discreet little hotel just outside Winchester. Rooms by the hour, if you get my drift. They were seen together on more than one occasion. The hotel owner will swear to it.'

I shivered, pushing my hands into my pockets. 'You're going to print with that?'

'Yep. I've had it approved by my editor.' He held up his hands to dramatise the headline. 'Gordon Tolfree's secret mistress. Did she kill herself when he ended their affair and sacked her?'

31

I liked to think that Mrs Siddons would have kept her seat anyway. She won the election with a clear majority over the other candidates. But I couldn't help wonder if Kevin's article had influenced the result.

'Surely no one will vote for Gordon Tolfree after this?' Millicent had said when she'd tossed the latest edition of the *Hampshire Chronicle* onto the kitchen table.

'I don't think it will make any difference,' Ursula announced after reading the article. 'He won't be the first man to have had an affair with a younger woman. Most of those who plan to vote for him probably still will, though it might dissuade a few women.'

She passed the paper over to me, and I flicked through the pages. It didn't just reveal Gordon Tolfree's affair with Rachel Lacey, it also implied he was indirectly responsible for her death. With no evidence to back this up, I wouldn't have gone to print with such an article and I knew Elijah wouldn't have either.

While I was pleased with the local result, the national repercussions of the election were unsettling. When Prime Minister Andrew Bonar Law had fallen ill earlier in the year, Stanley

Baldwin had taken over and decided to call a general election to try to strengthen his grip on the party. His plan failed. Although the conservatives retained a majority, Labour and the Liberals had gained enough seats to produce a hung parliament.

It was hardly a resounding success for the Liberals, but this didn't stop Mrs Siddons from holding a lively Christmas party to thank her election campaign team.

Local supporters were treated to a ride over to Grebe House in a chauffeur-driven Daimler, courtesy of Horace Laffaye. On arrival, they were greeted by the sight of a beautifully decorated Christmas tree in the hall – the scent of pine mingling with festive spices as maids handed out glasses of hot mulled wine.

The carpet had been rolled up in the reception room and a gramophone played the latest jazz tunes. Percy was attempting to teach Ursula some of his favourite dance moves while Daniel and Millicent waltzed demurely across the floor, holding each other close. Daniel was a gentle soul who could be rather shy at times yet he always seemed comfortable with Millicent.

By contrast, Ben seemed far from relaxed. Constance, wearing a fitted midnight blue silk dress that accentuated her slender figure, had cajoled him onto the dance floor. His posture was rigid as a sergeant major as he held his arm stiffly around her waist. Despite looking handsome in casual flannel trousers and a smart blazer, you could still tell he was a policeman.

Constance's deep blue eyes, which many men, including Percy, had swooned over, gazed longingly at him. However, Ben's expression told me he couldn't wait for the dance to end.

I smiled at the sight of Elijah and Horace, who'd managed to keep hold of their glasses of brandy and cigars despite having sunk into the depths of one of Mrs Siddons' squishy red velvet sofas. I went over to join them, feeling blessed to be surrounded by so many good friends.

When I'd come back to live in Walden after the war, I'd been unsure if it was where I wanted to be. My father had persuaded me to return by talking Elijah into giving me a job at *The Walden Herald*. As my career in journalism hadn't exactly taken off in London, it had seemed as good a place to start as any.

Since then, I'd rekindled old friendships and made new ones and now felt that Walden was my home. Or at least I had, until the disturbing reappearance of Archie Powell. Anger flared whenever I thought of his intrusion into my life.

Before I could dwell on the problem, Percy grabbed my hand and dragged me onto the dance floor.

'I think we'll soon be hearing wedding bells.' He nodded towards Daniel and Millicent.

'Don't bank on it,' I replied.

'You're such a spoilsport,' he panted, still out of breath from his exuberant dance with Ursula. 'Don't you ever think about settling down? Getting married and having children?'

'No,' I said bluntly. Percy was three sheets to the wind already and needed no encouragement.

'I do. Especially since Harry died. You can't keep being...' He seemed to have lost his thread. 'Young. You can't keep being young. You have to be old one day.'

'You don't say.' I heaved him away from an oncoming couple as he lurched off course.

'I'm jiggered,' he gasped, coming to an abrupt halt. 'Let's go somewhere we can talk.'

Reluctantly, I allowed him to lead me out of the reception room and down the corridor to Mrs Siddons' famous hothouse. The room was as opulent as its owner, filled with orchids and other exotic blooms in jewel-like colours. Vivid greens mingled with ruby reds and topaz yellows – the colours of the flowers as overpowering as their pungent odour.

Percy pulled me towards him with one hand and held a sprig of mistletoe above our heads with the other. I stood on tiptoe, kissed him on the cheek and backed away.

He kept hold of my hand. 'Do you remember the first time we went to the cinema together?'

I smiled as I thought of the picture house we'd gone to on The Strand. Percy had bought me a box of chocolates and then proceeded to eat most of them as we watched a swashbuckling Douglas Fairbanks save a simpering Mary Pickford. I'd let Percy choose the film as I'd made him sit through the Pathé News reels before it started. Afterwards, we'd walked hand in hand over Waterloo Bridge.

'Yes. It was fun.' That afternoon, thanks to Percy, I'd felt young and carefree, something I hadn't experienced in a long time.

'Can't we turn the clock back?' he pleaded. 'I made a mistake when I said I was in love with Constance. And you made a mistake when you ran off with that fella whose name I can never remember.'

I sighed. 'Those weren't mistakes. They were part of growing up.'

'Yes.' He pounced on this. 'You're right. And now we're more mature and ready to settle down.'

It sounded as if he was talking about decades of thwarted love instead of a few years of close friendship.

I sank into a wicker chair. 'You seem to think marriage brings happiness.'

He knelt on the floor beside me, looking horribly as if he were about to propose. 'It does for some people.'

'But not for everyone. Millicent isn't happy. She loves Daniel and she loves being a teacher. Why does she have to choose?'

'I agree that's unfair.' He grasped my hand. 'And I'm not saying I have all the answers. But I... well, I—'

'Percy.' I cut him off, afraid of what he was about to say. 'You're just feeling sad because of Harry's death. You're not ready to settle down yet and neither am I. I don't want to get married. Not to you or anyone else.'

He pouted but seemed to relent. 'If you change your mind, I demand first refusal. I'll be extremely miffed if you run off with some young fella who catches your eye.'

'I'm not planning on running off with any fella, young or old.'

I thought ruefully of Marc. We couldn't carry on seeing each other. It wasn't fair to anyone.

'Good.'

Then, in typical Percy fashion, he leapt to his feet, all maudlin notions of romance forgotten. 'I'm famished. Let's eat. I think I spotted a dish of cold salmon in lobster mayonnaise. Mrs Siddons knows the way to a man's heart.'

With relief, I followed him out of the hothouse and along the hall to the dining room. While Percy worked his way around the heavily laden buffet table, I sat next to Ben, who'd been more restrained in how much food he piled on his plate.

'Is there a way you can check when someone arrived in England from France?'

He wiped his mouth with a napkin. 'I never have to worry about making small talk with you, do I? Who is it you're snooping on now?'

I smiled, stealing a vol-au-vent from his plate. 'Grace Evans. Rachel Lacey's sister. Do you know when she arrived in England?'

He shook his head. 'Superintendent Cobbe got her address in London from Mrs Crow, Rachel's landlady. A local constable was sent to the address to break the news of her death. That would have been a day or so after it happened. If I knew how she travelled to England, I could make a few telephone calls and find out the exact date.'

I finished the vol-au-vent and borrowed his napkin to wipe my mouth. 'I'll try to find out. Superintendent Cobbe has interviewed her, hasn't he?'

'He spoke to her when she visited the Royal Hampshire County Hospital in Winchester to identify Rachel's body. Why? What's brought this on?'

'I just get the feeling there are things about Rachel we don't know – and that her sister isn't telling.' As I said this, I realised I'd landed myself in hot water.

He placed his plate on the table and stretched out his legs. 'How do you know Grace Evans?'

'Tilly Crow, Rachel's landlady, gave me her address too.' I was aware I was making things worse. 'Rachel owed three months' rent, and as Grace lived near my grandmother's house, I said I'd call on her and mention it.'

'And what were you doing talking to Rachel Lacey's landlady?'

'Mrs Durling gave me her address...'

He rolled his eyes, and I decided it was time to shut up.

'Superintendent Cobbe knows you've been sniffing around, along with a journalist from the *Hampshire Chronicle*. Don't overstep the mark,' Ben warned. 'And tell us anything you find out.'

'I will, I promise.'

He pulled a face to indicate he didn't entirely believe me. 'There's something that the superintendent has agreed I can share with you, although it's not for publication. You remember Gordon Tolfree wouldn't tell us who he met for a drink after

work on the day of Rachel's death? It turns out it was Archie
Powell. They were seen deep in conversation at the bar of The
Westgate Hotel.'

32

Christmas Day had always been a quiet affair when it was just me, my father and Lizzy. Katherine was obviously used to it being a more social occasion.

I only attended church for propriety rather than having any religious belief, but I always visited St Martha's on Christmas morning to lay flowers on my mother's grave. After the morning service, from which Archie was mercifully absent, Elijah and I joined Horace in his Daimler and were chauffeur driven to 9 Chestnut Avenue. I soon discovered Horace and Elijah weren't the only guests who'd been invited for morning drinks.

When Reverend Childs arrived, I suspected Katherine was trying to smooth ruffled feathers after the altercation at the carol concert. She succeeded, and the vicar accepted a glass of sherry and politely chatted with Horace and Elijah.

Mrs Siddons turned up in full festive finery, wearing a gorgeous red silk dress, ruby drop earrings and a black fur stole that had Lizzy swooning. Even Ben and Sid dropped in for a coffee and a mince pie while they were on their morning rounds.

Only Ursula and Millicent were missing as Daniel had driven them to Kent to stay with Reverend Nightingale in Faversham.

We enjoyed a late lunch after all the guests had departed, with the exception of Elijah, who joined us for roast goose and all the trimmings, followed by Lizzy's brandy-laden Christmas pudding.

'I have some exciting news,' Katherine announced after coffee had been served. 'My brother has written to say that Smugglers Haunt is now legally mine.'

During the summer, Millicent, Percy and I had travelled to Devon for my father and Katherine's wedding and been enchanted by the white-walled villa that overlooked Smugglers Cove. It was there that Marc and I had been reunited.

Smugglers Haunt had belonged to Katherine's first husband, and she should have inherited it after his death. But her brother, a solicitor, had been forced to take legal action to prove his sister was the rightful owner.

'We've decided to motor down and see in the new year there. Why don't you come with us?' my father said to me. 'You'll be on your own with Millicent and Ursula away.'

As tempting as it was, I shook my head. I couldn't leave Percy when he was in such a state. And I was worried about Freddie.

'I can't at the moment, but I'd love to visit soon. Perhaps at Easter or during the summer holidays. Could Millicent come too?'

'Of course, she can,' Katherine said. 'I want you to treat it as a second home.'

This was an enticing prospect. A villa on the south coast of Devon that we could visit whenever we wanted. I couldn't wait to tell Millicent. And Percy. In the summer, he'd taken lodgings at a rather exotic boarding house called the Jewel of the Sea. I was sure he'd be delighted to reacquaint himself with his former landlady, Miss Emerald Dubois, and the crates of illicit spirits and tobacco she kept hidden in the smugglers' cave at the back of the property.

After chatting into the evening, Elijah offered to walk me home, and we strolled along Chestnut Avenue, feeling the effects of too much food and wine.

I pulled my new three-quarter-length winter coat around me, enjoying its warmth and fashionable cut. I hadn't been able to resist wearing it home and was carrying my old overcoat in a bag.

Elijah gave me a sidelong glance. 'A new coat and an invitation to stay in a seafront villa whenever you want. Having a stepmother isn't such a bad thing after all, is it?'

The coat had been a Christmas present from my father and Katherine, and as soon as I'd pulled aside the wrapping paper and felt the soft blue fabric, I'd known it was my stepmother who'd chosen it.

I had to admit Elijah was right. It had taken me a while to come to terms with my father's second marriage and now I wondered what I'd made such a fuss about.

He lit a cigarette. 'Why did Percy drag you off at Mrs Siddons' party?'

I smiled. No doubt Horace had asked him to find out what was going on.

'To tell me we're not getting any younger, and it's time we settled down.'

Elijah snorted with laugher. 'Drunk, was he?'

'Very. He seems to think marriage is the answer to everything.'

'It can be if you find the right person.'

I realised that Elijah had found the right person. Yet, for him, marriage was impossible. I'd come to understand the hopelessness of forbidden love during my time as a hospital volunteer during the war. Wounded and dying men had asked me to write letters to loved ones on their behalf – and the true nature of their relationships had been obvious despite the guarded language they'd used.

I decided to move away from the grim topic of marriage to the safer subject of murder.

'Superintendent Cobbe told Ben to let me know that the person Gordon Tolfree met for a drink on the night of Rachel's death was Archie Powell. They were seen in the bar of The Westgate Hotel.'

'What time?'

'Seven o'clock.' I knew what he was thinking. Archie had been seen in the cathedral for the prince's service at two in the afternoon. It was unlikely he'd been the one to drive the car into Christmas Close and on to Walden and then return to Winchester in time for his drink with Gordon. It was possible, though it would be cutting things fine. 'He may not have driven the car but he was still in close proximity to both Rachel and Harry's murders.'

'Hmm.' He sounded doubtful. 'Why did Cobbe say Ben could tell you about Tolfree and Powell's meeting?'

'To warn me. According to Ben, he's worried the pair might be plotting to get back at me.'

'It's the one thing they have in common.' Elijah drew on his cigarette and breathed out with a hissing noise. 'Why don't you go to Smugglers Haunt with your father and Katherine for New Year? I can manage in the office.'

'I want to find out more about Harry Hobbs and Rachel Lacey. For Percy and Freddie's sake.'

'It's not your job. Leave it to the police.'

'I am,' I protested.

'You're not, and I don't blame you. But be careful. There's

something very off about this – the method of killing, for one thing.'

He was right. Injecting someone in the arm with cocaine was an unusual way to commit murder.

'I'm going to see the first night of the pantomime with Katherine tomorrow evening.'

He chuckled. 'I don't envy you that experience. Is there a killer in the cast of *Cinderella*?'

33

After watching Gordon Tolfree's charity production of *Cinderella*, all I could say for certain was that the cast certainly knew how to murder a script. It was entertaining, although not always for the right reasons.

Katherine and I arrived early at Christmas Hall to bag decent seats. We joined the Baverstocks, who'd already claimed three chairs in the front row. Clifford had a newspaper in hand, evidently not expecting the pantomime to provide much in the way of entertainment. Hetty and Percy were eagerly awaiting Freddie's appearance, though I suspected for different reasons. Hetty produced a tin of sweets from her bag, which she would pass along the row at regular intervals.

When Freddie shuffled onto the stage, in yellow tights and a painted-on moustache, he looked as if he'd rather be anywhere else in the world at that precise moment. Given what he was wearing, this was understandable.

His young, frightened face emphasised the age difference between the prince and Cinderella. I wasn't sure why someone had decided that drawing a thick black line in burnt cork above his top lip would make him appear older. It didn't. When he took Jennifer Tolfree's arm and led her into the ball-room, he looked like he was escorting his mother to a tea dance.

It was a good job that Gordon Tolfree had been cast as a grumpy ugly sister. No acting was needed as anger emanated from every pore of his heavily made-up face. He barked his lines so loudly, no acting was required from his wife to shrink back from him convincingly.

Oliver Miller did a fair job as the other ugly sister. By that, I mean he managed to deliver his lines in a coherent but toneless manner. When he had to display an emotion, he'd adopt the same constipated expression each time to convey it.

As the wicked stepmother, Nancy Miller was more nervous than nasty. She gabbled her lines at such speed it was difficult to know what she was saying.

Although Freddie looked petrified, he at least managed to remember his lines – unfortunately, not the order in which they should have been delivered. As words tumbled from his mouth, his expression would suddenly change. I knew him well enough to know when he was thinking: *Damn, wrong scene.*

I tried desperately not to giggle, but it didn't help that I was sitting next to Percy, who was making strange squawking noises of supressed laughter. Hetty kept handing him toffees, possibly in an attempt to glue his mouth closed.

Bridget Durling was the star of the show, prancing across the stage in a silvery tutu, waving her wand at all and sundry. She was clearly having the time of her life, granting wishes with gusto, dressed in a beautiful glittering costume that made her look younger than Cinderella.

Towards the end of the performance, it was apparent some-thing was beginning to go wrong with the set changes. The cast would glance at each other in panic, seeming unsure where to stand or where to find certain items.

I remembered Jack Archer was acting as the stage manager, responsible for moving scenery, placing markers, and setting out props. I suspected he was indulging in a backstage tipple and getting drunker as the pantomime wore on.

The glitches were never more evident than in the final scene when the prince places the slipper on Cinderella's foot and declares he's found his bride. It was obvious the cast were confused by the layout of the stage. While Freddie had to root around in search of the slipper, the rest of the actors and actresses jostled each other, trying to identify their positions.

After Freddie finally managed to shove the slipper onto Jennifer Tolfree's foot, he stepped backwards straight into a thunder-faced Archie, playing the baron.

Percy snorted with laughter and Hetty nudged him in the ribs.

Cinderella spun around in ecstasy, her enthusiastic overacting leading to one of the most bizarre moments in what had already been the strangest show I'd ever seen. Clasping her hands to her bosom, she rushed into the arms of her father, the baron, screeching, 'My prince, my prince.'

I wasn't sure if this was due to confusion at the unfamiliar stage layout or wishful thinking on Jennifer's part. Possibly a combination of the two. Archie muttered something in her ear, turned her around, and shoved her in the direction of Freddie.

Jennifer rallied, yelling, 'My prince, my prince,' for the second time, and hurled herself towards a bewildered Freddie. Unprepared for the force of her embrace, he was unable to steady her, and Jennifer's flailing hand smacked him hard across the mouth. Smearing his painted moustache down his chin, she slid to the floor, her wig landing on the stage just before she did.

The stunned silence that followed was broken only by the sound of Freddie muttering, 'Oh dear,' as he touched his bleeding lip.

'Poor Freddie. That woman was out of control,' Hetty said in a whisper loud enough for the entire hall to hear.

Percy was now red in the face and hiccupping.

Then, to everyone's relief, the curtain descended to loud applause and boisterous laughter. When it rose again, the actors who were still upright attempted to form a line for their final bow. By now, even this simple act was beyond them.

Gordon leant heavily against the scenery, massaging his temples, while his wife sat breathless where she'd fallen. Bridget Durling danced up and down, frantically waving her wand as the rest of the cast huddled together, bobbing their heads self-consciously.

When the applause had finally died down, Katherine wiped the tears from her eyes and said she was going backstage to congratulate the cast on their extraordinary performance. Unable to face another encounter with Archie, even in his ridiculous costume, I stayed with the Baverstocks.

Clifford scratched his head. 'I thought it was supposed to be a pantomime, not a farce?' He'd been so riveted by the performance he hadn't so much as glanced at his newspaper.

'It's the first night,' Hetty replied, gathering up sweets from her lap. 'You've got to expect a few teething troubles. Freddie looked so handsome until that mad woman clouted him. All the girls will be swooning after him.'

'Mother. No girl will go near him if she's had the misfortune to see him in those tights.' Percy was wiping his eyes with a handkerchief. 'Good job he's coming to live with me. He won't be able to show his face in Winchester after this.'

'He's got a place at the Architectural Association School of Architecture,' Hetty told me. 'Percy's going to take care of him.'

I smiled, wondering if London was ready for two Baverstocks.

I was about to reply, when I caught sight of Kevin Noakes seated in the back row. Unfortunately, Hetty saw him too, and insisted we go over to say hello.

Clifford and Percy tried to whisk her away, but they weren't quite quick enough. Before they could bundle her out of the door, she'd told Kevin how much she was looking forward to reading his review of Freddie's charismatic performance.

'Don't worry,' Kevin assured her. 'He'll definitely be getting a special mention.'

Satisfied with this, Hetty hugged me, slipped some sweets into my pocket, and allowed Clifford to escort her from the hall.

After the Baverstocks had left, I flopped down into the chair beside Kevin, who was still chuckling to himself as he scribbled in his notepad. I wasn't sure if he was laughing at the pantomime or his write-up of it.

'Best one yet,' he announced, which made me wonder what I'd been missing all these years.

'I can't wait to read your review,' I said, still feeling overwhelmed by what I'd just witnessed.

'It'll be a corker.' With a flourish, he finished what he was writing, then turned to say in an undertone, 'I spoke to some chaps I know from Morn Hill. Oliver Miller wasn't called the fixer because of his skills as a mechanic. It was because he could fix you up with anything you wanted, from cars to cocaine.'

This roused me from my *Cinderella* stupor. 'Have you been to the police?'

He shook his head. 'These men won't speak to the police. As far as they're concerned, Miller wasn't doing anything wrong. These types of drugs weren't illegal at the start of the war.'

'They are now.'

'You can't compare an army camp in wartime to civilian life today. Cocaine, morphine and opium were in demand. Some of these men took drugs. Maybe some still do. I don't know, and I didn't ask. They're leading different lives now and they don't want their families or employers to find out about past misdemeanours.'

I could understand his reluctance to cause trouble for these men. But it didn't seem fair that Oliver could carry on as normal when Rachel and Harry had lost their lives, possibly because of his drug dealing.

And then there was the question of Gordon Tolfree. How much did he know about Miller's activities?

34

Kevin Noakes was right. I had never seen so many motor cars in my life. Rows and rows of them – sedans, tourers, sports cars. They filled the forecourt and covered an adjacent field.

Marc had written to say that he'd discovered Ian Fitzherbert was the owner of Fitzherbert's Motors in New Cross, and I'd replied, asking if we could go there.

When I got to Waterloo, he was waiting for me outside in his motor car. As I jumped into the passenger seat of the tiny Austin Seven, the niggling feeling I was being watched crept over me. I hadn't recognised anyone on the train, and glancing back at the station steps, I couldn't see any familiar faces.

My unease dissolved as we drove out of the centre of London and onto the quieter roads of New Cross. It felt exhilarating to do something with Marc other than stroll around a park. When we got to Fitzherbert's Motors, we walked arm in arm, like any other couple looking to make a purchase.

Marc's usually serious face was transformed by his boyish enthusiasm for the motor cars. It reminded me of when we'd first met and how I'd been drawn to his inquisitive brown eyes and warm smile. Although he'd had the assurance of a much older man, there'd also been something innocent in his curiosity and delight in the unfamiliar country he'd found himself in.

When we met again in the summer, the intervening six years had changed him. After his time in the Resistance, he'd served in the Belgian Army and then returned to England to settle in Devon with Annette. I often wanted to ask him about those war years, but I knew better.

It was a chilly morning, and the warmth of his arm linked in mine made me long for us to go somewhere private, where we could curl up together away from prying eyes.

Then I felt Marc tense, and he said, 'That's Ian Fitzherbert.'

I looked to where a tall, aristocratic man was getting out of a chauffeur-driven Daimler.

Marc pulled me behind a large Vauxhall van. 'I didn't expect to see him here. His office is in Soho. He has managers to run his businesses.'

'Does he know you?'

'No. And I'd like to keep it that way. It's possible he might have seen me in court. I'd rather not make his acquaintance if I can avoid it. He's always on the lookout for solicitors to represent his lackeys. It appears suspicious if he always uses the same ones for his dubious acquaintances.'

'He's younger and more upper class than I expected.'

I wasn't sure what I thought he should look like. A swarthy villain, perhaps, with slicked-back hair like in the gangster movies. Yet Ian Fitzherbert was thin, elegant and barely in his thirties.

'He's from an aristocratic family. One that's lost all their inherited wealth. It's rumoured Fitzherbert wasn't prepared to give up his lavish lifestyle, so he built up an empire that's a mixture of legitimate businesses working in tandem with his not-so-legal enterprises.'

'Cocaine dealing?'

'He has rich friends with expensive habits. It's said he supplies drugs to half the aristocracy, including some members of the royal family.'

I couldn't help thinking Rachel Lacey would have been way out of her depth in such company.

We sauntered amongst the cars furthest away from the showroom forecourt until a soft drizzle began to fall. Marc was wondering if we could make it back to where the car was parked without being noticed when we saw Ian Fitzherbert leave.

After the Daimler had pulled away, I told Marc I wanted to visit the showroom and strike up a conversation with the manager.

'Be careful,' he warned. 'I'll wait for you in the car.'

With Marc out of the way, I spent a few minutes examining the sports cars parked on the forecourt directly outside the showroom, aware that a wiry man in a bright yellow blazer and matching tie was watching me through the window.

When I went inside, under the pretence of admiring a magnificent and extremely long Rolls-Royce, he sidled up to me.

'That's our most expensive car. And probably a little too big for a lady to handle.'

I gazed at it longingly. 'I can't afford to buy it, but I bet you I could handle it. I'm considered to be a pretty decent driver.' I could almost hear Elijah and Robbie's howls of laughter at this statement. 'I'm from Tolfree Motors. I've just started there.'

His eyes narrowed. 'Miller's new girl?'

'That's right.'

'You're not here to pick anything up, are you?' He glanced around as if checking no one could hear us.

'Oh no. Mr Miller just told me to familiarise myself with the place. It's very impressive.'

It would be too soon for Oliver to trust anyone else with his secrets, and this man would know it.

The man regarded me warily. 'Will you be doing the collections in future?'

I shrugged. 'I'm not sure. Mr Miller said it takes time before he delegates that job.'

He nodded, seeming satisfied. 'Shame about Rachel. She was reliable, and Mr Fitzherbert trusted her. Miller said he'd be doing the next pick-up himself.'

I nodded. 'He mentioned he had a buy-to-order model to collect.'

'Good,' he said, evidently relieved Oliver was taking care of things. 'It'll be ready for him on Friday. I won't be here, but my receptionist will have the keys. Maybe I'll see you again once you've learnt the ropes.'

'I hope so.' I smiled and left the showroom, strolling casually across the forecourt and out to the road where the Austin Seven was parked.

'What's the betting there'll be cocaine hidden in the car Oliver Miller is collecting?' I said, after relating the conversation to Marc.

'Tell your policeman friend what you know, and don't go anywhere near Oliver Miller or Tolfree Motors.' Marc reached out and took my hand in his. 'Okay?'

I nodded, the warmth of his touch and the concern in his voice bringing a lump to my throat.

For a while, we sat listening to the gentle patter of rain on the canvas roof, enjoying being so close to one another in the privacy of the tiny car. The world outside looked cold and unwelcoming, and I longed to pull him towards me, desperate for a few moments where nothing else mattered except the two of us.

But I was aware of the impropriety of the situation and so was Marc.

Eventually, he let go of my hand, his eyes heavy with regret. 'Do you want me to take you back to Waterloo Station?'

I shook my head. 'Could you drop me off in Hither Green? I should go and see my aunt and grandmother. Katherine invited them to spend Christmas with us, but Gran refused. She can be a little...' I tried to find a diplomatic word '...trying.'

'It must be hard for her. Having lost her daughter and seeing your father with someone else.'

Coming to terms with my mother's tragic death had been difficult for the whole family. Somehow my father and I had managed to move forward with our lives, but my grandmother stayed resolutely in the past. Her bitterness caused her to shun any pleasures, which sadly removed much of the fun from my aunt's life.

'How was your Christmas?' I asked, knowing that polite conversation was keeping us on the right course. If we drifted into anything more intimate, it would be hard to come back from. 'Did your parents enjoy their stay?'

He smiled. 'They loved being driven around London. And it was fun to show them the sights.'

'You must miss them.'

'Not as much as Annette. With no family of her own, she's become close to them. She's lonely here.' He sighed. 'They kept talking about how lovely it would be if we returned to Belgium. Especially if we had children.'

My heart lurched. 'What will you do?'

'I don't know. I'm happy here. But I have other people to consider.'

He parked on a quiet road near Mountsfield Park, and we sat in silence for a while. I wanted to be brave and tell him we had to stop seeing each other. Perhaps he wanted to say that too. But I sensed neither of us was ready to face that final conversation yet.

'You will let me know when you come to a decision?' It was the best I could do.

'Of course.' He pulled me towards him, and we embraced for a long time. Then, without speaking, we drew apart, and I got out of the car and watched him drive away.

As expected, lunch with Gran and Aunt Maud was a tricky affair. Gran insisted I tell her how we'd spent Christmas Day, which allowed her to make barbed comments about our frivolous conduct.

In her view, my father was weak and let his new wife spend too much of his money, even though I pointed out that Katherine had money of her own. Gran remarked that Mrs Siddons' dress sounded vulgar, the vicar was unprincipled, and Elijah drank far too much. I couldn't argue with this last statement.

My aunt was clearly in need of some time away from my grandmother, so after lunch, we went to the Park Cinema on Hither Green Lane to watch the comedy film *The School for Scandal* with Queenie Thomas and Basil Rathbone. Afterwards, we had tea and scones at a café in Mountsfield Park, and I told her about the amateur production of *Cinderella*. She was still wiping away tears of laughter when I kissed her goodbye and hopped on a bus, intending to go to Waterloo Station.

But I only got as far as Lewisham high street before I hopped off again. Through the window, I'd seen Grace Evans going into Dolly's Hair Salon. This was too good an opportunity to miss.

I wanted to find out how and when she'd travelled to England but couldn't think of a plausible excuse to call on her again at Longbridge Court.

I hurried across the road, hoping Dolly wouldn't comment on why I was back so soon. When I pushed open the glass door, I saw Grace seated on one of the cushioned chairs by the reception desk.

She scowled as I walked in, but before she could say anything, Dolly hurried over to give me a hug.

'Iris, how lovely. If you can wait half an hour, I'll be able to fit you in for a shampoo and set, and we can have a good chat.' She winked at me. 'Are you off to that jazz club with your young man?'

'Maybe,' I said, returning the wink. I'd once told Dolly about Percy and the Foxtrot Club, and now, every time she saw me, she asked if I was seeing him.

She laughed and waved a floral smock at me before bustling away. I sat down and pretended I'd only just noticed Grace was there.

'Hello again. I should have known by your hairstyle that you come to Dolly's.' I touched the ends of my bobbed hair. 'She's been cutting my hair since I was a teenager.'

After hearing my exchange with Dolly, Grace seemed less wary. 'Oh yes. You mentioned you used to live near here.'

'I usually pop in to see Dolly when I come up to Hither Green to visit my grandmother. She does the sharpest bobbed cut around. The salon in Walden won't even attempt it.'

Grace smiled. 'I was afraid I wouldn't be able to find anywhere as good as my hairdresser in Nice. I needn't have worried.'

This was the opening I'd hoped for.

'I'd love to go to Nice,' I said. I had, in fact, been there the previous year. 'My father said he'd take me. We were going to cross from Dover to Calais, then catch a train to Paris and change at Gare Du Nord for the train to Nice. Is that how you travelled?'

'I took the train to Gare Du Nord and then on Le Havre. It was easier to get a ferry from there to Portsmouth. My trunks were sent separately, and I took a train from Portsmouth to Waterloo.'

That line went through Winchester.

'Did you plan to stop off and see Rachel before going on to London?'

She hesitated. 'That had been my original intention. I wish I had now. But she wrote to say she'd be busy at work and would come up to see me once I'd settled in. She'd rented the house in Lewisham and made sure it was ready for me.' Grace pulled out a handkerchief. 'When I heard the knock at the door, I thought it was her. But it was the police, telling me she was dead.'

35

'You expect me to ride my bicycle to London to catch a big city drug dealer moving cocaine in a fast car?' Ben sank into a chair and stretched out his long legs.

Elijah sniggered, and I had to smile at the image.

'Not exactly.' I placed three mugs of coffee on Elijah's desk. 'The Metropolitan Police are probably already aware of Ian Fitzherbert's connections. Couldn't you get someone to stop the car?'

Ben shook his head. 'Superintendent Cobbe is unlikely to ask them based on your information. Who told you about this Ian Fitzherbert?'

'A solicitor I know. The manager at the showroom said Ian Fitzherbert had trusted Rachel Lacey and thought she was reliable. In her absence, Oliver Miller is doing the pick-ups himself. It's the perfect opportunity to find out if he's the one behind the drug dealing. Couldn't someone search the car when Miller arrives back in Winchester?'

Elijah scrutinised me over the rim of his coffee mug. 'What's the name of the solicitor who's been telling you this stuff?'

I evaded the question. 'Apparently, it's well known that Ian Fitzherbert runs legitimate businesses but also has links to criminal organisations that deal in drugs and prostitution. He pays the legal fees for petty criminals who have been caught dealing his drugs. Reputable solicitors try to avoid him while others are happy to take his money.'

Elijah grunted and reached for his cigarettes. 'I thought I told you to leave things to the police. You shouldn't have gone to Fitzherbert's Motors on your own.'

'Lots of people go there to look at the cars, even if they can't afford to buy them.'

'But you didn't just go and look at the cars, did you? You told the manager you worked for Tolfree Motors.' Ben finished his mug of coffee and stood up. 'I'll mention what you've told me to Superintendent Cobbe, though I don't think he's going to be thrilled about it.'

'One other thing.' I followed Ben out to the main office. 'Grace Evans took a ferry from Le Havre to Portsmouth. It sounded like it was before Rachel's death. Could you find out exactly when she arrived in England?'

Ben shook his head in disbelief. 'You don't want much, do you?'

* * *

I'd arranged to meet Kevin at lunchtime on Friday in the Old Rectory Café. I figured that if Oliver Miller had to catch the train to London, get over to New Cross to collect the car, and then drive it back, he wouldn't arrive in Winchester until the afternoon.

'When's this car likely to get here?' Kevin winked at Florrie as she set a plate of chips down in front of him. She gave me a cursory nod when I thanked her for my ham sandwich, saving her smile for Kevin.

'I don't know. I'm guessing sometime this afternoon.'

'Still on for tonight?' he asked.

'What? Oh, sorry,' I mumbled through a mouthful of sandwich when I realised he was talking to Florrie.

'Can't wait,' she replied, giving me a sharp look before going to serve another customer.

Kevin turned his attention back to me. 'You think Superintendent Cobbe is going to arrest Oliver Miller?'

'I'm not sure. I'm going to wait around for a while to see if anything happens.'

'I'll hang about with you. I just want to know if it's worth getting Terry, our photographer, to come along.'

'I walked from the railway station to Tolfree Motors before I came here. There's a police car sitting at the end of the road.'

His eyes lit up. 'I'll get Terry.'

That afternoon, Kevin, Terry and I headed to the Brewers Arms, a pub on the corner of City Road, and bagged a table next to the window. The mystery of the stolen Wolseley still bugged me as I looked across at Tolfree Motors. Oliver Miller hadn't noticed it was missing until after he finished work on the seventh of November. He said the car was always parked around the back of the building, so if anyone had driven it away during the day, they would have risked him seeing them through the large showroom windows.

Gordon, Oliver and Rachel would all have had keys to the showroom and known where to find the keys to the Wolseley. Tilly Crow mentioned that Rachel had left Crows' Nest early that morning at around six-thirty when it would still have been dark. She could easily have taken the car without being seen and left before Oliver Miller arrived. But why? And how did it end up in Walden?

At that moment, a red three-door 1924 Sunbeam tourer turned the corner into City Road. It was an eye-catching motor car, and Oliver Miller looked like he was enjoying driving it. He didn't even seem to notice the police car parked at the end of the street as he swung onto the forecourt of Tolfree Motors.

Gordon Tolfree emerged from the showroom as Oliver Miller got out of the car and the two men stood back to admire the gleaming red paintwork. Then Oliver leant in through the driver's door and seemed to be pointing out different features to Gordon. They didn't immediately notice the police sergeant and constable heading towards them.

Kevin, Terry and I watched transfixed as the two policemen began to search the motor car. Gordon Tolfree stood motionless, his mouth hanging open, while Oliver Miller glanced around as if weighing up his chances of escape.

When the young constable pulled a large brown paper parcel from under the front passenger seat, Kevin and Terry leapt out of their chairs and ran to the door.

I stayed where I was to observe the chaotic scene unfold from a distance. Terry quickly positioned his camera and began to snap. He moved in to get a photograph of the sergeant holding the parcel and then stepped back to capture the moment the constable led Oliver Miller to the police car.

Minutes later, a grinning Kevin and Terry strolled over to the pub, leaving Gordon Tolfree staring in disbelief as the police car drove off with Miller inside. Then, as if aware he was being watched, his eyes flicked towards the pub window, and his gaze met mine.

For a brief moment, I thought he was going to stride across

the road to confront me. But he just shook his head and turned to walk back into the showroom.

36

It was late in the day, and Elijah and I were just finalising that week's edition when we heard a heavy tread on the stairs. It didn't come as a complete surprise when Gordon Tolfree stormed into the office.

'I do not deal in drugs. And if you say I do, I'll sue you for libel.'

Elijah didn't bother to get up from his desk. 'I'm not in the habit of publishing rumour or speculation. Oliver Miller has been arrested for possession of cocaine. That's what I'll be printing.'

'Everyone will think I knew what was going on.' Gordon paced up and down, unable to stand still.

'And did you?' Elijah asked.

'Of course I bloody didn't.'

'Sit down, Mr Tolfree. Why don't you have a drink?' Elijah nodded in my direction, and I stood up and fished the whisky bottle and two glasses from the filing cabinet.

I placed the whisky in front of Elijah, picked up my coffee and moved to a chair in the corner.

Gordon stood with his hands on his hips, his eyes darting between me and Elijah as if he suspected we were trying to catch him out. 'Why would I want to drink with you?'

'Because I think we both want the same thing. To know who's guilty and who's not.'

Elijah poured two shots and pushed one across the desk.

Gordon's hands dropped to his sides, then he slumped into the chair I'd vacated. He reached for the whisky and took a large gulp.

Elijah sipped his own whisky, then picked up his cigarettes. He offered the packet across, but Gordon waved it away.

'What is it that concerns you, Mr Tolfree?' Elijah asked.

'I'm fed up with newspapers printing lies about me,' he barked. 'I've come to warn you that if you dare take the same approach as the *Hampshire Chronicle*, you'll be hearing from my solicitor.'

Elijah leant back in his chair and lit a cigarette. 'I believe the article you're referring to alleged that you had an affair with Rachel Lacey and subsequently dismissed her from your employ.'

Gordon was silent. He knew as well as we did that both of those facts were true.

'Did you sack Rachel from her job?' Elijah asked.

'She was selling cocaine,' he yelled. 'I sell motor cars and make good money from it. I don't deal in drugs. Of course I bloody sacked her.'

'Even though you'd been having an affair with her?' I said.

I didn't want to antagonise him, but I did want to hear his version of events.

Gordon Tolfree turned to me with a snarl. 'Everyone knows you went off abroad with some bloke. So don't you dare sit in judgement on me.'

'I'm not,' I replied. 'I just want to find out what happened to Rachel Lacey and Harry Hobbs. People will only stop accusing innocent people when the real killer is caught.'

'She's right, Mr Tolfree. The gossip and speculation will only end when someone is charged with murder.'

Gordon reached for his whisky glass, then put it down again. 'I liked Rachel. And she liked me. At least that's what I believed.' He took a deep breath. 'In hindsight, perhaps she was playing me for a fool. Keeping me sweet so I didn't suspect what was going on.'

Was that true, I wondered? Mrs Durling thought Rachel had been lonely and wanted someone in her life. I knew what that felt like. I also knew it could lead you to behave unwisely.

Victoria Hobbs had said that Gordon and Rachel were good together. As far as I could see, there had been no need for Rachel to become Gordon's mistress. She'd done it through choice, although perhaps his wealth had been an enticement.

Elijah was watching Gordon closely. 'What made you suspect she was dealing in cocaine?'

Gordon sipped his whisky, seeming hesitant to answer. Eventually, he said, 'Archie Powell.'

Elijah and I exchanged a bewildered look. I felt a flicker of anticipation. Were we finally going to discover a link between Rachel and Archie?

'How did Mr Powell know about the cocaine dealing?' Elijah asked.

'He didn't know the exact details, but he heard things when he was in Winchester Prison. Inmates shared information on where they could get hold of drugs. For the most part, Archie ignored the talk. He acknowledges we all make mistakes and he doesn't believe in sitting in judgement on his fellow men.' He cast a disparaging glance in my direction as he said this.

I ignored the jibe. 'He heard something about Rachel Lacey?'

He shook his head. 'Not by name. Someone said cocaine was coming into Winchester through a car dealership. That's when Archie began to listen. He heard there were cars coming down from London with cocaine hidden inside and being delivered to Tolfree Motors.'

'When did Mr Powell tell you this?' Elijah drew heavily on his cigarette.

'Shortly after his release from prison. We met to discuss ideas for the cathedral's war fund.' He avoided looking at me when he said this, and I guessed the war fund wasn't all they'd talked about. 'After that, I started keeping a closer eye on Rachel. She was the one who mainly did the pick-ups and she sang in that dodgy bar.'

'Did you notice anything suspicious?' I asked.

'Nothing. The cars were all clean when I searched them. Of course, I realise now that Miller had probably got there before me. So I had a chat with a friend of mine who owns The Westgate Hotel. All the local reporters drink there and he knows everything that goes on in Winchester.'

'And what did you find out?'

'That if you wanted cocaine, you should have a quiet word with the manager of the Blackbird Bar. The place where Rachel worked as a singer.' It was clear by the emotion in his voice that he was still shocked by her betrayal.

'So you sacked her.' Elijah leant across the desk and topped up Gordon's glass.

Gordon nodded slowly. 'I had no choice. I had to remove any connection my business might have with drug dealers.'

'How did Rachel react? She must have been upset.' I imagined she would have been furious at having to take all the blame.

'She was at first. Tried to deny everything. Then she admitted it and said she'd leave. I could have gone to the police with what I knew, but I didn't want to get her into trouble.' He rubbed his eyes. 'I still cared for her. And believe it or not, I did want to do right by her, even though she'd hurt me. Since meeting Archie, I have tried to be a better Christian.'

I had to suppress a growl.

Elijah shot me a warning glance. 'You had no idea about Oliver Miller?'

Gordon shook his head as if he still couldn't believe the deception. 'Not a clue. Now I feel guilty for placing all the blame on Rachel. If I'd known...'

'No point in what-ifs,' Elijah advised.

'I suppose not. Rachel and I agreed it would be best if she left to start a new life in London. I was still paying her, and she had until the end of the year to sort herself out.'

'But she died before that could happen,' I commented. 'Who do you think murdered her?'

He slammed his empty glass on the table and stood up. 'Miller and whoever he was getting those bloody drugs from. I've told Superintendent Cobbe what I think. Rachel must have known too much, and they wanted her out of the way. Same goes for Harry Hobbs. Oliver Miller was his brother-in-law. Harry must have found out something.'

'I believe you could be right, Mr Tolfree,' Elijah said, stubbing out his cigarette.

Gordon nodded and strode from the office, marginally less angry than when he'd arrived. Whether that was due to the whisky or having aired some of his grievances, I wasn't sure.

'Well? What do you make of that?' Elijah swung around in his chair to look at me.

'I think he was telling the truth,' I replied.

'So do I. And I get the impression that, despite his initial bluster, Gordon was glad to get his feelings about Rachel off his chest.'

'He could always have confided in his pal, Archie, who we now know was responsible for Rachel losing her job and her lover.' I got up and went over to the window. There was a light dusting of snow on the road outside, and I could see the footprints Gordon Tolfree had left on the pavement below. 'Archie also spent time with Harry, apparently helping him overcome his demons. Look how that turned out. How long will it take before people realise Archie Powell isn't the good Christian he pretends to be?'

37

'Oliver Miller's been charged with possession of cocaine. Superintendent Cobbe is talking to the Metropolitan Police. He wants to gain enough evidence to charge him with distributing the drug.'

Ben was our next visitor that evening and he poured the dregs of the coffee pot into a mug while I cleared up the office.

'Ian Fitzherbert will probably provide Oliver Miller with a good solicitor,' I said, attempting to clean the coffee stains from Elijah's desk.

Ben picked up his mug so I could wipe underneath. 'The Metropolitan Police know about his connections. They're happy that two of his dealers have been charged even if they can't get to Fitzherbert himself.'

'Two?' I queried.

'The manager of Fitzherbert's Motors has been arrested too.'

'And Tolfree?' Elijah lit a cigarette and tossed the match into the ashtray I'd just emptied.

'There's no evidence he was involved. Superintendent Cobbe

is still digging but he's inclined to believe Tolfree genuinely didn't know anything about the drugs.'

'So where does that leave us with the murders of Rachel Lacey and Harry Hobbs?' Ash fell from Elijah's cigarette onto the clean desk, and he quickly brushed it into the ashtray before I attacked him with a damp cloth.

'No further forward, I'm afraid,' Ben replied. 'Miller could have slipped out of work without anyone noticing on the afternoon Rachel was murdered. Or perhaps this Ian Fitzherbert got one of his cronies to do it.'

'The manager at Fitzherbert's Motors told me that Ian Fitzherbert had liked Rachel and considered her reliable. If anything, he might have intended to keep using her when she was in London.'

'What about Harry Hobbs' murder?' Elijah puffed meditatively on his cigarette as he sat back in his chair. 'I think Tolfree could be right. Harry might have found out his brother-in-law was dealing drugs.'

'I can't see why Oliver would kill Rachel,' I replied. 'She was planning to go away and start a new life. And whoever killed Harry must have killed Rachel as well. It's unlikely two people have been walking around with syringes full of cocaine.'

'Unless someone decided to copy the method of killing,' Ben said. 'It has been known.'

I frowned. 'That's what I can't understand. Why use cocaine? And why leave the car by Tolfree's house with cocaine in it? It's like someone wanted to draw attention to the drug dealing.'

'So if not Tolfree, Miller or Fitzherbert, who are we left with?' Elijah said.

I leant against the door of his office. 'Archie Powell or a vengeful woman.'

Elijah mused on this. 'Let's put Mr Powell to one side for the moment as he still doesn't have a clear motive. Which vengeful woman do you have in mind?'

'Jennifer Tolfree, Nancy Miller or Victoria Hobbs. Each one might have cause to be angry with their husbands and Rachel.'

'Hmmm. Jennifer Tolfree could have killed Rachel because of the affair, but what reason would she have to kill Harry? Nancy Miller doesn't really have a strong motive for murdering anyone except her husband, and even then, I get the impression she's the type that would stand by him. Victoria Hobbs is a possibility,' Elijah agreed. 'She could have been angry with Rachel and her husband.'

'It's just a theory,' I said. Victoria was my least favourite suspect, though Elijah was right. She was the only one with a plausible motive for both murders.

'I'll add another woman to your list.' Ben pulled out his pocketbook. 'Grace Evans arrived in England on the day Rachel was murdered. Her ferry from Le Havre docked in Portsmouth at ten o'clock on the morning of the seventh.'

'That must be significant,' I said, although I didn't know why it should matter. Something about Grace niggled me; I just wasn't sure what it was.

'I suppose she could have taken the train from Portsmouth to Winchester, though she would have needed to know where her sister was going to be. Unless she'd arranged to meet her at the hall. But what motive does she have?' Elijah stubbed out his cigarette and began to button up his jacket.

'Maybe Rachel had an affair with Grace's husband?' I suggested. 'She seemed to like older men and he was twenty years her senior.'

Elijah shook his head. 'Unlikely. How would she manage to have an affair with a sick man recuperating in Nice while she was living in Winchester? And if that were the case, Grace would hardly have invited her sister to come and live with her.'

'I'm still confused about that. Tilly Crow thought Rachel had written to her sister, asking if they could share a house in London. Yet Grace told me she was the one who'd proposed it to Rachel.'

Ben shrugged. 'So what does it mean?'

I didn't have an answer to that. I flopped into my chair to consider what I knew from my meetings with Grace Evans. My feeling that something wasn't quite right about her was growing stronger.

'I don't like that look.' Elijah eyed me warily as he rose from his desk and stretched his back. 'What are you thinking?'

'Except Gordon Tolfree, no one really benefited from Rachel's death. And he doesn't seem to have hated her. He just wanted to avoid any scandal – from their affair and her drug dealing. Yet her murder only served to bring both to light.'

'So what are you saying?' Ben pushed back his chair and took his cup over to the sink.

'That Rachel was the scapegoat in all this. She was the one to suffer the repercussions of the affair and the cocaine dealing. Yet others were more responsible. It was probably Oliver Miller who introduced her to cocaine during their time at Morn Hill. After the war, he was the one who recommended her for the job at Tolfree Motors and that's how she ended up couriering drugs for Ian Fitzherbert. She must have come to realise how dangerous Fitzherbert was. Perhaps she turned to Gordon Tolfree, hoping he might provide a way out. Instead, he found out about the cocaine and dumped her. She had every reason to want to get away.'

'You believe she killed herself?' Ben shook his head. 'The pathologist doesn't think that's likely.'

Nor did I. Another idea entirely was forming in my mind. But I had no idea how to find out if I was on the right track.

Then a thought struck me. I leapt up, grabbing my coat from the hatstand and plucking my satchel from where it was hanging over the back of my chair.

'Where are you going?' Elijah called as I headed to the door.

'Just to Robbie's. I want to ask him something.'

He looked relieved. 'As long as that's all it is. Don't go traipsing off anywhere on your own. This mystery isn't solved yet. And Archie Powell's still out there.'

I nodded and hurried out of the office, leaving Elijah and Ben to finish clearing up.

It was bitterly cold outside and snowflakes floated in the air. All was silent apart from the clicking of my shoes on the pavement.

Then I heard another set of footsteps. They sounded close by and moving at speed. I glanced over my shoulder and saw a figure in a black cloak striding up Queens Road.

I turned onto the high street, hoping to find it filled with people, but there wasn't a soul in sight. All the shops had closed for the day and the only light came from the intermittent streetlamps.

Looking over my shoulder again, I saw the figure had just turned the corner and was heading in my direction. I guessed who it was and hoped that he was simply on his way to visit the church.

I hurried on, knowing that even if R. Roper Photographic Studio was closed, Robbie and his family were likely to be upstairs in their flat.

The footsteps behind me continued and, to my annoyance, I saw the figure had walked past the turning for Church Road. Even at my frantic pace, I knew he'd soon catch up with me.

Cursing under my breath, I swung around and barrelled straight into the broad chest of Gordon Tolfree.

He reached out and placed his hands on my shoulders to steady me.

'You should be more careful, Miss Woodmore.'

My breath caught in my throat and it took me a moment to recover from the collision. I stepped away from him, only to walk backwards into the black-clad figure.

Archie's hands replaced Gordon's on my shoulders and he gave me a wolfish grin.

38

'Are you following me?' I snarled.

Archie held up his hands in protest. 'I was on my way to the church.'

'It's down there.' I pointed towards Church Road.

He smiled. 'When I saw how deserted the high street was, I decided to make sure you got home safely. It's not the sort of night for a *lady* to be out on her own.' His emphasis of the word clearly demonstrated he thought I was anything but a lady.

'What do you want?' I snapped at Gordon Tolfree, who was blocking my path.

'To end this hostility,' he said, stepping to one side. 'I was just coming back to see you and Mr Whittle. I wanted to invite you both to a New Year's Eve party Jennifer and I are holding at Sycamore Lodge. We'd like to put all this unpleasantness behind us and start the new year on more cordial terms.'

'I think Mr Tolfree has made an extremely magnanimous gesture.' Archie inclined his head sycophantically towards Gordon. 'Perhaps we should follow his example and show each other a little more understanding.'

I ignored him.

'I'll pass on the invitation to Mr Whittle,' I said curtly to Gordon before brushing past him.

I tried to walk at a normal pace to show I wasn't in any way perturbed by my encounter with them, but I let out a long breath when I reached R. Roper Photographic Studio. There was a light on in the shop and when I tapped on the glass door, Robbie appeared from the back.

'I'm not taking you for a driving lesson at this time of night,' he grumbled as he let me in, closing the door behind me. 'We're about to have supper.'

I smiled, feeling safe inside the shop. Had Gordon and Archie intended to accost me? I guessed not, as they couldn't possibly have known I'd leave the office at that time. Gordon probably had been on his way to issue his invitation and no doubt Archie had seen an opportunity to scare me and taken it. I pushed them both from my mind and focused on what I'd come for.

'I just want to look at some photographs from last year's pantomime. Do you have any? You said you'd been roped in before by Jennifer Tolfree to help at their press days.'

Robbie's brow furrowed. 'I can't remember. What was the show last year?'

'*Little Bo Peep.*'

He sniggered. 'Oh yes, that's right. Lots of silly hats and sheep.'

I followed him through the shop and into the studio. 'Do you still have copies of the photographs?'

'Somewhere. Ellen will know. Why?' He went to the foot of the stairs and shouted for his wife to come down.

'I'm curious to see what Rachel Lacey looked like.'

'Was she in it?'

'She played Little Bo Beep.'

He rubbed his chin. 'Pretty girl, as I remember, wearing a frilly shepherdess costume and carrying a crook.'

Ellen appeared, wiping floury hands on her apron, and Robbie asked her about the pictures. She went over to a huge wooden cabinet and began pulling open drawers. It seemed to take an age for her to examine sheets of photographs only to put them back again.

'Here it is.' She plucked out a folder. 'Winchester Pantomime. Christmas 1922.'

Robbie peered over her shoulder. 'That's it.' He took the folder from her and rifled through the pictures. 'That's Rachel Lacey.'

He pointed to a young woman wearing a wig of blonde curls beneath a high, round-brimmed bonnet that was tied beneath her chin in an elaborate bow.

Robbie handed me another photograph. This time, Bo Peep was standing outside Winchester Cathedral smiling and waving, presumably at the people who'd come along to buy tickets for the pantomime.

When I'd been going over what we knew of Rachel's life, it had occurred to me that while Grace had nothing to gain by killing her sister, Rachel had everything to gain by killing Grace.

Rachel had no money, no job and no lover. Grace no longer had a husband but she had inherited his money. I remembered her saying her husband was a man of independent means, which meant that on his death, she'd become a woman of independent means.

I thought of the family photographs I'd seen on the mantel-piece of 3 Longbridge Court. In one of them, the two sisters had been wearing hats and smiling broadly at the camera. They'd appeared to be around eighteen at the time.

I tried to recall the image as I scrutinised the two grainy

pictures of Bo Peep. Eventually, I gave up and handed the photographs back to Robbie. If I was honest, it could have been either sister under that bonnet. I simply couldn't tell.

'What are you looking for?' Ellen asked.

'I was just curious to see Rachel Lacey,' I replied, too embarrassed to share my theory with the Ropers.

I left them to their supper, wondering if I was being ridiculous to even think it. But I couldn't let go of the idea.

Was it possible that the woman calling herself Grace Evans was in fact Rachel Lacey?

39

I caught the early train to Waterloo the following morning and took a bus to Lewisham. I got to Dolly's Hair Salon just as she was opening up.

As I walked along the high street, she emerged from the salon holding a wooden sandwich board proclaiming:

The most up-to-date ladies' styles, permanent waving and hair colouring.

'Iris. Back again so soon.' Dolly peered at the strands of hair peeking out from under my cloche hat. 'Is it not straight?'

'It's perfect, as usual.' I touched my locks, glad they were hidden by the hat. I'd barely run a comb through them before leaving the house. 'I wanted to ask you about something.'

Dolly placed the board on the pavement and ushered me inside. 'Talk to me while I set up.'

I followed her into the back room, which smelt of perming lotion and laundry soap – a row of freshly washed floral smocks hung from a row of hooks on the wall.

'It won't take long. When I was here the other day, I was chatting to a lady I know. Mrs Evans.'

'Poor lady. Lost her husband and her sister. Only young. A widow in her twenties. Enough of them since the war.'

'I noticed her bob cut was similar to mine.' I trailed after her as she laid out combs and scissors in each of the booths.

'My signature cut.' Dolly proudly waved a pair of lethal-looking scissors at me. 'It's earned me a few bob, if you pardon the pun. People come to me from all over London. And you still travel all the way up from Hampshire.'

It was true. No one could cut a bob as precisely as Dolly.

'How did Mrs Evans hear about you?'

'She's local and needed a haircut urgently. Turned up with her hair in a terrible state. Looked like she'd cut it herself.' Dolly sniffed. 'I don't think much of hairdressers in France if that's the best they can do.'

'When was that?'

'Last month, I think. Yes, I'm sure it was some time in November. Shall I check my book?'

'Yes, please.'

I followed Dolly to the reception desk, where she lifted a large record book from under the counter and flipped back through the pages.

'Here she is. Mrs Grace Evans. Her first visit was on the eighth of November. That's when I styled it into a bob cut for her. She's come in a few times since then for a wash and set. When you saw her the other day, she wanted it trimmed before she went away.'

The eighth of November was the day after Rachel's death. 'Do you know where she's going?'

'America. She said she needed a fresh start. Who can blame her after what she's been through? I doubt I'll be seeing her again.'

'Did you dye her hair?'

'No, though someone had. It wasn't her natural colour. I can always tell. Natural hair has different tints to it – you can see them in the light. The brown was too uniform. Not a bad job but definitely dyed.'

'Could she have had long blonde hair and then cut and dyed it herself?'

'I suppose so.' Dolly stopped what she was doing to consider this. 'Yes. Now I think about it, she'd look better as a blonde. It would suit her colouring. Lovely blue eyes and milky complexion.'

'Thanks, Dolly.'

'Take care of yourself, love. And don't go getting into any trouble,' she called as I headed out of the door.

I hurried along Lewisham high street, past the clock tower towards the park. A van was parked at the end of Longbridge Court. Behind it was a taxi.

Two men emerged from number three carrying a large black trunk between them. Grace Evans appeared, wearing a calf-length red-belted overcoat and matching red felt hat with a bow. She said something to the men, and when they nodded, she reached into her purse and handed them some notes.

I kept my distance and watched her get into the waiting taxi. When it drove around the corner, I hurried over to number three as the men came out carrying a second trunk.

'Has Mrs Evans left already?'

'You've just missed her. She's on her way to Waterloo Station.'

'She's going abroad, isn't she?'

'That's right. America. Taking an ocean liner from Southampton.'

'Perhaps I'll catch her at Waterloo.'

'You might. She was hoping to get the boat train, though she was cutting it fine.'

I thanked them and headed back to the high street in search of a taxi. I was unlikely to reach Waterloo before Grace's train departed, but it was worth a try. If not, I'd just have to head home and report what I'd discovered to Ben, although I feared it would be too late by then. No doubt, the ship would have already set sail for America – along with the truth about Rachel Lacey.

When I reached Waterloo Station, I realised it would be pointless searching for Grace. The concourse was packed, and I had to push my way through throngs of people to get to the ticket office. I examined the departures board trying so see which platform the boat train would leave from.

Then I spotted Grace's red felt hat. It was quite distinctive with a ribbon around the crown tied into a large bow at the back. She was standing at the end of a queue that snaked towards the ticket office. Unsure what to do, I waited for a couple of other people to go ahead of me before I joined the line.

Grace kept glancing at her watch and then back at the crowded concourse. I stood to one side, hoping she'd keep looking past me. She was carrying a small valise in one hand and a handbag was strapped over her shoulder.

When she reached the counter, I heard her ask, 'Have I missed the boat train for Southampton?'

'I'm afraid so. It's just pulling out now.'

'When's the next one?'

'There's not another boat train until this afternoon. But there's another train to Southampton at ten-thirty. It's a stopping service, so it will take longer.'

'That's fine. I'll have a first-class ticket, please.' She reached into her handbag and took out a purse.

'Single?'

'Yes. I won't be coming back.'

I pulled my deep-crowned cloche hat low over my eyes and kept my head down as she took her ticket and scurried past me. I checked my watch. The ten-thirty would leave in ten minutes.

I stayed in the queue, desperate for it to move faster. When I eventually reached the desk, I asked, 'Does the ten-thirty to Southampton stop at Walden?'

When the man said that it did, I upgraded my return ticket to first class and asked if there was a public telephone nearby.

'There's a kiosk in the alcove over there.' He jerked his head towards the waiting room.

I took my ticket and hurried across to it, annoyed to see it was occupied. I glanced pointedly at my watch to no avail; the man simply turned his back on me and carried on his conversation.

When he finished, I rummaged in my purse for any remaining coins. What with the taxi ride and upgrading my third-class ticket, the morning was proving to be more costly than I'd anticipated.

I asked for the station house in Walden and waited impatiently for the operator to make the connection. To my relief, Ben answered.

There was a long silence when I explained what I suspected.

'You never met Rachel Lacey, did you?' His voice was laden with scepticism.

'No, but—'

'And you say you're not completely certain from the photographs you saw?'

'No. I...' At that moment, I heard the announcer say the next train to Southampton would shortly depart from platform five. 'I have to go. The ten-thirty train is about to leave.'

'Iris, don't—'

I set the mouthpiece down and hurried out to the concourse, heading for platform five.

40

I scurried along the platform and saw the red bow of Grace's hat as she moved amongst the throng of people. When I saw her disappear into one of the first-class carriages, I slowed my pace and my breathing. I didn't have much time to decide what I was going to do or say.

When I reached the carriage, I saw that she was the only passenger inside. With no idea whether she was a murderer or not, I hopped in and sat on the upholstered bench opposite her. She started in surprise at the sight of me and her eyes widened in panic and confusion.

'Wha... what are you doing here?' she stammered.

'Going home. I live in Walden.'

'Oh yes, of course.' She glanced out of the window and along the platform. 'Are you on your own?'

I had no choice but to admit that I was. The fact that she'd asked the question, alerted me to the danger I was in, and I wondered if I should try to stop the train. However, this woman could genuinely be Grace Evans – and I could be making a big mistake.

As the train moved off, she seemed to relax a little, though she was still watching me warily. Given the two visits I'd made to her home and my all too convenient appearance in Dolly's Hair Salon, this wasn't surprising. She must have realised this was no coincidence.

All I could do was to engage her in conversation and hope she revealed enough for me to determine if my theory was correct.

'I went along to the first night of the pantomime.' I smiled. 'It was certainly a show I won't forget in a hurry.'

I saw the spark of curiosity I was looking for and proceeded to describe the unfortunate mishaps and eccentric performances of the cast. The ruse worked.

She couldn't hide her amusement, and I could tell from her expression I wasn't recounting the antics of a group of people who were strangers to her. She could picture the scene and the characters.

Her cackle of laughter when I described Jennifer Tolfree rushing into Archie Powell's arms and then colliding with Freddie confirmed my suspicions. The glee on her face was unmistakable.

Realising her error, she became more serious. 'I'm sure they did the best they could under the circumstances.'

'You must be glad you weren't part of it,' I said, realising I was going have to show my hand if I wanted to find out more.

'I didn't feel able to go along to support them,' she replied cagily.

I nodded. 'I understand. It would be too risky for you to return to Winchester in case someone recognised you.'

Her face remained impassive, and she didn't answer immediately. Her eyes rested on mine, then she said, 'What is it you think you know?'

'I think that you borrowed the Wolseley from Tolfree Motors

on the morning of the seventh of November and drove to Portsmouth to pick up your sister, Grace Evans.'

She didn't reply, and I saw her glance towards the internal door of the carriage. The noise of the guard outside, talking to other passengers, was reassuring.

'Don't worry, Gordon Tolfree's been arrested,' I lied.

This had the desired effect, and Rachel's mouth fell open.

'For murder?'

'He must have seen you drive into Christmas Close. Did you take Grace there to show her the pantomime sets and costumes?'

She nodded convulsively. 'Grace used to love dressing up in Mother's costumes. I knew she'd adore the ball gown. She always fancied herself as a leading lady even though she had no talent for acting.'

'And Gordon mistook her for you?' I prompted. Now I was certain I was talking to Rachel Lacey, I realised why Harry Hobbs had been so convinced of Gordon Tolfree's guilt. It was because Rachel had told him what Gordon had done. Or at least her version of events.

'We both had long blonde hair.' Her hand rose automatically to her short brown locks. 'She tried on the costume and then went outside to the porch to smoke. I had no idea Gordon was there. Grace's arms were bare, and he must have jabbed her with the needle. When I found her, she was dead, and he was driving off in the car.'

'That must have been very frightening.'

'I was petrified and in shock. I knew I was in danger if I stayed in Winchester, so I took Grace's case and left.' Her eyes flicked upwards to the small valise printed with the initials G. E. resting on the luggage rack above her head. 'I jumped on a train to London and went to Longbridge Court. What else could I do?'

Inform the police of your sister's murder was the obvious answer to that. Instead, I asked, 'Why did you pretend to be her?'

'I knew I'd be safe if people believed I was dead. I needed Gordon to think I was dead. You, of all people, should know what he's like.' Her fingers gripped the strap of the handbag on her lap. 'You lied – pretending to be a friend of mine. Something you're very good at, according to Gordon. He was forever moaning about you, Constance Timpson and Sybil Siddons. How you conspired to destroy his father.'

'We didn't. Redvers Tolfree destroyed himself.'

'I know that now. But I was naïve when I first started seeing Gordon.' Her face hardened. 'Then I realised he was a chip off the old block. He was as bad as his old man. Even worse. He's a murderer.'

'You pointed me in his direction.' I thought back to how each time I'd visited Longbridge Court, Rachel, as Grace, had subtly tried to implicate Gordon Tolfree.

She gave a slight smile. 'I knew you'd be suspicious of him. And you were right to be.'

'Why did he want to kill you?'

She waved her hand dismissively. 'He was angry. About the cocaine.' She stopped, then added, 'I guess you know about that?'

I nodded.

'Gordon thought I was responsible for everything.'

'He didn't suspect Oliver Miller?'

She shook her head. 'If I took the blame, Oliver could carry on with the racket. It was safer for both of us that way. We weren't dealing with nice people.'

I presumed she meant Ian Fitzherbert.

With a trembling hand, she took an elegant silver cigarette case from her handbag and held it open across the aisle. When I shook my head, she lit one for herself before returning it to her bag.

Judging by the expensive cigarette case and lighter, and the cut of her red overcoat and hat, I guessed that Rachel hadn't been shy about spending the money in her sister's bank account.

'I did use cocaine, I admit. And I did pass it on through the Blackbird Bar.' Her hand shook as she raised the cigarette to her lips. 'I didn't want to do it, but they made me.'

I wasn't sure this was true. Rachel Lacey didn't strike me as the type of woman who did anything she didn't want to do.

'Is that why Gordon ended your relationship? That was cruel of him,' I said sympathetically.

'Do you know, at one point, I actually believed we were in love?' She gave a bitter laugh. 'I thought he was going to leave his wife for me, not that he ever said as much. At the time, it didn't matter. He was rich, and we had a good time. I used to enjoy our nights together. Then he suddenly became all pious. It was going fine until he found God. Or to be more precise, Archie Powell. That man thinks he is God.'

'True.' I nodded in agreement.

'He's a piece of work, isn't he? Attractive, but not to be trusted. What is it he wants?'

'Respectability. Archie likes people to look up to him. He feels I took away his elevated position.'

'So that's why he and Gordon got together.' Her eyes narrowed as she drew on her cigarette. 'Yes, that makes sense. I'd be careful if I were you. Look what happened to Harry.'

'What did happen to Harry?' I asked.

She breathed out a long plume of smoke, taking her time before answering. 'He was working at that church in Walden, and I think he must have seen Gordon driving the car home after he'd killed Grace.'

I didn't mention the fact that Gordon couldn't have been the one to have driven the Wolseley into the clearing by Sycamore Lodge. The most likely person to have put it there was Rachel herself in order to implicate him. I suspected her plan had nearly backfired when Harry had seen her, and she'd had to convince him her life was in danger to stop him from going to the police.

'You don't think Harry took an overdose?' I said.

'No. Not Harry. Sometimes, when he was in one of his moods, he'd come to the bar, and I'd share my cocaine with him, but he was never a regular user.'

'You were fond of him?'

Her large blue eyes filled with tears. 'Nothing romantic. We just used to have fun, that's all. Victoria didn't approve. At first, she suspected there was something going on between us, then she guessed he was taking cocaine. She was another one who was quick to put the blame at my door. Little did she know her respectable brother was the real drug dealer. That always made me laugh.' Suddenly, a thought seemed to occur to her and she asked, 'What's happened to Oliver?'

'The police found a large quantity of cocaine hidden under the passenger seat of a new Sunbeam he'd picked up from Fitzherbert's Motors.'

I didn't mention that I'd put them on the scent of it.

She winced. 'Nasty. That won't go down well.'

'I wonder why he killed Harry at the church.' I was curious to hear how she'd pin this on Gordon.

I remembered the road atlas I'd seen when I'd visited Long-bridge Court. I'd thought at the time it must have belonged to Rachel rather than Grace as it contained street maps of Alder-shot and the surrounding area, including Walden. It would have shown the location of St Martha's Church, and Rachel must have known that Sycamore Lodge was nearby.

'I think Gordon arranged to meet Harry there, saying he could get him some cocaine. I suppose it was easier for Gordon to tackle Harry when he was on his own outside the church.'

I thought it unlikely Gordon Tolfree would have chosen to kill a man so close to his family home.

'He's a dangerous man,' I said. 'You were wise to escape.'

Rachel seemed pleased by this. 'I was, wasn't I? You see why I had to do it? It wasn't just Gordon. Ian Fitzherbert took a shine to me. He assumed I'd carry on working for him when I moved to London. I had to get away.'

'It was a clever plan.'

Encouraged by my praise, she told me how she'd changed her hairstyle to avoid being recognised. In her version of events, the idea to become Grace had only occurred to her when she'd reached London and found all her sister's trunks had arrived at the house.

Now I knew her secret, she seemed compelled to tell me how she'd managed to cover her tracks. It sounded like the riskiest moment had been when the police arrived to inform her of the death. She hadn't enjoyed going to the county hospital to identify her sister's body or being interviewed by Superintendent Cobbe. But after that, she'd been left in peace. Until I'd shown up at her door.

As she spoke, I noticed that her mannerisms had changed. Before, when I'd visited Longbridge Court, I was seeing Rachel impersonating Grace. Now I was seeing the real thing.

'It must have been terrible for you to have found your sister's body at Christmas Close and then to have had to view it again at the hospital.'

'It was heart-breaking.' Rachel raised a handkerchief to her eyes but I didn't notice any tears. Not like the genuine emotion she'd shown over Harry.

When I asked what Grace had been like, she began by describing what a caring woman she'd been. Yet when she talked about the war years, it was clear she felt her sister had let her down by leaving so soon after their mother's death to volunteer as a nurse in France. And again, when the war had ended, and Grace hadn't returned to England, I could sense her resentment at being abandoned for a second time.

I caught glimpses of a vulnerable woman who'd been hurt by others, particularly Gordon Tolfree. Her venom was most apparent when she talked about him and described the way he'd treated her. Surprisingly, she showed little resentment towards Oliver Miller, probably recognising he was in too deep to behave any differently. But she'd evidently expected more from her former lover.

Listening to her story, I became aware of Rachel Lacey's curious personality. Or personalities. Like an actress, she took on different characters. On the one hand, she gave me the impression of being a self-centred young woman who cared little for the feelings of others. On the other, she displayed genuine affection when she spoke of Harry Hobbs and Tilly Crow. Although she'd left Crows' Nest owing three months' rent, after my first visit to Longbridge Court, she'd been true to her word and used her sister's money to send Tilly a cheque for what she owed.

By the time the train pulled into Walden, it was obvious to me that at some point Rachel Lacey had decided the only person she could rely on was herself. And to hell with anyone who got in her way.

'Are we at Walden Station already?' she asked, feigning surprise. Throughout the journey, she'd repeatedly glanced at her wristwatch, and I was sure she knew exactly where we were. And how long it would be before she was safely on board a ship heading for America.

'Where are you off to?' I asked, picking up my bag from the seat beside me and making a show of preparing to disembark.

As the train slowed, I faced a dilemma. I was certain that Rachel had killed Grace Evans and Harry Hobbs. Should I stick with her and try to stop her from leaving on the ocean liner? But how would I be able to do that? And what reason could I give for staying on the train?

She smiled. 'I'm going a long way away. Make sure Gordon Tolfree and Archie Powell get what they deserve.'

'I will,' I promised, though the sound of the train screeching to a halt drowned out my words. I peered out of the carriage window and, through billowing smoke, spotted Ben in the distance, talking to the station master.

I gripped the door handle, waiting for the smoke to disperse. When it did, I was astonished to see Superintendent Cobbe striding along the platform. I almost smiled when I recognised the two people by his side.

I hopped out of the carriage and held the door open, allowing the superintendent to peer inside.

'Could I ask you to step down from the train, Mrs Evans?' His tone was polite, but it was clear this was an order.

I heard Rachel gasp, and when she emerged from the carriage, she gave me a look of pure loathing.

Bridget Durling stared at her in horror. 'Oh, Rachel. How could you do it?'

Freddie's eyes were round with astonishment.

'That's Rachel,' he muttered to no one in particular.

Superintendent Cobbe nodded at Ben, who stepped forward and gripped Rachel's arm.

Snapping a pair of handcuffs onto her wrists, he said, 'Miss Rachel Lacey. I'm arresting you on suspicion of the murder of Mrs Grace Evans and Mr Harry Hobbs.'

41

'What made you suspect?' Elijah lit his cigar and placed the green onyx lighter back on the glass table next to a matching ashtray.

Not for the first time, I wondered how he managed to avoid dropping ash or spilling coffee over Horace's expensive furnishings, yet I had to scrub both from his desk at the end of each day.

'I was trying to work out who gained the most from Rachel's death,' I replied. 'The answer was Rachel herself.'

'Her sister's money and a new life.' Horace leant forward in anticipation. I hadn't been surprised by my invitation to dinner and knew what was expected of me.

Ben listened in amusement. He'd received Horace's call too, and we'd strolled around the lake to Heron Bay Lodge together, knowing we'd be treated to a decent meal with expensive wine. We agreed that there were worse ways to spend an evening, and we hadn't been disappointed.

Dinner had consisted of fried fillets of sole, followed by mutton cutlets royale and petit fours to finish, accompanied by champagne and claret. Elijah and Horace were now comfortably seated side by side on the sofa with their brandy and cigars.

Ben and I were settled in a pair of armchairs by the fire, a pot of coffee and two delicate porcelain cups and saucers on the table between us. We knew we were the after-dinner entertainment.

'Oliver Miller offered Rachel a job at Tolfree Motors to help him collect and distribute the drugs he was getting from Ian Fitzherbert. As her sister had decided to settle in France with her new husband, I suspect Rachel felt she had little choice but to accept the offer.' I paused to pour the coffee.

Ben stepped in. 'It's likely she already had knowledge of what Oliver Miller was up to from their time together at Morn Hill. She may even have been involved in dealing drugs herself during the war.'

'At some point, Rachel began an affair with Gordon Tolfree. In hindsight, he seems to think she was keeping him sweet, so he didn't suspect what she and Oliver Miller were up to.' I passed a cup to Ben, then sunk back into the highly cushioned armchair.

Horace chuckled. 'No doubt, at the time he thought it was due to his irresistible good looks and charm rather than his money.'

'From what Tilly Crow and Victoria Hobbs said, Rachel did genuinely like him. She believed that one day he might even leave his wife for her. It was obvious she expected more from him than she got.'

Ben nodded. 'Thanks to Archie Powell, Rachel lost her job and her lover.'

'She was hurt that Gordon had turned against her. And angry at being made the scapegoat as it was Oliver Miller who was running the show. But it was too risky to tell anyone about his involvement. If she took the blame, the operation could keep going with Gordon none the wiser.'

'I'm surprised Miss Lacey didn't vent her anger at Mr Miller,' Horace commented.

'She knew he was in the same predicament as her. They were both in too deep with Ian Fitzherbert and were afraid of him. Over time, they must have become aware of the extent of his criminal network. Ian Fitzherbert liked and trusted Rachel and expected her to carry on working for him in some capacity when she moved to London. She was trapped and needed a way out.'

'And her sister provided the solution,' Elijah remarked.

'I have a feeling the seeds were sown when Rachel went to France for Grace's husband's funeral. Rachel had lost her job at Tolfree Motors and her future looked bleak while her sister had just inherited her husband's estate and was planning to move to London. At some point, Rachel realised that if she became Grace, she could escape from her problems and have enough money to start a new life in America.'

'Superintendent Cobbe has spoken on the telephone to Grace Evans' housekeeper in Nice,' Ben said. 'She told him that Rachel wrote to her sister to ask if they could live together when Grace returned to England. According to the housekeeper, Mrs Evans wasn't keen on the idea but felt it was her duty to take care of her sister.'

I sighed. 'When Grace agreed, her fate was sealed, as Rachel began to put her plan into action.'

'So she took the car from Tolfree Motors and went to meet her sister from the ferry when it docked in Portsmouth on the seventh of November?' Horace was a stickler for detail and would want to understand the precise sequence of events.

'She'd done a lot of preparation before this,' I explained. 'Rachel had persuaded her sister to wire her money so she could rent a house for them in London. She chose 3 Longbridge Court in Lewisham as it's quite secluded. Grace had her trunks sent ahead and travelled to England on the seventh of November with only a small valise.'

'And Rachel was waiting for her at the dock,' Elijah said grimly.

'Rachel drove Grace to Christmas Close to show her the pantomime sets and the costumes. She said her sister always fancied herself as the leading lady and loved dressing up in their mother's costumes when they were children. She'd turned on the gas fires to warm up the dressing room and managed to persuade Grace to try on the ball gown. Probably after she'd given her drugged tea. Jack Archer noticed that the gas ring in the office had been used.'

'The tea was laced with barbiturates. The pathologist thought they were likely to be Rachel's own sleeping pills,' Ben said. 'It would have been impossible to get her sister to ingest enough barbiturates to kill her, but the dose made Grace drowsy enough to enable Rachel to inject a shot of cocaine. The ball gown had short puff sleeves, so Grace's arms were bare, and a puncture mark was found in the vein of her left elbow.'

'Cocaine was a drug Rachel knew well,' I continued. 'The simplest way to deliver a fatal dose is intravenously. Once Grace collapsed, she dragged her out to the porch for Jack Archer to find.'

'Did they look alike?' Horace asked.

'Similar, but not identical. That's why the costume, staging and timing were so important. Rachel wanted Jack to be the one to find Grace. She knew he'd be in the pub until it closed at three o'clock and a bit the worse for wear when he arrived at the hall. He has poor eyesight, and the cocaine overdose distorted Grace's features and made her skin blue. She was laid face down with her blonde hair spread out around her head. Rachel's cigarettes and lighter were lying next to her on the ground.'

Horace tutted. 'How cruel.'

'Her hate seemed to stem from the resentment she'd felt at the way Grace had treated her after their mother's death. She'd felt abandoned by her.'

'It was well planned,' Elijah commented.

'Rachel told me on the train that the idea to impersonate her sister had only occurred to her when she got to London after Gordon Tolfree had supposedly killed Grace. She said she went to Dolly's Salon to get her hair cut and dyed. Grace hadn't been in England since the war and few people knew what she looked like. But Dolly had already told me that Rachel turned up on the eighth of November with badly cut hair that had already been dyed brown. I suspect Rachel did it herself in the dressing room at Christmas Hall.'

'So she left her sister lying dead in Christmas Close and became Grace Evans. But why move the car?' Elijah asked. 'Why not just leave it where it was?'

'Because she needed to get away fast and couldn't risk travelling from Winchester railway station. Someone she knew might have seen her. Changing her long blonde hair to a short dark crop would fool most people, but not if they saw her face close up. Far safer to go from a quieter railway station like Walden.'

'And incriminate Gordon Tolfree in the process.' Horace tutted again.

'At some point, it occurred to her to dump the Wolseley near his house, leaving some cocaine in the glove compartment for good measure – hoping to lead the police investigation straight to Gordon's door.'

'Hell hath no fury like a woman scorned,' Horace observed.

Elijah frowned. 'That piece of vindictiveness led to the death of Harry Hobbs. I'm guessing he saw her driving the car down Church Road to Sycamore Lodge.'

'She had no idea he was working at the church in Walden. He would have recognised the Wolseley and gone to see who it was. I expect she told Harry the same tale she told me. That Gordon was trying to harm her and had killed her sister by mistake. She had no choice but to run away as she was frightened for her life. I suspect that when the vicar saw the lights of Harry's van pulling away, Rachel was inside, and he dropped her off at the railway station.'

'Why did Harry point you in the direction of the car,' Horace enquired.

'He was following Rachel's lead. When we asked him why he was so convinced it was Gordon Tolfree, he said he'd tell us when he had proof. That's probably what Rachel had said to him. I imagine she begged him to keep her secret, promising to reappear and tell the world the truth when she had enough evidence to put Gordon Tolfree behind bars.'

Horace swirled the brandy around his glass. 'Instead, she reappeared and killed him.'

I nodded. 'She knew he wouldn't stay silent forever. Harry must have told her he'd be working at the church for another few weeks and his presence there gave her the opportunity she needed. I think she took the train to Walden and waited in the woods nearby until Harry was alone. It probably wasn't difficult to persuade him to have a drink and take some cocaine with her for old times' sake. Once he was under the influence, she was able to inject him with the syringe.'

'And leave one of Gordon Tolfree's business cards in the van,' Ben said. 'The writing on the card is like her handwriting, although with so few words, it's difficult to prove.'

Elijah savoured his brandy thoughtfully. 'Not an easy case for Cobbe to bring to court.'

'We've been gathering evidence,' Ben replied. 'Rachel is still claiming that her sister was killed when she went outside to smoke. But when Superintendent Cobbe spoke to the Evans' housekeeper, she told him that Mrs Evans never touched cigarettes as she believed they were detrimental to the lungs. She also said she'd helped Mrs Evans to pack and arranged for her trunks to be sent ahead to the house in Lewisham. Rachel had written to say she was going to pick up her sister from the ferry port and that the car she was borrowing wasn't large enough to hold much luggage.'

'You've got to hand it to her.' Elijah waved his cigar, seemingly unaware we were all watching for any ash to fall on the leather Chesterfield. 'It's an audacious plan.'

I breathed a sigh of relief when he placed it safely in the ashtray with no spillages.

'Rachel had confidence in her ability as an actress,' I said. 'Apart from going to the county hospital to identify her sister's body, she didn't have to set foot in Winchester again. She was the one who'd rented the house in Lewisham on her sister's behalf and she only planned on staying there until she could book her passage to America. Once she was there, I don't think she would have continued to call herself Mrs Evans. I'm sure she would have found a more glamorous stage name and tried to find work as an actress.'

'But she only got as far as Walden.' Horace raised his brandy glass in a salute to me.

'Thanks to Ben. How did you get Superintendent Cobbe to come?'

Ben grinned. 'I'll admit, I was cursing you when I phoned Winchester police station that morning. I expected him to say, "Tell Miss Woodmore she's been reading too many penny dreadfuls". And he did.'

Horace and Elijah chuckled.

I wasn't offended. Under the circumstances it was a reasonable response.

'I agreed with him,' Ben continued. 'And said it sounded far-fetched to me, too. But... if we let Grace or Rachel go to America, we'd never be able to prove it one way or the other.'

'Very true,' Horace said approvingly.

'The superintendent told me to delay the train if necessary as he needed to find someone who knew Rachel Lacey. He drove to Christmas Close, where Mrs Durling and Freddie were clearing up after the pantomime.'

'Hence, we were subjected to this rather extravagant headline by Mr Noakes,' Elijah said, holding up a copy of the *Hampshire Chronicle*.

Handsome Prince and Fairy Godmother Identify Cinderella as Killer

was splashed across the front page.

Accompanying Kevin's exclusive interview was a photograph of '*local landlady turned detective*'. It showed Mrs Bridget Durling, in her fairy godmother costume, smiling and waving her magic wand. Freddie stood beside her, dressed as the prince, complete with yellow tights and painted-on moustache above a swollen lip. He stared directly into the camera with an expression that suggested his life couldn't get any worse. I imagined Hetty pasting the picture into her scrapbook.

Ben smiled at the image. 'Perhaps Walden can get back to normal in the new year. Going into 1924, I'd prefer the town to be a little less like New York. Let's leave stolen cars, cocaine and murder behind in 1923.'

I noticed Elijah and Horace exchange a glance.

Horace steepled his hands under his chin. 'I'm afraid, we've got some bad news.'

Elijah drew on his cigar and let out a long breath. 'You know Reverend Childs encouraged the Walden Women's Group to work with the committee of Winchester Cathedral's Great War Fund?'

'Yes.' Apprehension crept over me.

'It was because the fund has bought Mill Ponds,' Horace announced.

I drew in a breath. 'Why? What do they want with Mill Ponds?'

'They plan to use it as a hostel for unemployed and disabled ex-servicemen. It's going for a knock-down price as no one else wants it.' Elijah gazed morosely into his brandy glass. 'Nathan Cheverton took what the church offered.'

I turned to Horace. 'Can't you stop them?'

He shook his head. 'I may have influence in a number of quarters, but I'm afraid the church answers to a higher power.'

'No,' I groaned, knowing exactly where this was leading.

'I don't see what's so bad about it.' Ben hadn't yet made the connection. 'It seems like a good idea to me.'

'I'm afraid they've appointed Archie Powell to manage the hostel due to his experience setting up Creek House in Deptford.' Elijah looked at me with concern. 'He's moving to Walden to live at Mill Ponds.'

42

'I'd like to thank you for finding out the truth about Rachel Lacey.' Gordon Tolfree stood with his chest thrust out and his legs spread wide. 'It's a huge relief to me and my wife that I'm no longer the subject of gossip and slanderous newspaper speculation.'

I was tempted to point out that when the case came to court, Gordon's name wouldn't just be appearing in the *Hampshire Chronicle*. The national newspapers would report on every aspect of the sorry tale and the Tolfrees were likely to find themselves the topic of many a conversation. Still, why spoil the party?

'I knew that woman was trouble. But to think she could do that. To her own sister and poor Mr Hobbs.' Not a single strand of Jennifer Tolfree's elaborately arranged hair moved when she shook her head in disbelief.

'Don't dwell on it, my dear.' Gordon patted her arm. 'It's best to put the past behind us. Including that unpleasant business with my father.'

I hadn't wanted to attend the Tolfrees' New Year's Eve party for many reasons. The main one was standing a few feet away from me. Archie Powell had his arm around Victoria Hobbs' shoulder, and I didn't like the way her deep brown eyes were gazing up at him.

But curiosity, and – I had to admit – loneliness had driven me to Sycamore Lodge. Millicent and Ursula were still in Kent, my father and Katherine had gone to Smugglers Haunt, and Elijah had chosen to decline the Tolfrees' invitation and spend a cosy evening in with Horace instead.

I thought of Marc and wondered what he was doing. Had he taken Annette out to dinner? Perhaps they'd gone to a party with friends. Or they could be celebrating at home together.

'With God's help, 1924 will be a better year for all of us.' Jennifer's eyes drifted to Archie as she said this. He was wearing a well-cut dinner suit and she wasn't the only woman casting discreet glances in his direction.

'Hear, hear.' Gordon raised his glass with a rigid smile. 'I'd like us to put aside any differences we may have had and start again.'

'Of course.' My smile was as forced as his as I lifted my glass, but I had no desire to bear grudges.

Gordon seemed happy with that, and he and Jennifer drifted away to attend to their other guests. When I looked around the room to see if I could spot any of my friends, my eyes met Archie's. He was watching me with that familiar insolent smirk, as if he knew what I was thinking.

The Tolfrees were nowhere to be seen, so I placed my empty glass on the drinks table and slipped out of the room. I'd see the new year in alone with a sherry in Ursula's book room.

The driveway to Sycamore Lodge was lit by flickering gas lamps, which illuminated the swirling mass of snowflakes. I pulled my coat tighter around me and walked quickly away from the house and down the track to Church Road.

As I neared the churchyard, I could hear soft footsteps behind me. I didn't slow my pace. I knew who was following me and had no desire to make it any easier for them to catch up.

I was level with the old wooden bench at the side of the church where Harry had lain frozen when Archie called my name. I didn't bother turning.

'Why don't we celebrate the new year together, Iris?' he said when he reached my side. 'After all, I'm going to be part of your life again in 1924.'

'Why are you here, Archie?' I kept my eyes fixed on the road ahead, refusing to look at him. 'Why don't you go to a place where no one knows your past?'

'Because I've atoned for my sins.' He stood in front of me, forcing me to stop. 'And I have nothing to be ashamed of.'

'We both know that's not true,' I replied, drawing back from the smell of alcohol on his breath.

'I paid a heavy price,' he hissed. 'Thanks to you.'

'Missing your cassock?' I sneered at the black woollen cloak he was wearing over his dinner suit.

For a moment, I thought he was going to strike me. Then he stepped aside to let me pass.

'You've made your peace with Gordon. Why can't we do the same?'

'Because he's never fired a gun at my friends.'

He gave an exasperated sigh. 'With or without your blessing, I'm going to make Walden my home. And I think I'm going to be very happy here.'

I turned on him. 'Do you? I wouldn't be so sure of that. There are too many people around here who'll be a constant reminder of what you did. They know you for what you are.'

He dismissed this with an arrogant wave of his gloved hand. 'Any past misdemeanours will be forgotten once the hostel is established. You saw what I achieved at Creek House. You even wrote articles praising my work. Mill Ponds will be on a much grander scale. I'll be able to help more men take back control of their lives.'

'I don't deny that you've helped many people, but you've harmed others.' I glanced up at his sculpted jaw and intense eyes. 'Particularly women who don't conform to your way of thinking.'

'I don't deny that I've made mistakes.' The lascivious smile returned. 'Perhaps you were one of them.'

'I'm sure I was,' I replied. 'You were certainly one of mine.'

'One?' He smirked. 'How many have you made? I'd love to hear all about your present indiscretions.'

I ignored him and turned sharply onto the high street, quickening my pace.

With his long stride, Archie had no problem staying level with me. 'It will be good to be busy again. I've had too much time on my hands recently. You should be pleased I'm going to be occupied. It means I won't have as much time to keep an eye on you.'

I felt a thud in my chest. 'Why would you want to keep an eye on me?'

'Because I know what you're like, remember?' His tone was mocking. 'Always the non-conformist. The rules don't apply to you, do they?'

'Is that why you've been spending so much time in Walden? I think you'll find our small town very dull.'

'I admit, I've found your trips to London far more interesting.'

I exhaled sharply, then cursed myself for reacting.

'I see you've caught on at last.' He sighed with malevolent satisfaction. 'Yes, I'm talking about your relationship with Marc Jansen. It's strange that you always meet with just him and not Mrs Jansen.'

'He's an old friend,' I muttered, trying to sound calm.

'Hmm. From what I've seen, he's more than a friend.'

'How do you know his name?' I hated having to ask but needed to discover his source of information.

'After one of your clandestine meetings in St James's Park, I followed him back to his offices in Holborn. It wasn't difficult to find out who he was.'

I winced as I remembered all the times I'd felt I was being watched. Not willing to give Archie the satisfaction of seeing or hearing my distress, I told myself to keep walking and say nothing.

'What would your father say about your relationship with a married man?' Archie said, feigning moral outrage. 'And your beloved Mr Whittle and Mrs Siddons? Do your friends, Percy and Millicent, know of the affair? I'm sure they'd be interested.'

My throat tightened, and my breath became shallow. I wanted to swing around and slap the smug smile from his face. Instead, I kept walking, staring straight ahead, determined not to give him the reaction he wanted.

When I reached the turning for Victoria Lane, I realised by the silence that I must have left him behind. I was tempted to look back to see what he was doing but managed to stop myself.

'Happy New Year, Iris,' he called after me. 'I think 1924 is going to be full of surprises.'

ACKNOWLEDGEMENTS

I'm a frequent visitor to the beautiful city of Winchester, and I enjoyed giving it a central role in this book. Thanks to Winchester Heritage Open Days, I was able to research and explore many of the places I write about, including the *Hampshire Chronicle's* offices (though they've moved from their original location on the high street), Winchester College, Abbey House, P & G Wells Bookshop, The Great Hall of Winchester Castle, Jane Austen's House on College Street, and The Westgate Hotel.

Nestling among the real locations of Curle's Passage, Cathedral Close, Kingsgate and St Swithun Street is the fictional Christmas Close.

The Prince of Wales did visit Winchester on 7 November 1923 when he was presented with the Freedom of the City, and I have accurately depicted his itinerary for the day in this book.

As ever, I'm indebted to the numerous people, books, libraries, museums and archives that contributed to my knowledge of this period.

I'd like to thank the following people for their continued support: my parents, Ken and Barbara Salter – my father particularly for his help with historical research; Jeanette Quay for being my sounding board and filmmaker; and Barbara Daniel for advice and encouragement.

Thanks to my very patient editor, Emily Yau, and all the other brilliant members of the Boldwood Books team.

ABOUT THE AUTHOR

Michelle Salter writes historical cosy crime set in Hampshire, where she lives, and inspired by real-life events in 1920s Britain. Her Iris Woodmore series draws on an interest in the aftermath of the Great War and the suffragette movement.

Sign up to Michelle Salter's mailing list for news, competitions and updates on future books.

Visit Michelle's Website: https://www.michellesalter.com

Follow Michelle on social media:

X x.com/MichelleASalter
facebook.com/MichelleSalterWriter
instagram.com/michellesalter_writer
BB bookbub.com/authors/michelle-salter

ALSO BY MICHELLE SALTER

The Iris Woodmore Mysteries

Death at Crookham Hall

Murder at Waldenmere Lake

The Body at Carnival Bridge

A Killing at Smugglers Cove

A Corpse in Christmas Close

Standalone

Murder at Merewood Hospital

Poison
& Pens

POISON & PENS IS THE HOME OF
COZY MYSTERIES SO POUR YOURSELF
A CUP OF TEA & GET SLEUTHING!

DISCOVER PAGE-TURNING NOVELS FROM
YOUR FAVOURITE AUTHORS &
MEET NEW FRIENDS

JOIN OUR
FACEBOOK GROUP

BIT.LYPOISONANDPENSFB

SIGN UP TO OUR
NEWSLETTER

BIT.LY/POISONANDPENSNEWS

Boldwood

Boldwood Books is an award-winning fiction publishing company seeking out the best stories from around the world.

Find out more at www.boldwoodbooks.com

Join our reader community for brilliant books, competitions and offers!

Follow us
@BoldwoodBooks
@TheBoldBookClub

Sign up to our weekly
deals newsletter

https://bit.ly/BoldwoodBNewsletter

Printed in Great Britain
by Amazon